One Year in Retirement and 25 Short Stories

Martin Green

iUniverse, Inc.
New York   Bloomington

One Year in Retirement
and 25 Short Stories

iUniverse books may be ordered through booksellers or by contacting:

iUniverse
1663 Liberty Drive
Bloomington, IN 47403
www.iuniverse.com
1-800-Authors (1-800-288-4677)

ISBN: 978-1-4401-5249-8 (soft)
ISBN: 978-1-4401-5250-4 (ebook)

Printed in the United States of America

iUniverse rev. date: 6/23/2009

FORWARD

During the past three years—2006, 2007 and 2008—I self-published three volumes of collected short stories.. All of these stories had first been published in magazines, the first few in "literary" publications, the bulk of them, after I'd become more technically attuned, in on-line magazines. My original goal was to have 100 published stories appearing somewhere. Online magazines continued to publish my stories and when the number passed 150 I revised my goal upward to 200. At the same time, I wanted to write a longer piece of work. I considered a novel but, this would be pretty time-consuming and at my age I don't have much time to spare. I decided instead to write a "fictionalized memoir." I chose the year 1991, the year after I retired, to write about. In this way, I could write it one month at a time. When I finished, I called it, not too originally, "One Year in Retirement."

Why a "fictionalized" memoir? Well, a straightforward account of any one year in my retired life (prior life as well) would be pretty dull. Most of the events I describe did happen but not all in that one year. The most glaring example is having surgery for an enlarged prostate. I did have this surgery but not until some years later..

I had another reason for writing "One Year in Retirement." I wanted to put into it some of the things I'd learned about how to handle going from work to being retired. As I wrote, I realized that what I'd learned wasn't that much. Nevertheless, I've tried to put a few helpful things in the book, sometimes explicitly, other times implicitly. I hope the book will be somewhat instructive, if only because it reports the missteps I made and the misconceptions I had.

Aside from the longer piece, I had 25 short stories I hadn't collected before and putting these together with "One Year in Retirement" makes up a volume about the same size as the previous ones. Here it is. As stated before, all of my stories are fiction and the phrase "fictionalized memoir" speaks for itself. In spring 2009 I did reach the 200 stories published mark and went a bit over. I may be the oldest writer still having stories published on the internet. I don't know how many short stories I have left to write, and at my age I don't know if I'll be able to write another longer piece. So this volume, plus the previous three, make up my body of work to date and, if nothing else, puts it into a somewhat more permanent form than otherwise. As in previous volumes, the publication a short story appeared in is shown in parenthesis after the title.

ONE YEAR IN RETIREMENT
Prologue

"So now that you're retired, what are you going to do?" This was the question most asked at my retirement/birthday party (and also the subject of this memoir)..

Retirement. For most people, the promised land. But also uncharted territory. I retired at the end of 1990. As my birthday happens to fall on December 30th, my official retirement day was Friday, the 28th, two days before my 61st birthday I'd worked 27 years in various research capacities for agencies of the State of California. I'd analyzed masses of data, conducted mail and telephone surveys, worked with computer programmers, learned how to use a personal computer myself, provided information to the media, State managers, and legislators, and written dozens of reports. I'd also sent and received thousands of memos, the activity employed most by State paper-pushers to convince themselves they're doing something useful, sat in on too many boring meetings to count, been yelled at by self-important legislative aides, had projects scuttled by budget cuts, contended with some of the worst managers in State service, and, because I finally had a good agency head, worked two years longer than I'd intended. It was time to go.

On my last day, I didn't do any actual work. No wise remarks, please. State employees, most of them, do actually work, or try to. I'd spent the last few weeks trying to get everything up to speed. I'd even compiled a notebook on how to run the agency's rickety computerized information system, put together haphazardly over the years like a house built by different contractors, none of them very capable, and liable to tumble down at the slightest breeze. Keeping this system reasonably upright was the chief responsibility of my position..

I'd already had my retirement lunch, about which more later. My office mate Art Chang, took me to a Chinese restaurant for lunch. I thought the food was terrible, but he meant well so I pretended to like it. In the afternoon, I was presented with a birthday cake and everyone in the agency, led by our chief, Dr. Harriet George, and our Assistant Chief, Dr. Denny Morgan, gathered around to sing "Happy Birthday" to me. Their singing left something to be desired, but, like Art Chang, they meant well and I appreciated their effort. In some of my previous State jobs, nobody would have even noticed that I was leaving. I finished packing up and left for the light rail carrying a boxful of stuff I'd accumulated in the two years on my last job. I was done.

In one of his novels, C.P. Snow describes a young man leaving his job; I believe it was a civil service one. He'd been miserable there, but at the moment of leaving he experiences nostalgia and regret. I hadn't exactly been miserable as a civil servant but I hadn't been ecstatic either. As is the case with most people, it wasn't my life but a job that had enabled me to live my life.. It had enabled me to get married, buy a house and raise a family; in other words, live a typical middle-class life in our country in the twentieth century. Now that I was done with work, it would provide pretty good health benefits, by no means great, and a pretty decent, definitely not a great, retirement. The really good State retirement was reserved for elected officials, even those whose conduct was so bad they were thrown into jail. Looking back, I regretted I hadn't been able use more of whatever abilities I had (the State had no interest in the abilities of its great mass of employees) and hadn't been able to accomplish more. But it was too late for that now. As I've said, I was done. It was on to retirement.

The following evening, Saturday, I was relaxing, probably reading a book, in our living room when the doorbell rang. Our younger son Steve said it was Chuck, the boy who delivered our newspaper, the Sacramento Bee, there to collect for the month. I pulled myself out of my chair and got the checkbook; I didn't want to have Chuck standing out in the cold. When I opened the door it wasn't Chuck. A group of friends and neighbors had gathered for a surprise retirement/birthday party my wife Sally had spent the last few weeks arranging. Unlike some parties of this type, this one was really a surprise.

I was also surprised by the number of presents I received. Most were bottles of wine in fancy wrappings. There were a couple of books. The biggest gift was from our next-door neighbors, Arnie and Mary Segal, two tickets to the upcoming production of *Les' Miserables* at in the new downtown convention center. Arnie was one of my tennis buddies; we'd played together for years at our local swim and tennis club. I knew the tickets had to be expensive. Maybe I should have considered retiring earlier.

Later on, our older son Jack, who as usual had gone out somewhere, came over to join the party. Jack was at that time 23 and a junior at Chico State college, home for the holidays. He hadn't finished college yet for a variety of reasons and we weren't even sure if he'd go back for his senior year. Steve, our younger son, was 18 and going to our nearby community college. As with Jack, the plan was for him to go there two years and then finish up at a four-year college.

I started this Prologue with the standard question asked of me at the party: "So now that you're retired, what are you going to do?" My standard answer was that I hoped to be playing more tennis. I knew this was an evasive response. I did hope to be playing more tennis, but I couldn't be doing this all the time. Like most people, I'd spent the better part of my life working, five days a week, eight hours a day. If nothing else, this had provided a certain structure to my life.

Yes, I had other interests besides tennis; I liked to read and write for one thing. But I wasn't the type who had a workshop in the garage and I did yard work only out of necessity. The truth was that I really didn't know what I was going to do to fill in all those hours I'd spent working I knew I should have given this more thought, but I hadn't. I'd been too busy wrapping up things at work; at least, this was what I told myself. So the thought of retirement was a little scary. I'd heard that for wives of new retirees the thought might be even scarier. They'd have their husbands loafing around the house and getting underfoot all day.

I'd venture a guess that most new retirees feel the same way I did at that time, a little scared of the future. No office to go to. All right, it was a State office, but still it was in effect my second home. I'd get there around eight o'clock and have a coffee and a blueberry muffin I'd pick up in the building cafeteria. I checked my calendar to see what calls I had to answer, what meetings (if any) I had to attend and what projects were due. I had a computer, but this was in the days before all business was conducted by e-mail. I usually had some kind of report to prepare for Dr. George as I was considered to be a good "writer." At least I could write a simple declarative sentence. I could also look at a mass of numbers and usually be able pick out anything of interest in them, usually that costs had exceeded projections. Most days I spent some time with the programmer who kept, or tried to keep, our information system going, giving him encouragement and telling him what a great job he was doing. I knew which people at the data processing center to call when we had a rush job to do and needed priority in getting onto the computer. I also knew people in other departments I could call upon for information. Now all this would be gone.

Before going on to January and my first retirement day, a little about my circumstances at the time. First, like almost all Californians I know, I'm not a native. In my case, I'm a New Yorker, from the Bronx. Many World War II vets who were stationed in California or just passed through liked it and moved there. My "war" was Korea, then called a "police action." I was drafted the fall after graduating college. The Army, in a rare wise move, sent me to Europe, not Asia, to forestall the Communist menace. When I returned to New York, my first job was with an advertising agency. I wanted to be a copywriter and create great ad campaigns, but so did all the other young people in the agency. As stated, I had a certain knack with numbers and so was assigned to the agency's research department. Advertising was a glamour industry then and at first I was happy that I'd found a place in it, although dealing with sales and advertising figures every day was anything but glamorous.But after a while I found I didn't like it, not necessarily the work I was doing but the business itself.. In an ad agency, I felt, beneath all the hustle and bustle and supposed good fellowship, ran an undercurrent of fear. The fear was that a client could always leave and if enough clients left there went the agency.

I also didn't particularly like New York. Maybe this was partly because I wasn't earning enough to be able to afford living in my own place. Advertising may have been a glamour industry but the starting salaries it paid were pretty dismal. Every day I took the subway from the Bronx down to Grand Central Station in Manhattan, trying to do the New York Times crossword puzzle while holding onto a strap and trying to keep my balance in a car full of jostling people. I liked some of my co-workers at the agency, but most of them seemed intent on only one thing, getting ahead, no matter what the cost. And, as I've said, there was always the underlying fear from one day to the next that your job and possibly the entire agency might be gone.

All in all, New York seemed like a big, crowded, noisy, dirty city. It was also becoming, at that time, a dangerous city. I'd grown up in it and that was fine, but when I thought about it I found it hard to imagine bringing up a family there and this was what I eventually wanted to do. I'd met a fellow from San Francisco, a UC Berkeley grad, while in the Army and he was always telling me what a great city it was. I contacted him and he told me to come on out.

I did and camped out in his place for a while. I'd hoped to find a non-advertising job, but after a couple of months of looking I had to settle for one in another ad agency. I'd already been type-cast. But I moved into my own apartment. I bought my first car (in New York, nobody I knew owned a car) and learned how to drive. I thought life in San Francisco was a big improvement. Still, there was always that fear of having my job disappear. After a year at this agency, I had a review and was given a raise, but it wasn't much of one. And any promotion seemed far off in the future. Several people at the agency told me that my best chance of getting ahead was to look for a job in another agency. I didn't want to have to keep jumping from one ad agency to another in order to get ahead.

I saw an ad for a State job in the paper. It would do no harm to inquire, I thought, so I sent a letter. I didn't know it but this particular agency was desperately trying to fill research analyst jobs. I had an interview and was hired on the spot. The pay was a little below what I was making at the agency, but in six months I could take an exam and advance up to the next job level, where I'd be making more. Then there was health insurance and retirement benefits. I wasn't terribly concerned with these at the time, but I knew they were there. Above all, there was job security. I knew that with the State I couldn't be called into someone's office, as had happened with several friends of mine, and be told the agency was cutting back and they were being let go. At least at that time this was the case.

As I've mentioned, I couldn't imagine raising a family in New York. I was of the 50's generation so I planned to get married, some day anyway, and have a family. In San Francisco, I met Sally, an occupational therapist, originally from Georgia, now working in an Oakland hospital. Probably sooner than I'd expected, we married and life took another turn. I transferred to Sacramento to accept a promotion and because that's where we could afford to buy a house, then around $20,000, which today sounds unbelievable. Then we had our two sons and life took still another turn. Sally got an occupational therapist job in Sacramento, then, after Jack was born, stayed home until Steve started kindergarten. She then went to work part-time as a teacher's aide and was currently working at a nearby office taking catalog orders for J.C. Penney.

We had moved from our first (starter) house to a larger one in a suburb of Sacramento called Carmichael. The larger house, three-plus bedrooms, was 25 years old. As anyone who's ever lived in a house of advanced age knows, some appliance is always breaking down and something—a fence, a door, a gate— always has to be fixed. I've mentioned that in New York nobody I knew owned a car. As I lived in the Bronx and went to high school in Manhattan I rode the subway there for four years If you had sons growing up in Carmichael, that meant getting them cars as soon as they could legally drive so they could get to their high school and also to their summer jobs. So, besides an aged house, we had three cars to maintain, a 1984 Camry Sally and I drove, a 1980 Mazda for son Jack and one of those little green Hondas common at that time for Steve. We also had two cats, the venerable Binky, who'd been a member of our family for years, and Mickey, a younger cat, who'd joined us two years ago...

On Sunday, the 30th, I had my 61st birthday. Since we'd had the big party the night before, we didn't do anything special. On Monday, New Year's Eve, our sons both went out somewhere while we went to across the street to a little party one of our our neighbors gave every year. We played cards and other games while worrying about what our sons were doing. Luckily, whatever it was, they survived and were there on Tuesday, New Year's Day, for Sally's traditional roast pork and black-eyed peas Southern New Year's dinner. . On Wednesday, January 2nd, the important event was that I slept in and didn't go to work. Retirement had begun.

JANUARY

I would like to start out by saying that my first day of retirement was a significant one. But no, I didn't wake up with a light bulb going on as I suddenly realized what I wanted to do with the rest of my life. I had no epiphanies. I didn't rush to my desk and start a long-buried novel. I didn't have any world-shaking ideas, like an iPhone or an iPod. I didn't resolve to dedicate the rest of my life to helping my fellow man, or even to save the whales. In fact, I don't really remember what I did that first day. I do remember though that one of the things I did and continued to do through the month of January was to catch up on my sleep.

I know there's supposed to be no such thing as catching up on your sleep. Once you've had a sleepless night, that's supposed to be it. My body thought otherwise. In the past 27 years working for the State, whose hours began at 8 AM, I'd get up at 6:15 every morning. My morning routine was to wash, brush teeth, dress, have orange juice and an instant breakfast, then walk to the bus stop to take the bus to my office. In the last few years, it was take the bus to the light rail station, a transportation improvement that made getting downtown 15 to 20 minutes longer. When I got off the bus, or the train, I walked to my building, went to the cafeteria as described to get my coffee and a blueberry muffin (our cafeteria had delicious blueberry muffins, which I missed), then it was up to my office to look at my calendar and start the day.

Now, with no office to go to, I slept in, usually to ten o'clock, rose, had a leisurely breakfast of juice, cereal with fruit, possibly a coffee cake, coffee, then a second cup of coffee while I finished reading the newspaper and did the daily crossword puzzle. This (except for the blueberry muffin) was a considerable improvement over my early morning work routine. But then there was the question: what to do for the rest of the day?

There was an exception to my new leisurely life style one morning in the first week of January. Sally, who was awake and out of bed to go to J.C. Penney, came into our bedroom and roused me. It was nine AM. I had a call from Rochelle, my senior clerk. A data processing problem had come up. She described the problem. I gave her instructions on how to get around it, I hoped. I also asked her not to call before ten unless it was an extreme emergency. Rochelle called again that afternoon. The problem had been resolved. I hoped my old agency could get along without me. At the same time, I had to admit I felt a little pleased that they had to call upon me for my expertise.

I've mentioned that I was a little scared of what I'd be doing with all the extra time on my hands. I guess I spent a good deal of time in the house that January but I wasn't one of those husbands who got in the way of their wives; at least not yet. For one thing, I had to organize my new office. Our older son Jack had returned to college in Chico and my new office was to be in his old bedroom. First,. with the help of our younger son Steve, I moved my old roll top desk from our bedroom, making Sally happy as it took up a lot of space, to Jack's room. I also put a new bookcase in the room. With the consultation of Steve, who was an early computer "whiz," I'd bought a computer and a printer. Again, with Steve's help, I set up the computer, or, I should say, he set up the computer while I looked on. I spent a lot of January afternoons in my office, "putting my papers in order," which usually meant throwing away a lot of stuff. Binky and Mickey took a great interest in what I was doing and looked on with approval as I disposed of all the junk I'd been keeping around for years. While I was doing all this, there were still times when I felt at a loss for something to do.

Since they're important actors in my first year in retirement, just a little about our sons, Jack and Steve. Jack had grown from a plumpish child into a tall, athletic teenager. He tested high and could have been in "gifted child" classes had he wanted. As it was, he held his own in his classes without studying too much until hitting senior year in high school and that's when "senioritis" hit, with a vengeance. He started cutting classes, stopped studying at all, his grades crashed and for a time it seemed he wouldn't be able to graduate. We also suspected that at this time he was experimenting with marijuana. In short, Jack had gone from average kid to being a rebel, though in what cause we had no idea..

After a lot of talking on our part, Jack somehow managed to do well enough to get his diploma and then went to our community college for two years, getting barely passing grades. We asked around and it seemed that of all the four-year State colleges he might be able to get into the best was Chico State. It had the reputation of being a party school, but the parents of all the kids who'd gone there told us it also had a good academic program. It wasn't too far away, about a two-hour drive, and Jack would be away from Sacramento and certain of his friends who we felt were not exactly a good influence on him. So, after he'd been accepted, Jack, over his objections, went off to Chico State.

If we'd thought that a change of scenery and being on his own would change things, we were overly optimistic. Once away from home, Jack let his hair grow long and grew a beard, making him look like a throwback to the hippie days of the 1960's. He also seemed to be constantly on the verge of flunking out, something which he professed not to care about. As he told us repeatedly, he didn't see what good college was anyway. So that was Jack in 1991.

If Jack was our "bad" son, I suppose, in classic style, Steve was our "good" son. He wasn't athletic, he wasn't a top student and he didn't have many friends. When he was eleven, his best (I won't say his only) friend moved away and it left him in a funk. Out of desperation, we'd gotten him a computer, from Radio Shack (one of my data processing friends at the agency had recommended it). To our pleasant surprised, he took to it like the proverbial duck to water. In a short time, he was writing his own programs and eventually he even put together his own computer to replace the Radio Shack one. Right now he was in his second year at our community college, doing fairly well in his classes and planning to apply to a number of four-year colleges in the spring. Needless to say, he was going to major in computer science.

Aside from my indoor project of "organizing" my office, I had an outdoor project. We'd had a very cold December and some of the plastic pipes of our back yard watering system had cracked. I've already indicated I wasn't a gung-ho handyman, but these had to be fixed before spring and, being retired, I had no excuse for not at least trying my hand at repairing them. This meant measuring, sawing, trying to fit pieces together and visiting handyman stores (before Home Depot and Loew's), where I attempted to explain what I needed. For me, this project was a major undertaking and possibly it was a good thing I had this to occupy me.

Sometime in mid-January, I undertook something else. Like many seniors, I was going to take advantage of being retired to go back to school. The community college our sons went to was only a ten-minute drive away and gave a whole variety of classes, ranging from car repair (which I could have used) to plumbing (ditto) to reading the classics and writing. On this morning, I drove to the college to see if there were any courses that sounded interesting and that I could sign up for.

I found that several thousand other people, or at least it seemed that many, had also come to sign up for classes. Most were regular college-age students, some were middle-aged and a few were old folks like me. Every time I tried to get into a class that sounded attractive, I was told that it was too late, the class was already filled up. I ended by getting into a Shakespeare class (you could always learn something from Shakespeare, I told myself) that met one morning a week. .

What about tennis? If December had been unusually cold, January was unusually warm, with nice sunny days almost the entire month. I'd been a member of our local swim and tennis club since we moved to Carmichael; in fact, the proximity of the club was one of the reasons we moved there. The boys could walk just around the corner to the club. They took their first swimming lessons there and then, when they got older, tennis lessons. This was in the 70's, during the big tennis boom. Almost everyone in the neighborhood, it seemed, was taking up the game, wives as well as husbands. I'm sure that two or three of the subsequent divorces among people we knew had their start in conflicts on the tennis courts. Sally, I'm happy to say, never seriously took up the sport..

As for myself, as everyone else was playing, I figured I might as well, too.Growing up in the Bronx, I'd been a pretty good handball player, but I'd never touched a tennis racket. In fact, tennis was considered a sissy sport and if anyone ever appeared with a tennis racket on our street I'm sure it would have been wrapped around his neck I'd played handball when I lived in San Francisco until one morning I woke up with a terrific pain in my left shoulder. The doctor I saw told me it was bursitis. He gave me a cortisone shot and that took care of it, but I was leery of playing handball again. In handball, you hit the ball with your left as well as your right hand. With tennis, I'd be using only my right arm so I didn't have to worry about the bursitis flaring up again..

I took a few introductory lessons and started to play. Tennis might not be handball, but it was a good workout and I liked the tactics of the game. In time, I became a passable doubles player. As in handball, I seemed to have a knack for discovering the other players' weaknesses and, being pretty competitive, I never hesitated to exploit them.Over the years I gained the reputation of being a tough tournament player, winning a number of trophies, plus t-shirts, mugs and other such prizes. Such success that I had came about, I think, because most of the other club members got too excited about playing in a tournament and, as they say on the sports page, pressed too hard. I tried to remain calm and to, again as they say, play within myself. Of course, in club tournaments, which were almost always doubles, having a good partner was also helpful. In any case, playing tennis became my chief form of exercise. I'd never liked working out on machines in a gym.

I usually played doubles at the club with my next-door neighbor Arnie and two other neighbors; Charlie Combs and Mike Snyder, we were dubbed "the fearsome foursome." We played Saturday mornings and, when weather permitted, one night a week. It so happened that January that year had almost perfect tennis weather. Instead of the winter fog and rain that was typical of Sacramento, it was mostly sunny and warm. So I was ready to go. Now that I was retired, playing just twice a week didn't seem enough. Unfortunately, my three tennis buddies were all still working and I didn't know of any other club members who were retired so I could play with them at the club during weekdays.

When I had occasion to drive downtown to work I passed Carmichael Park, where I always saw some old-timers on the tennis courts early in the morning. On the second week of January I drove to the park, getting there at nine, and, sure enough, two of the six courts were already occupied. I'd brought a basket of balls (the basket was a birthday present from my sons) so I went to a third court and started to practice serving. After a while, two elderly gentlemen came over, one short and ruddy-faced, the other tall with a white moustache, and asked if they could join me. They introduced themselves as Jeff and Maurice. They told me they expected their friend Sam to come along soon and after we'd hit around for a few minutes he did, a slim, fit-looking oldster. We split into doubles teams, I had Maurice for a partner, and played a couple of sets, splitting them 4-6 and 6-4; these old guys were pretty good.

As I was to learn, a dozen or so of these old guys came to Carmichael Park regularly. They all knew each other and the park was to them pretty much what my club was to its members. Maurice was known as the "Mayor," because he functioned as the "club" president, allocating players to the courts to keep the sides competitive. The players were of all kinds. Maurice was a retired lawyer. Jeff had been a jusge. Sam had been in television. Among the others was a lawyer, a dentist and a few other former State workers. They were a friendly bunch and so I became a member of the Carmichael Park club.

Because the weather was so good all through the month, I had more than my fill of tennis; in fact, not using great judgment, I overdid it. As I'd grown older, like most club players, I'd succumbed to the aches and pains inherent to playing the game. These included sprained knees and wrists, sore shoulders and occasional groin pulls. Now, playing so much during the month, I experienced what tennis players feared the most; I felt a twinge in my elbow. This was the usual first sign of that most dreaded injury of them all, tennis elbow. Needless to say, still not using great judgment, I didn't stop playing, as I should have. I took an anti-inflammatory pill before going to the courts and iced my elbow afterwards.

While I was organizing my office, trying to repair the broken plastic pipes, starting to read Shakespeare and playing too much tennis, other things were going on in the outside world. Going back to the previous year, the UN passed a resolution telling Iraq to get out of Iraq by January 15th. On January 16th, Iraq hadn't left Kuwait, so the war officially began. On the domestic front, the Governor released his budget, which called for a big increase in State college fees, not good news. It also had cuts in State spending and a few added taxes. Also, on Sunday, January 20th, my New York Giants had beaten the San Francisco 49ers 15-13 on a last-minute field goal to win the NFL championship and get into the Super Bowl. The next Sunday, the Giants beat the Buffalo Bills 20-19 as the Bills missed a last-minute field goal. For the next year, I could talk about the defending Super Bowl champs, the New York Giants.

Meanwhile, something that was to become an even more important activity in my retirement than tennis had, like the Iraqi war, been set into motion during the previous year. I've said "more about my retirement lunch later." On the big day, Sally drove downtown and picked me up at my office. The lunch was in mid-December and it was, to my surprise, at the venerable, and expensive, Firehouse restaurant, in Old Sacramento. Almost everyone in my agency, a relatively small one to be sure, was there. Dr. George made a nice speech about my repairing the agency's once all-but-broken data system. My friend Art Chang presented me with a plaque having something to do with my lite rail ridership. My senior clerk Rochelle, on behalf of the agency, made a little speech, then gave me a gift card to one of Sacramento's large department stores, for a pretty good amount.I think I've indicated that I was a little cynical about my State experience, but I have to admit that at the moment I was touched. It was rare in State service to have your efforts appreciated. I stood up and told my former co-workers this.

I now have to introduce Jean Zeiger, the first teacher whose aide Sally had been. As Sally had stopped being an aide (the job was stressful), so Jean had stopped being a teacher to open up a gift shop downtown. The shop hadn't panned out and Jean was having a close-out sale. After my retirement lunch, we drove there and Sally bought a few things. Jean is one of those super-energetic persons who put the rest of us to shame. She bicycled thousands of miles on weekends and she and her husband had bicycled all over Europe. I knew she'd be doing something after the shop had closed so I asked about her future plans.

She said she knew Karl Engel, the editor of the Sacramento Press, which was a weekly alternative newspaper, and had talked to him about working there, whether it would be writing or something else, she didn't know. She asked me what I'd be doing after I retired and I gave her my standard answer about playing more tennis. Jean asked if I'd be interested in doing something at the Sacramento Press. I replied that I might be. She took my phone number and said she'd pass it along to Karl Engel. Well, we all know what happens when someone says he or she will pass along your phone number. Nothing. It's like someone saying, "Let's do lunch." You say, "Sure," and you never hear anything about it again. I was pretty confident I'd never hear from Karl Engel. In this, I was to be mistaken.

I knew about the Sacramento Press because it was one of several free publications that appeared in a stand in the lobby of my State building. Since it was free, I'd pick it up every so often to read at lunch. The paper was published downtown and was mostly concerned with downtown issues. Karl Engel was against bigger buildings, more developments and anything that would bring more traffic. He wanted the downtown "neighborhoods" to be left as they were. He also had the typical "liberal" outlook; he was concerned about the problems of gays, minorities and the homeless. And of course he was opposed to the upcoming Iraqi war.

It wasn't until I read a little book by Karl Engel (that he sent me a few years later) that I found out a little more about the Sacramento Press. He writes that he got a degree in journalism in New York in 1972. He couldn't find work as a reporter in San Francisco so came home to Sacramento in 1974. Further on, he describes himself as an ex-busboy just fired from an Old Sacramento restaurant for punching the headwaiter, who had a few thousand dollars, no personal or professional entanglements, so, what the hell, why not follow up on a friend's suggestion to start a newspaper in Sacramento? This was in 1975.

As might be inferred from his comment about punching a headwaiter, Karl Engel was a bit of a character. Even though I didn't know about this incident, I, along with most who knew of him at the time, regarded him as part of the downtown scene. He was a small man with glasses and a beard and piercing blue eyes behind those glasses. Wearing old clothes that looked as if they came from a thrift shop and an old, misshapen hat, he pedaled around downtown on a rusty bicycle delivering the Sacramento Press to various news stands. I wondered if Jean had formed a bond with Karl Engel because they both rode bicycles. In any case, Karl Engel didn't seem the kind of person likely to call me. As I wrote above, in this I was to be mistaken.

On Monday, January 14, I spent the morning going to the supermarket, the bakery, the drug store and to Ace hardware to get the stuff for fixing the plastic pipes. When I returned home, I had a phone call. It was Karl Engel of the Sacramento Press. He'd gotten my number from Jean Zeiger. He wanted to know if I was interested in doing some "reporting." No, he wasn't interested in anything involving the State, about which I might conceivably have some knowledge. He didn't have any suggestions about what I should report about. He'd leave that up to me. I put down the phone. Well, at least he'd called. I had lunch, then went out to the back yard to work on those pipes.

In the last week of the month, I had another call from my (former) senior clerk, Rochelle, this time at 10 AM. The computer run to produce cost and utilization tables for the last quarter had been made, finally, but there were problems with some of the tables. I told her I'd call Art Chang and talk it over with him. I reached Art in the afternoon and we had about an hour's discussion. The problem appeared to be that some of the counties reporting had made changes in their tapes and evidently the programs we used hadn't allowed for them. We agreed on what had to be done and then another run would be made. I had mixed feelings about this incident. It was a little annoying having to deal with something like this after I'd retired. At the same time, it was again nice to know that I was still needed. .

I had some other communications from the State during that week. I received a nice check for unused sick leave and vacation time. This was another of the few good things the State did for its employees. Your sick leave and vacation days accumulated from year to year and if you were sparing in your use of them you were paid for the balances left when you retired. The check was welcome as Steve's Mazda had needed a brake repair during the month. Also, I received the estimate of my Deferred Compensation, at that time kind of a State 401K. Again, this was a good thing the State did; you could defer part of your pay up to a certain amount and the State matched that amount. I'd deferred up to the maximum and the Deferred Comp at retirement came to a goodly amount.. I arranged to have it paid in monthly amounts for the next ten years, or until the time I had to start withdrawing from our IRA's. Money, as I'd soon found out, when the bills kept coming in, was as important to have in retirement as when you were working and had a monthly paycheck..

On the last day of the month I finally finished with the plastic pipes in the back yard. This was the moment of truth. I turned on the water and stood back. The sprinklers sent out their sprays of water. The pipes didn't break. Success. This might have been even better than the Giants winning the Super Bowl. The next day, February 1st, after a month of dry weather, it rained.

FEBRUARY

In the first week of February, I started my Shakespeare class. The teacher, Mr. Schroeder, was an older man, although younger than I was, who said he'd studied at Stratford-on-Avon and had acted on the local stage. He also acknowledged to being an expert on Shakespeare. Our first play was going to be "The Merchant of Venice."

During that week we had a call from our son Jack in Chico, telling us he needed more money for his text books. He was coincidentally also taking a course in Shakespeare. He didn't like it. He felt the same about his courses in general and couldn't wait to get out of Chico. When we'd visited the college before Jack started his classes there, we found that it had a nice campus placed right in what seemed to be a nice little college town. We liked it. All of the kids we knew who'd gone to Chico had also liked it. Jack might have been the only student who ever went there that hated it.

Meanwhile, our son Steve was busy applying to four-year colleges. His grades were pretty good, not great, and we thought he had a good chance of getting into San Diego State, which was supposed to have a respectable computer science program. He was also going to apply to Cal Poly, another school with a well-regarded computer science program. Of course, the college with the top-rated computer science program was UC Berkeley. We didn't think Steve had much chance there as we'd heard that only students with a 4.0 average, or at least close to it, were accepted. But Steve wanted to apply there anyway so we told him to go ahead.

The rain that had ended January didn't last very long. The next Monday morning I went again to the Carmichael Park tennis courts. The first time I served I felt a sharp pain in my elbow. I immediately said I couldn't play any more. A few minutes later, I went over to an empty court and tried to serve again, very gently. Again, the sharp pain. No doubt about it, I had tennis elbow. My State health plan was a large HMO. When I got home I called, not my regular HMO doctor, but another HMO doctor, Dr. F—, who lived in our neighborhood and was a member of our swim and tennis club. He didn't come to the club very often but was a very good tennis player. He seemed to think a cortisone shot would help, as it had helped with my bursitis, and referred me to still another HMO doctor. I called and made an appointment. I was learning one of the basic truths of being retired, and therefore of being an old guy. Now that you had the time to play tennis (or whatever sport you engaged in) your aging body wouldn't let you.

Later that week, Sally and I made a trip to downtown Sacramento. We went to the fairly new downtown library first, then browsed around the stores in the Downtown Plaza. We had lunch, then drove to a bagel store near to my old State building. I had a coupon so we bought a dozen bagels for ourselves and another for the people in my old office.

We had coffee with Rochelle and another woman from my old office in the building cafeteria. My coffee was on the house, courtesy of Tina, one of the cashiers, who gave me a big hug when we come in. After, we went up to my old agency. Dr. Morgan, the assistant chief, was there. He told me that Dr. George had proposed paying me $50 for an hour's consulting time, or would buy dinner for Sally and myself. What do you know, like a retired business executive, I'd become a highly-paid consultant. I told Dr. Morgan I'd call and let him know.

That Saturday Sally and I went to see "*Les Miserables*" at the Community Center, using the tickets given me at my birthday/retirement party. Our seats were in the front row center of the Grand Tier, which was like the first balcony of a Broadway theater. "Les Mis" was at the time a new-type musical, with everything being sung, like an opera.. The production was very well done, the scenery was spectacular and the actors talented. Still, after it was all over, I couldn't have told you what any of the musical numbers were. I preferred the old-fashioned musicals of the forties and fifties when you came out of the theater humming the songs you'd just heard. No doubt about it, I was now a bona-fide old guy.

What had happened to the Sacramento Press? I suppose it indicates the importance I placed on it at the time that I'd waited almost a month before calling Karl Engel back and I sometimes wonder if I'd had done so if I hadn't been sidelined from playing tennis. In any case, I'd done some thinking about what I could write. The downside of all the nice dry sunny weather we were having and what everyone was talking about was that Sacramento was in a drought. We even had certain days of the week in which we were not supposed to water our lawns. I called Karl Engel and told him this seemed a good subject for a story. He seemed unenthusiastic but told me to write something and he'd see about printing it..

I took this as a go-ahead so called the Carmichael Water District. I told the secretary I contacted that I was a reporter for the Sacramento Press and that I wanted to do a story on how the water district was handling the drought. I tried to sound as if I knew what I was doing, like the reporters on TV and in the movies. I want that story, lady. The secretary was gone from the phone for a long time and I thought that my journalistic career might be over before it even started. But then she returned and told me I had an appointment to see the district's General Manager, a Mr. McGuffy, the following week. I said, "Thanks, babe": no, I thanked her politely, asked her for directions and jotted the date down on my calendar. Little did I know that history, of a sort, was being made.

On the appointed day, I drove to the Water District's office, located in a desolate part of Carmichael I'd never known about before. I'd equipped myself with a stenographer's notebook I'd just bought in the drug store for 98 cents and two ballpoint pens. I also had a blue binder with "State of California" printed on it that was left over from my old job. At the District's office, nobody asked me for my press credentials, which was good as I didn't have any. I was ushered into the General Manager's office within a few minutes and greeted warmly by Mr. McGuffy, who was an amiable man in his forties. If he was surprised to be interviewed by such an old guy, he didn't mention it. I didn't think that he'd been interviewed very often by any member of the press. Maybe I was the first one.

He was very much concerned about what troubles the drought might bring if it continued and gave me a whole host of facts and figures about the water district. To him, the drought was serious business, as serious as an earthquake would be to the entire state.. I stayed there for about an hour, busily taking notes on my steno pad, and learning more about the water situation than I ever wanted to know. Finally, I told him I had enough information for a story, asked him a few questions about himself and how he'd come to his present job, then I thanked him, he thanked me, and I left. Now all I had to do was write something.

When I returned home, I told everyone I didn't want to be disturbed (actually, no one was home except the cats) and immediately sat down at my computer. I wanted to start writing while the interview was still fresh in my mind. I didn't know it then, but this was a procedure I'd use with all of my stories. Binky as usual sat on the back of my chair; she liked to see what I was writing. Mickey as usual was up on the bookcase so she could survey the territory and make sure nothing could get at her. I looked over my notes and, after a few moment's thought, started in... My title, or headline, was "How One Water District is Coping with the Drought."

Of course, I knew nothing about writing a news story, but I did know that you should start with a "hook" to catch the reader's attention. So my first sentence was: "Never on Monday, or on any other day." I went on to write: "This is the prospect for outside watering facing hom-eowners in the Carmichael Water District if the worst possible scenario occurs this summer." I didn't know it. but I was following in a hallowed journalistic tradition, giving the reader the worst possible scenario. The story was 500 words and had quite a few quotes from Mr. McGuffy When I was done, I printed it out on my printer. In those olden days there was no such thing as e-mail, so I had to put the story in an envelope and address it to the Sacramento Press. I also put in a little cover letter and, to make sure, called the Press's office. Karl Engle wasn't there but I spoke to a woman named Anna, explained who I was and told her I was sending in the story.

Just as I was about to go to my Shakespeare class one morning later in the week, Karl Engel called. He said my water story was good and that he would use it. Actually, the draught was becoming big news and the Bee had a piece about it later in the month, but mine appeared first, I had a scoop. Karl Engle asked, presumably because I was now a water expert, if I'd like to go to some agricultural board meeting. The meeting was on a Saturday, my tennis day, and it was in some remote place an hour's drive away. I told him I would like to but I was really busy and couldn't do it, hoping that wouldn't kill my budding journalistic career. He grunted and hung up. Nothing had been said about my doing any other stories.

I was a little surprised at how my Shakespeare class was conducted. I'd expected Mr. Schroeder, the Shakespeare expert, to expound on the themes of the "Merchant of Venice" and possibly tell us how they were stilll relevant today. Instead, he showed us tapes of a BBC production, three in all, one tape per session. While we watched, he was off doing something, I don't know what. It seemed to me he had a pretty easy gig. In my college days, we didn't get to watch tapes; we had to read what we were studying. Bit I didn't mind watching the tapes; it was a good production. The actor playing Shylock.and the actress playing Portia were both excellent, and I recognized the actor playing one of Antonio's friends as a lead character in a spy series then showing on TV. Still, being old-fashioned, I did read the play. I wondered how many of my younger classmates did.

Sometime after the middle of February I went to see the HMO doctor I'd been referred to for a cortisone shot. She was a woman, quite a big, heavy-set woman. After I'd rolled up my sleeve, she produced a giant needle and, before I knew what was happening, jabbed it into my elbow. It hurt like hell. She assured me the pain would subside and I'd shortly be as good as new. The elbow continued to hurt for the rest of the day and then for the next week. This isn't what had happened when I'd gotten the cortisone shot for bursitis in my shoulder. So, instead of playing tennis, I had a painful elbow and could barely do anything for the rest of the month. Needless to say, the fine weather continued while I fumed but couldn't do anything about it. I'm afraid that for period of time I was the retired husband underfoot, complaining to Sally about my sad fate..

I wasn't the only one in my family to be in pain. When I retired, Sally and I agreed that we'd do some traveling. Both of us had been to Europe, Sally when she'd taken a year off after working in Bellevue in New York, I when I was stationed in Germany after being drafted during Korea. We'd planned a trip to somewhere in Europe, but then the Gulf War had started and we were a little leery about going abroad. My parents, who still lived in the Bronx, always spent part of the year in Miami, where they stayed in a "residential" hotel. Miami seemed as good a place as any to go to; neither of us had ever been there, it was a "tourist" city and we'd get to see my folks. We'd booked a flight for early March and made reservations for a ten-days stay at a hotel on the beach. Now my sister, who lived in Long Island, called. Her unwelcome news was that my mother had fallen and broken her hip.

I called my father that evening. My mother was in the hospital. They'd put a pin in her hip. She'd be in the hospital two weeks, then she'd have therapy to learn how to walk with the pin. Later, I called the hospital and talked to my mother. She was getting something for her pain, but her leg still hurt. No matter, she wanted to go home as soon as possible She didn't like hospitals. That sounded like my mother. Sally and I talked and agreed that we'd still go to Miami, although we'd probably do a lot less sight-seeing than we'd planned.(I should mention here that Sally's own parents had both passed away, her father at an early age from cancer just after we'd married and her mother a few years before.)

Later in the month, I drove down to my old State building to do my consulting bit. I had lunch with the Assistant Chief, Dr. Morgan, who told me the State, in line with the Governor's proposed budget, was cutting back and that the agency was having a hard time. After lunch, Rochelle, Art Chang and I adjourned to his office. We reviewed the notebook I'd compiled, which I'd thought clearly outlined the workings of the data system. Evidently, although it was perfectly clear to me, it wasn't that clear to others less familiar with the system and all of its little quirks.

. We went over the points that seemed to need clarification and Rochelle and Art took lots of notes. When we were satisfied with that, we went on to a couple of rush jobs Dr. George had ordered. Art and I put the programs needed for these jobs on the computer while Rochelle looked over our shoulders. By this time, it was almost four. I thought I'd contributed enough time and I wanted to beat the commute traffic home. Before I left, I stopped briefly into Dr. George's office. I didn't feel right about accept payment for my consulting services so we set a date for her to take Sally and me to dinner.

During the first half of February, there was a kind of phony Iraq war as various "peace" proposals were floated, by Saddam and by our good friends, the peace-loving Russians. Also, the usual "peaceniks' in this country had come out of the woodwork, lamenting our aggressive posture and predicting that thousands of our troops would be coming back in body bags. I suppose this sounds pretty familiar. On Friday, the 22nd, the radio reported that President Bush (the first one) had given Saddam an ultimatum to start pulling out of Kuwait by noon the next day and to complete the pull-out in five days. Later that day, television news had the usual rambling speech from Iraq rejecting the ultimatum, calling it shameless, and saying that Bush was an enemy of God and a friend of Satan. This too sounds pretty familiar. From one war to the other, Saddam stuck to the same script.

On Saturday night, Sally and I, with Steve, went to a local dinner theater; another one of my retirement gifts was a $50 gift certificate to it. The dinner and the play, something about Sherlock Holmes, were both okay, but also expensive as the total bill, even with the gift certificate, came to over $100. I guess that's why we hadn't gone there before. Driving back, I turned on the car radio and we found out that the ground war had started at 8 PM Eastern time. By Thursday, the 28th, after four days of the ground war, it was all over, for then, anyway. President Bush declared a cease-fire and the Iraqis accepted (supposedly) all of our terms. Little did we know at the time.

The Sacramento Press had a news stand at the community college and the next time I went to my Shakespeare class after sending in my water story, I took out a paper but no water story in it, just the usual stories about gays and the homeless. On Monday, the 25th, Karl Engle called. He wanted me to do another story, about a Russian family that was staying with a family in Carmichael. The Russian family had come over on some kind of cultural deal and went around singing peace songs. The lady in whose house they were staying had called Karl and he'd called me. I guess he considered me his Carmichael correspondent. He gave me a name and a number to call. So I was still a reporter.

I asked him if the water issue was out yet and he said it was. I went out to do some errands that morning, then stopped at the Carmichael library, which had the Sacramento Press. I looked into it. Yes, there was my water story, with a byline, by Martin Green. The library would let me take only two copies. As soon as I arrive back home, I showed my story to Sally. Just call me "Scoop" Green, I said.

The next morning I called about the Russian family and was invited to come right over. The Carmichael lady's home was a large and expensive-looking house on Winding Way, not far from the community college. She was not your typical suburban housewife. She was an art therapist (whatever that was), a teacher with a doctor's degree in education and a member of Grandmothers for Peace, although she wasn't a grandmother. It was on a Grandmothers for Peace tour of Russia that she stayed with the Russian family that was now staying with them The family consisted of a father, who was an architect, an artist and a former professional musician; a mother, who was a language school graduate who taught English; and a 14-year old son, who composed songs, played the piano and other instruments and, like my son Steve, was a computer whiz. Altogether, quite a group.

During their stay in Carmichael, the Russian family had appeared at various school assemblies, singing their peace songs, attended a number of conferences and had gone to the annual United Nations dinner in Sacramento, where they'd met then Mayor Anne Rudin and had received a letter of welcome from her. I thought it best in the midst of all this peace and harmony not to bring up the Iraq war. It took me two hours to get all the Russian family information down. Sometime during our session, the doorbell rung. It was a young lady who said she was a photographer from the Sacramento Press. She came in and took a lot of pictures. When everything was done, I went back home and, going to my computer and with Binky and Mickey looking on, wrote my story, calling it "Russians in Carmichael." I started it with:

> "You say potato,
> and I say kahrtophil;
> You say tomato,
> and I say parmeedohry …"

After this, I wrote: "The house guests being hosted by S—F—— and her family in their Carmichael residence are somewhat out of the ordinary," which was putting it mildly. Upon re-reading the story now, I see I also wrote: "The F—— household, in addition to two daughters, includes two dogs, two cats, three baby African gray parrots, three doves, several fish and one bunny." Luckily, all of these weren't in evidence; the people were more than enough. I continued to put down everything I'd learned and ended up with a story that I figured would take up three or four pages. Well, I thought, if Karl Engle thought it was too long, he could cut it down. He was the editor.

I mailed in the story that afternoon. The next week I got the Sacramento Press from the community college stand and my story, with a big picture of everyone, was on the front page. It continued on for three more pages in the back of the newspaper. I wondered what the Press readers, used to reading about downtrodden homeless people and gays and lesbians, thought of the F—— family and their Russian guests. When I got home, I immediately showed the paper to Sally and said, "Just call me Front Page Green." By the way, if you haven't guessed it already, the Sacramento Press, although it did pay its photographers, didn't pay its reporters for their stories; it was strictly volunteer work. So I had to be satisfied with the fame without the fortune.

Just before the end of the month, I went down to my tennis club and, very gingerly, served a few balls over the net. No pain in my elbow. We were going on our Miami trip in a week so I thought that was sufficient. I'd begin my tennis comeback after we got back. I was going to begin something else when we returned. Karl Engle called again and asked if I'd like to come down to the Sacramento Press office on Monday morning and do some editing. I told him I'd see about it when we returned from our trip to Miami. Just before we left, our son Jack called from Chico to tell us that Mazda he drove was making funny noises. I told him to take it into the shop to have it looked at. So there'd be another car repair bill to look forward to when we returned. Also, before we left, I called Art Chang. Everything seemed to be going okay, he said. So my role as a consultant seemed to be over. Maybe the agency could struggle along without me after all.

MARCH

We flew to Miami during the first week of March, arriving on a Tuesday evening. This was just about the time that several German tourists in Miami had been held up by, dare I say it without being accused of being a racist, black kids, robbed and in a couple of cases killed. Evidently the kids spotted the tourists by the kind of licenses on their rental cars, followed them on the highway, then rear-ended them to make them stopWhen we rented our car, a big guy (he was black) gave us a sheet of instructions on what not to do if we encountered any hostile natives, no matter what their color. One thing we should not do on any account, he warned us, was to stop if anyone hit us from behind. We should just keep going.

With this reassuring advice, we drove off for Miami, nervously looking in the rearview mirror for suspiciously acting vehicles. We made it to Miami unscathed, found the proper bridge to cross over to Miami Beach and drove up Collins Avenue, the main drag, passing what seemed like millions of hotels, some big and new, some small and old. Our hotel, when we finally came to it after what seemed like hours of driving, was one of the big ones but it looked pretty old. So did the staff. .The desk clerk looked like an octogenarian, at least, and "bellboy" was a misnomer for the white-haired man who rode up in the creaking elevator with us and who looked too frail to handle our bags. We'd had a long day and I didn't feel like any more driving so we had supper in the hotel's basement coffee shop. The waitresses were all elderly but heavily made-up ladies who sounded as if they'd retired to Florida from New York City. They were gruff but solicitous and when I told them I was a New Yorker one of them brought over an extra basket of rolls

The next morning we drove back down Collins Avenue to what I guess was downtown Miami Beach and found my folks' hotel. My father was sitting in a rocker on the front porch, waiting for us. He was at that time approaching 90 years old. He'd always been on the short side but broad and muscular. He'd been a plumber and I remember as a kid being impressed as he hoisted his tool box, which I couldn't budge, up onto his shoulders ever morning when he went to work. Now he looked even shorter and was less muscular but his hands were still large and strong-looking, workman's hands.

The residential hotel was an old building and, like our hotel, looked a little rundown. It had undoubtedly seen better days.. My father stood up and hugged and kissed Sally, whom he adored, then hugged me. We took an elevator to see my folks' room on the fourth floor. It was small, with a sofa-bed against one wall, a dresser, a couple of chairs facing the TV and a "kitchen area" with a table and chairs. It didn't seem like much but I guess it served its purpose as they'd been going to Miami every winter, staying six months, for as long as I could remember.

While we were there, several women stopped in to ask about my mother, all bringing something to eat for my father. After asking about my mother, they seemed eager for information about us. To them I wasn't an old guy, I was my folks' son out in California. They told us we had two beautiful children, not exactly the way I'd describe our sons. I realized they'd heard only the good things from my mother and father about their grandchildren, as we'd transmitted them. I wondered if Sally and I would eventually reach an age when our sons told us only the good things about our grandkids, if we had any.

It was then time to go to the hospital to get my mother, who was being discharged that day. I'd located Mount Sinai hospital on the map, my father not being sure where it was, and found it after only a false turn or two. My mother was sitting on a chair in her room. She didn't look too bad but said the place where they'd put the pin in her hip still hurt. We tracked down her doctor, who said this was normal and she might feel it for some time. My mother wasn't convinced; she was sure the doctor had made a mistake in his surgery. But she was ready to leave and get back to her home, her Miami one.

It took a while but we finally signed all the necessary papers. A nurse wheeled my mother outside and over to our rental car, and we managed to get her inside. I drove back to the hotel, going as slowly as possible so as not to jostle her. Getting her out of the car, into the hotel, then into the elevator and then into the room wasn't easy, but we managed it. When my mother was finally seated in an armchair, she said, "I had to fall and break my hip. Now I can't do anything."

"Don't worry," said my father. "I'll take care of everything.."

"And who's going to take care of you?"

This was a typical exchange between my mother and my father. They'd been married for 60 years..

After a while, we made out a shopping list and my mother told us where to find the store, a sort of semi-super market, where once a week the hotel van took them shopping. As we left, a couple of the ladies who'd stopped in earlier came by again and we left them talking to my mother.

We spent a pretty long time shopping as Sally kept thinking of things my mother and father could use. When we returned, my mother said it looked as if we'd cleaned out the whole store. We spent the afternoon visiting, showing my folks pictures of their grandsons and telling them of all their activities, only the good ones.

When it came time to have supper, Sally and I walked to Wolfie's, a well-known Miami Beach restaurant (Jackie Gleason, among other celebrities, had been a regular and a large picture of him was on the wall), just a few blocks from the hotel, and where my folks often ate. When we told the manager who we were he immediately asked about my mother. I told him she'd just come back from the hospital. We ordered cabbage rolls, one of my mother's favorites, to take out and brought these back together with a bagful of rolls and another of pastries, for which we hadn't been charged.

I have a pretty clear recollection of that first full day in Miami, but only some sketchy memories of the rest of our stay. I remember driving up and down Collins Avenue many times, thinking that there must be more hotels in Miami Beach than along any other strip in the world. Besides the other cars, I had to watch out for old people who suddenly decided to cross the street, without paying any attention to the traffic. I vividly remember one who materialized right in front of us, blissfully eating an ice cream cone, oblivious of my having to slam on my brakes or else both he and his cone would have been obliterated.

Over the course of the week, we met most of the other residents of the hotel. All were very short, shorter than my father, some less than five feet tall, as if they'd been hammered down; and maybe they had, by the Depression in the 1930's, by the concentration camps in Hitler's Germany (a few were actual survivors), and now by old age. In the afternoons, the residents gathered around the little hotel pool (I never saw anyone actually go in it), all sitting on their folding chairs, and exchanged gossip. They were all New Yorkers and a lot of the talk was about how bad things in that city had become. They also talked about how things in Miami were getting worse, including the hotel, the neighborhood it was in, the stores, the prices and even the weather. Like typical New Yorkers, they were all contentious, putting forth their convictions in loud voices, and there were some pretty heated arguments. Then, when it became hot in mid-afternoon and it was time to go inside they all parted as friends until the next day.

My mother improved daily, although she still complained about the pain in her hip and had trouble sleeping at night. We went shopping a few more times, the last time on our final day there to make sure my folks had everything they needed. A physical therapist, a large black woman, came from the hospital to put my mother through the prescribed post-op exercises. We brought some more meals from Wolfie's and the rest of the time Sally cooked something.

I remember that one day we took a break and stayed at our hotel. We went to the hotel's beach, which they bragged about in their brochure. We walked on the edge of the sand for a few minutes looking out at the ocean but a strong wind came up and we shortly retreated to our room. That was our one beach experience of the trip. Another day we drove around what was starting to be South Beach; it was known as the "art deco" area then and was being renovated. It had not yet become a swinging place and instead of having drinks at a sidewalk café we had ice cream cones as we strolled up and down, observing the strange-looking natives.

By the time we left Miami, my mother seemed to be recovering. My father assured us that he'd take good care of her. We hoped that by the time they returned to the Bronx in May my mother would be able to walk up to their first floor apartment and walk the few blocks to the stores. With this worry, we returned to Sacramento on Monday, March 8th.

Back home, we discovered that the weather had changed; it had rained almost all the time we'd been gone. I was glad my story about the drought had already appeared. We also found out that Jack's Mazda needed a new starter and Steve told us his computer needed a new mother board. Miami hadn't exactly been a vacation, but I was reminded why it had been good to get away while I was working. Even though I was now retired, it was still good to have a change of scenery, not to mention a respite from the steady stream of bills that kept coming, retired or not.

The morning after we returned, Karl Engle called. By this time I was no longer sleeping late and the days had gotten longer so I agreed to come down to the Sacramento Press office the next Monday to do some editing. Retirees traditionally do some kind of volunteering; I figured that, along with my writing, this would be my volunteer effort.. I also thought I might learn something about putting out a newspaper by being there on the spot. And I'd be getting out of the house once a week; while I was downtown, I could go to the new library there and keep in touch with my old office.

I had an idea for a possible story. A friend of mine named Ralph Foxx was a sculptor. He originally had a metalwork place and made, among other things, fences for residences and businesses. In fact, he'd designed and made the metal fence that had been put around the State Capitol. He also made sculptures out of metal and stone as a sideline and had placed a few of these in local galleries. Now he'd decided to become a full-time sculptor in metal, which

I considered pretty brave of him. His studio, or the building in which he worked, was in Carmichael. I thought a piece on Ralph would make a good story and also give him some publicity. I called Karl Engle and he said to go ahead with it. So I had another Carmichael story.

As it was still raining, which meant a delay in my tennis comeback, and I had the time, I wrote another piece, but not for the Sacramento Press. Sally had called my attention to s feature called "My Story" in the Neighbors section of the Sacramento Bee. Neighbors, as its name indicated, published stories about people and places in the various communities around Sacramento. Twice a week in our Sacramento Bee, we got the Carmichael Neighbors. For "My Story." people sent in pieces describing some interesting or amusing event in their lives. The important thi8ng is that those who had their stories printed received a princely $25. Now that I was officially a writer, it was almost incumbent on me to send something in.

When I was a teen-ager, I'd hitch-hiked across the country, from the Bronx to Idaho, to work one summer in the Forestry Service. A friend had worked there the previous summer and said it was a great deal. You were paid 60 cents an hour (remember, this was back in the 1950's), with time and a half on Saturdays. You also got your room and board and, as there was no place to spend your money, everything you made was clear. It sounded good to me so I went..

My story was about an incident when, after somehow surviving the summer, I'd started hitch-hiking back to the Bronx. I'd gotten a ride with two guys in a pick-up truck. When I climbed into the back I saw that it was filled with boxes marked dynamite. Uh, oh, I'd thought. Then it became even worse. The guy driving the truck was evidently drunk as the truck was swerving all over and eventually, somewhere in the mountains of Montana, the truck stopped, both guys got out and argued who was less drunk and should be driving. While they argued, I quickly got off, and after a while they drove away, swerving down the road. The end of the story was that after I walked several miles through the mountains trying to find a straight stretch of road where drivers could see me; finally, a car zoomed past, braked to a stop, I ran to it, got in and the driver, a teacher (sober) took me all the way to Iowa. I wrote the story and mailed it in.

The Sacramento Press was housed in an old white wooden building that needed painting. It was close to 16th Street and so easy to get to from the freeway. Inside, Karl Engle was at a desk; a woman who was introduced to me as Anna and whom I'd talked to one time when I'd called was at another desk, and a third desk was piled with papers. There were windows on two sides so that you could look out, and passers-by could look in. Further back in the room where there were no windows and up two steps were two tables with computers on them. A young man with long hair was seated at one table, hammering out something on his computer.

As I eventually learned, Anna was in charge of advertising for the newspaper. The Sacramento Press was free, so it depended on the revenue it received from advertisers to keep going. The young man at the computer was the person who put the paper together. Both were paid employees. Karl Engle wasted no time in small talk; he said he wanted me to do a column on things people could do in downtown Sacramento. I expressed my doubts, as in all of my years of working for the State I'd never really found anything to do down there. But, when he insisted, I told him I'd give it a try. I asked if our mutual friend Jean Zeiger was doing anything for the paper and he said she might do something on neighborhood activities.

After this, I sat at the one unoccupied desk, cleared the papers off and was put to work. The Press, in addition to its usual articles also had movie reviews, usually of foreign films shown at Sacramento's one or two art houses; play reviews, of local companies: and a variety of other pieces, such as doings in the gay and lesbian communities, the evils of city government and going vegan or finding joy in leading the simple life. The movie reviews were, I found, almost incomprehensible with references to directors, actors and film movements I'd never heard of. The play reviews were all laudatory, although reading between the lines it was clear that most of the productions were amateurish. The other pieces were almost all written with passion if not much regard to grammar or punctuation. I could see that the paper did need an editor.

I spent a couple of hours editing, trying to remember the rules of writing I'd learned in school many years ago. I tried not to make too many changes, just the ones I thought were absolutely necessary as I didn't want to alienate all of the other Press writers right away. I also took into account that these writers, like myself, were unpaid volunteers. In between editing, I talked a little with Anna, a heavy-set woman in her fifties, I guessed, who was friendly and who to9ld me she'd liked the stories I'd written. I learned she was heavily involved in community theater activities, making costumes, ushering and doing other behind-the-scenes work. Around noon I felt I could edit no more so I told Anna I was done, left and drove to Capital Park, where I found a parking space after circling around a few times,, then visited the Capital and the State Library, looking for ideas for a column on things to do downtown.

Later in the week, I went to Carmichael Park and played my first tennis in over a month. It was the middle, or the Ides, of March, but I'd remained idle long enough and was ready to take a risk, I played two sets, not serving too hard, and things seemed to be okay. Next Saturday morning I played with my doubles foursome—Arnie, Charlie and Mike, at the club. I served a little harder with no ill effects and Arnie and I won two sets out of three. Afterward, we sat around on the patio, which I considered the best thing about our club, as it was shaded by a big tree, and had our cold drinks. Arnie was a tall, lanky fellow, who was very good at chasing down balls, He taught psychology at the community college and had been helpful in getting Jack through there. . Charlie was a husky no-nonsense guy who worked in the State prison system. Mike was a financial analyst, a flashy but inconsistent player who could make a great shot one time, then flub an easy sitter the next. He was also the clown of our group, who "kidded" constantly while we played..

Another club member, John Anderson, came up to our table. "Hi," said Arnie. "Where's Pete?" John and Pete Wilson always played singles at the club on weekends and when you saw one you expected to see the other. I liked John, a pleasant guy, but had never especially liked Pete. Like myself, Pete worked for the State. But he'd been appointed to some high-level job while I served in the trenches and he never let me forget this. I think Pete felt that because he outranked me in the State hierarchy he should be able to beat me in tennis. He was a pretty good player and hard hitter, but I'd discovered early on his backhand was erratic, not unusual in club players. On key points, I always played to his backhand and almost always was able to draw an error. He'd get sore because he couldn't get a set off me..

"Hadn't you heard?' asked John.

"What?"

"Pete died last Thursday."

"You're kidding. I just saw you guys playing last weekend."

"That was just before he found out he had cancer. It had spread through his body. He went fast."

"How old was he?" Mike asked.

"He was 54."

"Geez, that's young." We all told John how sorry we were about the news. John said there'd be a memorial service the next week. Nobody asked him where it was. After John left, Mike said, "I had chemo a couple of years ago for my prostate. My PSA's down below 4.0 now. I hope it stays that way. I go in every six months "

"Yeah," said Charlie. "I had prostate surgery about five years ago; the old rotor rooter. Seems okay now, knock on wood." He rapped on the table.

"How about you guys?" asked Ralph.

"No," said Arnie. "Just a couple of basil cells I had cut out. PSA's good so far."

They all looked at me. "Nothing, except that lousy tennis elbow. Oh, I'm going for a blood pressure check next month.."

"Take it easy," said Mike. "You know all those guys who retire and then keel over, just like that."

"Don't bug him," said Charlie.

We talked for another half hour or so, mostly about our various aches and pains. When I got home, I took a shower, then told Sally about Pete. She said she was sorry to hear it and wondered if Jan, his ex-wife, would come to the funeral. Sally didn't especially like Pete either; she'd invited John, but not Pete, to my retirement/birthday party. Pete had left Jan to marry his secretary, who was about 20 years younger. That hadn't worked out either. After a year, she divorced him.

I usually go to sleep pretty easily, but that night I lay awake for a long time. I'd been shocked by John's news and had been surprised to hear that both Ralph and Charley had been treated for cancer. Loud-mouthed Mike and big tough Charley; it was hard to believe. I'd been thinking a bit about mortality ever since our trip to Miami. My mother and father had gotten so old. Mike may have been trying to bug me when he talked about all those guys retiring and then keeling over, but I knew one such guy, Stan Babcock, Bab, we called him. He'd looked forward to retirement more than anyone I'd known, always figuring out when he should go and how much of a pension he'd be getting. When he finally did leave, he was dead within a month. I'd been getting up more often in the night to go to the bathroom. I'd thought it was just getting older. Maybe it was something else. I wondered if I should ask my doctor for a PSA test.

Then my thoughts turned to Pete. Only 54, and he was gone. At least all those people in Miami had lived a long time. I still didn't think I could ever have liked Pete, but now I wished I'd been a little nicer to him, not done my best to beat him at tennis by hitting everything to that weak backhand. And if Pete had left his wife for a younger woman, maybe he'd sensed something and wanted one last fling. Who could know? I might call John tomorrow and find out about the memorial service.

After what had turned out to be a rather gloomy weekend, I went to the Sacramento Press office on Monday. I suggested to Karl Engel that I do my first column on the State Capitol and the State Library, but he had other ideas. He wanted me to do a column on "public art." He knew someone at the Sacramento Metropolitan Arts Commission and apparently the Commission had been sponsoring walking tours of public art on Saturdays. Now they were starting lunchtime walking tours on weekdays.

So I went over to the Commission's office and found Karl's friend, who had the title of Coordinator of the Art in Public Places Program. Well, I had never known such a thing existed; I was learning something. I was provided with material, including a map, that, I was told, would enable me to take a self-conducted preview of the tour and off I went. The art work was on the outside of the County Jail and Court Building, the County Parking Garage, and what was called the Riverview Plaza Building. There were also two sculptures in Plaza Park that I'd seen before and never remarked on, one dedicated to a gentleman who was a 19th-century banker, the other, I guess to be fair, to a 19th-century friend of labor. The tour took about an hour and, as I later wrote, gave me my day's exercise and worked up an appetite for lunch.

Later in the week, perhaps inspired by all this art, I went over to my friend Ralph Foxx's workshop It was a short drive from my house, in an industrial area off Fair Oaks Boulevard, and I was able .to locate it by the big sculpture in front. The workshop was filled with metal and stone sculptures, large and small. I was impressed. I was also impressed by the awards he'd won, Best of Show at the Carmichael Artist League Show, First Place for Best Animation and People's Choice Award. California State Fair Exhibits in 1989 and 1990, Best Animation and First Place at the National Orange Show in San Bernardino, 1990. I hadn't realized I had such a talented neighbor.

I spent over an hour there taking notes. When I returned home I went to my computer and, with the usual help from Binky and Mickey, wrote a fairly long piece, which I called "Metal Giants." I started with: "Turn right off Fair Oaks Boulevard into the W— Lane industrial area, drive past the usual auto repair, smog and body shops and there is the studio of

Carmichael artist Ralph Foxx. Although the studio is in the same type of corrugated iron shed as its industrial neighbors it isn't hard (even for this reporter) to find as in front is a huge stone and metal sculpture."

Further on, I wrote: "Ralph has not always been a full-time artist. For a number of years he ran an iron works business, which provided wrought iron grills for home decoration and protection …Among other large efforts during this period was the portable fence put around the Capitol building on the occasion of Queen Elizabeth's visit to Sacramento."

And: "Ralph Foxx is unique in several ways. He has developed his own style of sculpture, using materials found in junkyards and on coastal beaches. He has succeeded in becoming a full-time and self-supporting artist … Above all, he is that rare individual, a person who is doing what he wants to do." I wonder if, when I wrote this, I was comparing Ralph's career to my own with the State?..

That weekend Jack drove down from Chico. As usual, we didn't see much of him; he was out most of the time "hanging" with his friends. He still hated Chico even though one of his English teachers liked his writing and he might have something in the college magazine. We told him this was "great." That night he came home late, had forgotten his house key, and came in through the living room window, tearing the screen in the process. Not so great.

The next Monday I brought my Ralph Foxx story and my column on public art to the Sacramento Press office. I started my column by saying: "I was recently invited to the Sacramento Press office to do some 'important' editorial work. After I finished sweeping the floor and emptying out the wastepaper baskets, editor Karl Engle said he had another important assignment for me. 'We need a column on interesting things people who work downtown can do on their lunch hour.:

'In Sacramento? What interesting things?'

'How should I know?' Then, pointing his finger at the door and in a voice Stanley's editor must have used when sending him to Africa to find Livingston, he said, 'Go out there and find them.'"I ended the column with: "Is Karl Engle right? Are there interesting things to see and do in downtown Sacramento, just waiting to be discovered?" Then I asked readers to send in their ideas. None ever did.

On this Monday, I had a movie review, a local theater review and a strange column written by a local rabbi to edit. Around 11, Karl Engle asked me to go across the street to the coffee shop there and bring back a pot of coffee for the office. He evidently had a deal: they supplied the Sacramento Press with coffee and he gave them free advertising. I wasn't too enthused about doing this but at work I'd been in charge of the office coffee pot at various times so it wasn't something completely new. I said Okay and did it. The coffee was better than we'd had at the State.

At the end of March the Gulf War was over, but there was still fighting in Iraq. It was becoming apparent that although we'd gotten the Iraqis out of Kuwait, Saddam was still very much in control of his own country and that there'd be problems ahead. I'm sure no one thought at the time that in ten years we'd be invading them.

The memorial service for Pete Wilson was at a nearby church. A lot of people were there, including Pete's two ex-wives and quite a few members of our swim and tennis club. Pete's five children were there; I hadn't known he had so many. I also learned a few things about Pete I hadn't known . He'd been on his college baseball team and had been offered a tryout be some major league team. He was also a crack bridge player. All five of his children spoke, saying what a good father (despite the divorce) he'd been.

After the service, I talked to John Anderson. He seemed to still be in shock at Pete's untimely death. "Guess we should play a lot of tennis while we can," he said.

"Guess so."

At the time, I didn't know this was only the first of many memorial services I'd be going to in my retirement years.

APRIL

In the first week of April, Sally and I had finally had our dinner with Dr. George, in payment for my "consulting" work. It was at Wulff's, a restaurant that been started by two engineers at Aerojet and which I considered the finest in Sacramento. Sally and I had been there a number of times, going down their menu, item by item. The waiters weren't young people who told you, "My name is Joe and I'll be your server." They were all middle-aged gentlemen, dressed in dark suits, who were experts on food and wine. The tables were set a little too close together, but as no one ever talked loudly you could still have a private conversation.

Dr. George told us that the agency's information system seemed to be working, which I was happy to hear, but that money was short and they still hadn't been able to fill my position Dr. George was a great traveler; she'd been to Switzerland and Italy with a companion the year before and they'd had a great time. No, they hadn't gone on a tour; they'd rented a car and had driven all over. She was a woman in her fifties, rather stout, and I had a mental picture of her speeding along in her little European car going up and down the winding, twisting roads of the Alps.

During that week Sacramento had a big crime story. Some Asian gang kids invaded a Good Guys store and took hostages. The police eventually went in and some hostages were killed. Predictably, the family of at least one of the slain hostages was going to sue for millions.

On Monday, the 8th, I went down to the Sacramento Press office, as had become my weekly routine. I was busy editing when Jean Zeiger came in. She'd bicycled over with a piece she'd written on her neighborhood, which she gave to Karl Engle. They then went across the street to the coffee shop. I wasn't invited. At least, I thought, I wouldn't have to fetch the coffee pot. I've said that no readers ever wrote with ideas for my column. However, I did have a piece of mail, from a lady named Norma Eisenstein. She said she liked my writing. She was in some organization that invited foreign visitors to Sacramento and thought I should write a story about this. I showed the letter to Anna, who told me Norma Eisenstein was a big supporter of the paper and I should get in touch with her.

I left around noon and met my friend Al Chang for lunch. I declined his suggestion that we go to the Chinese restaurant; instead, we ate at the cafeteria in the Capital, which I'd discovered when doing my research for a column. It was open to the public and the food wasn't bad.. Art confirmed what Dr. George had said, that the agency was hurting for money and said he was thinking of transferring to another department. I was starting to think my retirement had come at an opportune time.

During the week, I called my Mother and she told me that she'd had what she called a "spell," where she'd felt dizzy and confused, but after a day or so it had gone away. I told her she should see her doctor about it. She said it was nothing. I said that if it happened again she should definitely see her doctor and she said, okay, she would. I also called Jack at Chico, who said the Mazda was running okay, but, as always, he complained about all the work he had to do. He said he'd finish out the term, but he didn't know if he'd go back for his final year. I told him we'd talk about it when he was home.

I'd read some article about the sandwich generation, the people who had children to put through school as well as aging parents who might require care. We weren't quite there yet, I thought, but my folks were getting along and, who knows, it might not be long before they couldn't look out for themselves. And who knew how long it would take for Jack to finish college, if he ever did. As for Steve, he was filling out applications for colleges in the State system, so there was another expense coming up.

I made another call. We had a former neighbor named Myra Lake. She was something like Jean Zeiger, a dynamo. When she'd discovered that her son, then in high school, was doing marijuana, she'd organized a group that distributed literature on drug use, provided speakers to schools and sponsored anti-drug legislation. When Jack had been in his "rebel without a cause" phase in high school, I'd spoken to her to gain some knowledge of marijuana and other substances. I thought she'd make a good story. She was agreeable and I made an appointment to drop over to her house the next week.

Around the middle of April, I received a letter from the Sacramento Bee. The "My Story" piece about my hitch-hiking adventures, or misadventures, had been accepted and would be printed. The letter asked me to call to provide some information. I called the Bee and gave my social security number (this was before the era of identity theft), address and phone number and some other stuff. Then I asked if the Bee accepted free-lance articles. The guy I talked to said they didn't but that their Neighbors section might. He gave me the name of a Neighbors "assignment editor" and a number to call. I called and the assignment editor, a woman whose name was Lois Bremmer, said they did take free-lance work when they needed fillers. I told her I was writing stories for the Sacramento Press. She said I should write something and bring it in. Oh, yes, I said, did Neighbors pay anything? Yes, they paid $50 a story. I'd definitely bring something in.

At about the same time, Steve received an even more exciting letter, this from UC Berkeley; he'd been accepted. I found it hard to believe; maybe he'd written a terrific essay or maybe his computer expertise had impressed them. Sally and I talked to Steve's councilor, who told us that UC Berkeley's computer science program was extremely hard and that it was entirely possible that Steve wouldn't be able to make it there. But Steve was nothing if not confident; so it looked as if we'd have a son at Berkeley. Of course, UC Berkeley, being in the State university system rather than a State college like UC San Diego or Cal Poly would cost that much more in tuition, not to mention room and board.

At my HMO appointment that week, my blood pressure, as it always did in a doctor's office, was high. I assured the doctor that it was no problem. He looked dubious but said nothing.I then asked him if he thought I should take a PSA test; he'd never mentioned doing this before.. He said, "Mmmm," and gave me the "finger test." He told me my prostate felt pretty large and that a PSA might not be a bad idea. He sent me to the lab, where a gray-haired woman stuck a pin in my finger and drew blood. I'd get the results in about a week, she said.

The same week I went to Myra Lake's house, expecting to be there about an hour. Instead, I was there for almost three hours. Some of the time was taken up by phone calls she had to answer, but most was spent taking copious notes about her many anti-drug activities, all of which she felt passionately about. I wondered if I could boil it down to a reasonable length for a story.

The next Monday I told Karl Engle about the possible Myra Lake story. He replied that he didn't print anti-drug stories. Taking drugs, he said, was an individual choice, not anyone else's business. I wondered how he'd feel if he had kids on something While I was doing my usual editing, a woman came into the office. I turned around and saw that she was middle-aged but attractive in a kind of dramatic way. What was someone like this doing in the rundown office of the Sacramento Press?. I soon found out. Anna introduced her as Nadia Davinsky and told her who I was. Nadia revealed that she did the movie reviews for the Press.

I braced myself as I'd been editing her reviews more and more in recent weeks. But she wasn't angry at my editing. She told me she appreciated my efforts; she sometimes felt so strongly that she got carried away and who could pay attention to such mundane things as spelling and punctuation. I was relieved. She invited to buy me a cup of coffee at the place across the street and, despite my protests, carried me off. She wasn't a woman you could easily say No to. Over coffee, she told me, in a foreign accent I couldn't identify, the story of her life, which was quite interesting. She was rich; now she was poor. She'd been married; the cad had betrayed her. She acted in local plays' nobody appreciated her. She was one of those women who like to touch you and soon she was holding my hand. I decided that I wouldn't tell Sally of this encounter. .

When I returned home, I looked at my Myra Lake notes and wrote a piece of 1,000 words. The next day I drove to the Neighbors office, which wasn't too far away, and met Lois Bremmer for the first time. She didn't look like my idea of an editor at all. She was a petite woman of about 40, with dark hair, a pleasant face and a soft voice. She read through my Myra story very quickly, then said Neighbors would take it. She didn't know when they'd print it; when they did I'd get paid my $50. First, $25 for the "My Turn" piece and now $50 for Myra; who said there wasn't big bucks in writing? It was a good thing Karl Engle hadn't wanted the Myra story.

Encouraged, I asked Lois Bremmer if she'd be interested in another story, about a group of old-timers who played tennis in Carmichael Park. I described some of the old-timers, trying to make them sound colorful, and she said to go ahead. Another possible $50, I thought. I'd go to work on it.

For my second Sacramento Press column, which had been given a title, "City Adventures," I wrote about two downtown fixtures that most people, except tourists, passed by without giving them a second look, the State Capitol and the State Library. In my exploration of the Capitol I'd discovered an exhibit on the 1906 and 1988 San Francisco earthquakes. The exhibit included a seismograph, for anyone who wanted to see if any earthquakes were then occurring in California. I also found a small photography exhibit called, "New Visions: Contributions by California Photographers, 1860-1960," which included photos by Ansel Adams. And in the basement, where I'd never gone before, was a 10-minute movie on the restoration of the Capitol and, in a room next door, an exhibit on more Capitol history.

The State Library, across the street from the Capitol, always had some kind of exhibit on its third floor. The current one was called, "Rival Cities: California's Two Panama Pacific Expositions, 1915-1916," and coming up were two exhibits, one celebrating the first overland trip to California by wagon train in 1841, the other on 19th century certificate art, membership certificates issued by fire-fighting, vigilante and patriotic groups, which had become collectors' items. The Library also had a Microform Reading Room, where you could look at microfilm of the Sacramento newspapers going back to 1851.

I managed to write almost 1,500 words about the State Capitol and Library, which I wouldn't have thought possible. I don't know if walking through them would qualify as a great downtown adventure, but at any rate I'd done my second column and maybe I'd given some useful information to a few history buffs.

My Shakespeare class continued; and, like the State Capitol and Library, I found it to be mildly interesting, although every so often I would, not setting a good example to my younger classmates, cut and go to Carmichael Park to play tennis. After "Merchant of Venice" we went on to "The Merry Wives of Windsor," which I found to be pretty boring and not too funny. But then we had "Taming of the Shrew" and Mr. Schroeder showed a video of a Central Park "Taming" called "Kiss Me, Petruchio," in which none other than Meryl Streep made her acting debut, opposite Raoul Julio, which was worth coming to class to see.

By this time, I was always on the alert for a possible story so I brought a copy of the Sacramento Press to class and afterward showed it to Mr. Schroeder. I asked if he'd be interested in my doing a story on him. He definitely was (I don't suppose teachers and local theater performers received much press coverage) and told me he'd bring his scrapbook to class the next week. When I mentioned this to Karl Engle the next Monday, he said the story didn't sound like a great one but I could go ahead with it.

I had another possible story. Karl wanted me to write something about the Sacramento art scene, this time not the public kind. He gave me the name and number of a local artist named Trudi Benton and told me to call her. When I did, she suggested meeting at a coffee houses, Rush Haven, nearby. I'd seen the place when driving by, but had never gone into it. Coffee houses, like this one and the one across the street from the Sacramento Press, were just then springing up all over and eventually I'd do a coffee house story for the Press and later on a couple for Neighbors.

Trudi was young, in her twenties, I'd say, and quite good-looking in a Bohemian way. This was the second time in recent weeks I was having coffee with an attractive woman. But early on she mentioned having a boy friend and she was, to my relief, very professional and business-like She was a dedicated artist. Her mother was an artist and art teacher, she told me, and she herself had started drawing at the age of two. Trudi specialized in making ceramic masks; she also made clay miniatures. In order to support herself, she was the "visual artist" for a mobile arts unit that went around to public schools and put on shows; she was the "art curator" for Rush Haven, which had pictures by local artists on its walls; and she did part-time waitressing.

On top of all this, she was going to Sacramento State college to get a degree in Fine Arts. I was impressed y her dedication and hoped that a story about her in the Sacramento Press might bring her some good publicity. After concluding the interview, I did ask for her phone number. No, it was nothing personal. She knew many other local artists and I thought she'd be a good source for future art stories. .

I had less luck with my attempt to do a story for Neighbors on the Carmichael Park tennis players. I'd go to the park armed with my trusty notebook and try to talk to the guys in between sets, but this just didn't work out too well. Unlike Mr. Schroeder, these guys didn't seem that anxious to see their name in print. I had to figure out some other way.

I'd learned a little something about writing newspaper articles by this time. Probably most important was that I printed people's names in big letters so that I could be sure I'd spelled them right. I didn't want anyone calling in to say I'd gotten his or her name wrong. For Neighbors, I referred to a person the first time by full name, then used the last name only. For the Sacramento Press, which was a little more informal, I sometimes used the first name, as I did for Trudi (somehow I found it hard to think of her as Ms. Benton). I tried to keep my sentences and my paragraphs short so the story wouldn't look like an intimidating mass of print on paper. When I quoted anyone I tried to make sure I was accurate; if I wasn't sure, I'd ask for a repeat and, when I thought it was necessary, I asked if it was okay to print that.

Another thing I started doing and kept on doing for the duration of my journalistic career was this: after an interview, when I was driving back, I tried to think of a first sentence to start my story and of what the "theme" of the story should be. For Trudi, I wrote, "Sacramento artist Trudi Benton is one person who's never had any doubt as to her vocation."

While all of this writing activity was going on, I was doing some other "retirement" things." Sally and I had decided that once a week we'd go out someplace to eat on the spur of the moment, sometimes to a pancake or waffle place for breakfast, sometime to some place for lunch and occasionally to a better restaurant for dinner. We'd also started going to movie matinees, which were much cheaper than going at night. And we always asked for a senior discount. I wasn't sure if the senior discounts started at age 60 or age 65 but the girls in the ticket booths, usually teenagers, never questioned our senior credentials. I suppose to them anyone over 30 looked old.

The PSA results, when they finally came, were inconclusive. My doctor had scribbled a note on the lab results to call him. He told me that he'd referred me to the Oncology Department and that someone would get in touch. He assured me that this was only a precautionary measure. I'd expected that the test was going to be just a routine one-time matter. Now, like the first-time offenders in all of those police procedural shows on television, I had been put, as they say, into the system, the HMO system. It might not have been Riker's Island, but I didn't feel too happy about it.

MAY

Writing a column about what to do in downtown Sacramento for the Press continued to be a problem. Having written columns about the Art Walk and the State Capitol and Library, I had no idea of what to do next. So I decided I'd just cruise around one weekday at lunchtime, try to talk to people downtown and see what I could pick up. I started by stopping in at an upscale men's clothing store in the Downtown Plaza and talking to the store manager. He had nothing of interest to report about his lunchtime activities as he said he always stayed inside his store to be available to possible customers. Not a promising start. But then I found out that he was president of the Downtown Plaza Association, and that a big renovation was starting next January to enclose the Plaza and make it a rival of the new Arden Fair mall.

He also directed me to the woman who was the Assistant Manager of Marketing for Downtown Plaza Associates, whose office was just across the way. This woman, let's call her Susan, was very friendly and proved to be a fount of information then and in the future, telling me about various events scheduled for the Plaza for the rest of the year. Susan was also on the Executive Board of the Sacramento Partnership, which was planning a big food fair at the Plaza in the fall. Her own favorite lunchtime activity, she told me, was shopping at Plaza stores; she felt guilty when she shopped elsewhere.

I then went to a large shoe store, whose manager and assisted manager were both excited about the planned renovation. The manager told me about his favorite lunch place, which, he said, had great deli, salads and pastries. The assistant manager's favorite place was a Chinese restaurant. I was picking up a lot of useful information, especially about places to eat.

I continued to talk to people, including a group of seven, who identified themselves as burnt-out State environmental specialists. I told them that, as a recent State retiree, I could appreciate how they felt. One of the group liked to bicycle to Old Sacramento on his lunch hour, and wanted more security for bicycles, having had two stolen. They all liked to the Farmer's Market on Wednesday's at Plaza Park (aha, another possible column), and they directed me to a muffin shop and to a place inside the Plaza for cinnamon rolls (more useful eating information). I also met a couple of people who worked for the County Arts Commission, and they told me about a few more events coming up downtown. So altogether it was a pretty productive walk; I'd gathered more than enough material for a column, found a source of information, Susan, for future columns, and learned about a lot of good downtown eating places. I also had Trudi as a source for art stories so I felt I was in pretty good shape. A large part of making my retirement job as a journalist easier, I was finding out, was the same as my State job, meeting people and making contacts.

I was kept pretty busy with the Sacramento Press in early May. On the first Monday, instead of editing, I was "assigned" to a story about the State's homeless assistance program being axed. I spent the morning trying to get through to the relevant State agencies and managed to get enough information to cobble something together. Then Karl had an idea for an issue on "urban heroes." My job, for some reason, was to find a couple of gay urban heroes. Again, I made some phone calls, one to a well-known gay activist, a Reverend Jerry Something, who called back and gave me the names of two guys who lived together and shared the same name. I made more calls and talked to one of the two guys in the morning and the other one in the afternoon.

I found out that this couple had been together for 22 years, the last 15 in Sacramento. One worked as a computer operator and the other was disabled so couldn't work full-time but did a lot of volunteer work. They were both active in various gay organizations and especially in raising funds to combat AIDS. They also assisted AIDS victims who were unable to leave home. When the "Urban Heroes" issue appeared, with pictures, I saw that these were two middle-aged guys, both balding, and that they had a cat.

In mid-month I received a card from my HMO, telling me I had an appointment to see a doctor regarding my prostate; the doctor was a surgeon. I of course had never met this doctor or even heard of him. This was typical of the impersonal way the HMO dispensed medicine. In fact, I wasn't sure if my own doctor, who I'd rarely seen up to that time, would recognize me if he saw me walking down the street.

The next time our "fearsome foursome" played tennis, I mentioned that I had a surgical appointment.. Charlie asked who the doctor was; I gave him the name. Charlie said, "Don't know that guy. I think you should ask for the guy who did mine, Dr. Volkman. He's the top surgeon there." Ralph chipped in to say that he'd heard of Dr. Volkman, and he had a great reputation. There was some more conversation about troublesome prostates, which I didn't find too uplifting. This was apparently a subject guys who had them could talk about forever.

I called the HMO and said I'd like to see Dr. Volkman, not the doctor I'd been assigned. The girl, following the usual HMO line, first said that I had to see the doctor I'd been assigned to. Then, after I'd objected to this, she said that Dr. Volkman was pretty well booked up and it might be a while, implying years, before I could get an appointment with him. I told her I was in no hurry. She said, grudgingly, I thought, that she'd look at his schedule and see when, if it was at all possible, she could fit me in. When I hung up, I thought, if I have to have surgery I might as well get somebody who was supposed to be good. And the fact that Dr. Volkman was so busy was possibly a sign that people other than Charlie and Ralph thought he was good. I'd wait. I didn't know it then but this was an astute policy. As you got older it was inevitable that you would need surgery for something or other. If you were a member of an HMO you usually had no idea of the merits of its doctors, surgeons or otherwise, and selecting a good surgeon was the most important element in ensuring a successful result. .

At about the same time, I had a call, an unexpected one, from the community college. It wasn't about my Shakespeare class. The girl said the Dean of Students wanted to see me. It was something to do with Steve. I asked if it was about his getting admitted to UC Berkeley. She said she didn't know. I made an appointment for the next afternoon.

The Dean's office was a pretty sumptuous one, I thought, for a community college. It was carpeted and had dark curtains, a number of chairs, two tables, a large bookcase and several paintings on the walls. The Dean himself sat behind a large desk, a man of about 50, with a hooked nose, small brown eyes behind steel-rimmed glasses and a bald head. I told him that I myself was a student at the college, taking a class in Shakespeare, to which he replied with a grunt.

He shuffled some papers in front of him, picked them up, peered at them through his glasses and then got to the point. What it came to was that Steve, with the help of a couple of his friends, had broken into the college's central computerized data base. I asked him how he knew that and he gave me a technical explanation; evidently, the college had security experts who'd created a "firewall" around the data base, some kind of alarm had gone off when it was broken into, and the intruders had left some sort of "footprint," which had been traced back to Steve's computer. I asked if he'd informed Steve or any of his friends about this. He said he had. Steve had said nothing to me..

The Dean said he couldn't begin to impress on me the seriousness of this "crime." The data base contained personal information, scholastic information and exam information. The boys could have broadcast all of this and created pandemonium. I asked if they had. He replied that the security people were still investigating. I told him that I'd talk to Steve immediately and that he'd be appropriately punished. I assured the Dean that nothing like this would ever happen again.

The Dean shook his head. This wouldn't be enough, he told me. He'd be meeting with an ad hoc committee to discuss the matter and decide on the penalty. It could be that Steve, and his friends, would have their grades rescinded and suspended, possibly even expelled, from the school.

This set off alarm bells. Would this affect Steve's admission to UC Berkeley?

—Yes, it very possibly could.

—But if the boys hadn't actually used the information?

—That's not the point. He made a rather long speech about how breaking into a data system such as the college's was a crime and that there was also the cost of repairing the damage, putting up the system again and developing more effective safeguards. He concluded by saying that all of this required considerable expense.

—When was his ad hoc committee meeting?.

—Hopefully, tomorrow. They weren't wasting any time.

I told him how much Steve wanted to get into UC Berkeley. He was basically a good kid. I would guess he'd just got carried away and wanted to see if he could do it. It would be a shame if this one prank would undo two years of hard work

The Dean didn't seem to be too impressed by this argument. We left it that he'd call me after the committee meeting. Meanwhile, I'd talk to Steve.

The first thing I did was go to Arnie's office. Luckily, he was in. I quickly told him about Steve's escapade and my meeting with the Dean.

—Yeah, the guy's a hard-ass, said Arnie.

—Is there anything you can do? You've known Steve since he was a kid. He's fixed your computer. Do you think you can talk to the guy?

Arnie told me he'd l see what he could do.

The next step was to go home and confront Steve. I had mixed feelings. On the one hand, I was furious. How could he do something like this? Right after getting into Berkeley, jeopardizing his entire future. Was he showing off to his friends? Or, as I'd told the Dean, had he just wanted to see if he could do it? But I didn't want to see his chance of going to UC Berkeley ruined by a thoughtless prank, no matter how stupid it was.

I found Steve in his usual place, in his room at his computer..

— I've just had a meeting with the Dean of Students

—Oh, yeah, that. What'd he say?

—He said you and your buddies hacked into the college's data base and you're in trouble, especially you.

—It was no big deal. Guys try to hack into data bases all the time. It's a challenge.

—Well, I guess you got in.

Steve shrugged. —I got lucky, made some good guesses.

—That's not the point. Do you realize you might have your grades rescinded and be expelled. And that will screw up UC Berkeley.

—You're kidding. We didn't do anything, just hacked in and then got out.

—Well, that was enough. There's also a cost to putting the data base back up again so nobody can hack into it.

—They don't expect me to pay that, do they? They should have done a better job in the first place.

—Steve, don't you realize that what you did was wrong?. It may even legally be criminal. I don't know. But you did something wrong. And why the hell did you do it just when you were admitted to Berkeley?

For the first time, Steve looked a little penitent. —I don't know, Dad. I guess I was stupid.

—To put it mildly.

—So what's going to happen now?

—The Dean's set up some kind of committee. They're going to look into it and then call me.

—Maybe I can tell them I'm sorry.

—That's a good idea. Why don't you write a letter of apology. Make it good.

I left Steve's room and went to look for Sally, who had to be told. What a mess. Were these things supposed to happen when you were retired? As I was to find out in future years, things like this always happened.

The next day we waited for the phone call from the Dean, but it didn't come. In the evening I went over to see Arnie. He'd talked to the Dean, but he didn't know if it had done any good. Like all good moralists, the Dean had asked: What if Steve was allowed to get away with this great transgression? The answer is that before you know it every student would be hacking into the college data basis. This, he implied, would shortly lead to anarchy and the end of Western civilization. I recalled my experiences as a kid when I'd ask some adult authority if I could do something. The answer was always: if I let you do it, then everyone would want to do it. The eventual outcome would be the same: anarchy and the downfall of Western civilization. So I knew the Dean's mindset; not good.

The next day I had an interview for a Sacramento Press story. There was no call in the morning and I didn't want to be sitting around waiting, as I had done the day before. I drove to Old Sacramento and parked in one of the garages and then found a restaurant called The Art of Spaghetti. It wasn't a restaurant story. I was doing a story on a charitable event called Laughs in the Park, sponsored by two young guys who'd made it big with a downtown comedy club and who also owned the restaurant. I found them in the restaurant courtyard, two 20-year-olds, with a third man, about 40, who introduced himself as Rob Rich, a public relations guy.

I spent about an hour with them, most of it listening to the two young guys banter back and forth; they thought they were pretty funny. With the thought of Steve's situation in the back of my mind I wasn't really in the mood for this; nevertheless, I automatically took my notes while sometimes laughing politely. I wrote in my story: "An hour spent with Bert and Ernie (not their real names) in the courtyard of their Old Sacramento restaurant, shows that they have the makings of a comedy team (with some work, guys) but they have wisely and profitably made a career of promoting other comedians."

When I returned home, I found that, as invariably happens, the Dean had called while I was gone. His message was that the committee had met and that he wanted to see me. I called his office and spoke to his secretary. The Dean was a busy man but I was able to make an appointment for early the following week. In the meantime, we'd have to wait and imagine the worst.

The next morning I was awakened by an early phone call, not from the Dean (my first thought) but from the Laughs in the Park PR man, Rob Rich. He was calling me about a job. No, it wasn't that, impressed by my professionalism at our meeting, he was offering me a high-paying position in his public relations firm. He was calling me about another non-paying volunteer job, to edit a magazine put out by an antique car museum. He gave me a name and number and said he'd told the museum people I'd call. I thanked him, hung up the phone, had breakfast, then went to Carmichael Park and took out my aggression on tennis balls.

The next week, the last one in May, I was in the Dean of Student's office again. I was nervous; he wasn't. He looked smug.

The committee had met and had discussed Steve's misconduct thoroughly. They'd agreed it was a serious matter. He went on in this vein for a good 15 minutes. I was tempted to tell him that, Yes, I got it, Steve's was the crime of the century. Finally, he got to the point.

The committee had agreed that Steve must be punished. Some had been in favor of rescinding his grades and contacting UC Berkeley. But they took into account that he'd been a good student, had no previous record of crime, and was definitely a computer expert. Also, no one had really been hurt by the incident. If the college was reimbursed for the expense Steve's hacking had caused they were willing to let his admission to UC Berkeley stand and hope that he would have learned a lesson.

I told the Dean that Steve had indeed learned a lesson, that he was truly sorry for what he'd done. I handed the Dean the letter of apology Steve had written (and I had polished). The Dean read the letter.

—I'm glad your son is showing remorse.

—About the college's expense; how much was it?

The Dean pursed his lips. —I believe $1,000 would cover it.

A thousand dollars; you've got to be kidding. I didn't say this aloud. —Are you sure it's that much?

—That's the minimum amount.

I thought quickly and came to a decision. Getting into UC Berkeley would cost another $1,000.

—All right. I can write you a check. I'll take it out of Steve's allowance. I didn't say this last aloud. A few minutes later, I left the Dean's office, feeling relieved, angry and extorted.

Back home, I summoned Steve and Sally to a meeting. I told them the news.

—So Steve can go to UC Berkeley?

—Yes, for a lousy grand. Steve, I'll expect it out of your first paycheck from Microsoft.

—I'm sorry, Dad. It was stupid.

—I'm glad you realize that.

—Thanks. I'll pay you back.

—Okay. But don't worry about that now. Just go to Berkeley and pass all your courses.

So that was that. I had other business at the community college. I went to my last Shakespeare class, returned Mr. Schroeder's scrapbook, together with a dozen copies of the Sacramento Press with the story I'd done about him in it and which he'd asked for.. I also went to the admissions office and signed up for a creative writing class I hadn't been able to get into for the spring term. This was an advantage of already being a student there. A few days letter I received a letter from the college; I was in the class. I thought that it was the least they could do.

JUNE

On the first weekend of June, Sally and I went to a lunch held by a group called the Suburban Writers. The group consisted of writers in the Sacramento area; I didn't know if you had to be published or not. We'd been invited by a friend of Sally's, who'd heard that I was now a writer. Most of the people there, I saw, were women. The main function of the lunch, it seemed, was to honor an elderly woman, whose name I didn't catch, who was both a writer and a writing teacher and who had published a number of romance novels. I thought the woman might make a good Neighbors piece so after the lunch I got her name and made a note of it for future reference.

On Monday, I went as usual to the Sacramento Press office and did my usual editing. I was a little nervous that the movie critic Nadine might come in, but Anna told me that she'd actually landed a part in a touring play and would be out of town for a while. That was good news. I mentioned the antique car museum to Karl, but he wasn't interested. He didn't like cars, old or new. I should have expected this from somebody who rode a bicycle. Once again, I was asked to go across the street to get coffee for the office. Once again, I was a little annoyed but said nothing. When I'd started going to the office on Mondays I'd thought that maybe I'd learn a little something about putting out a newspaper and also that I might get to know Karl Engel a little. After a few months, neither had happened. I did like Anna, the advertising lady, though.

The next day I called Lois Bremmer, my Neighbors editor. She said they might be interested in the antique car museum and that they were still interested in a story about the Carmichael Park tennis players. The next week I drove to the museum, which was out somewhere in south Sacramento, not a great location. I talked for about an hour with the lady who was museum's business manager. I decided I didn't want to take on the job, unpaid, of editing the museum's magazine, but I did write a piece about the museum, hoping that Neighbors would take it.I started by saying: "The best kept secret in Sacramento? A prime candidate is … " and then went on to describe the museum, trying to make it sound as attractive as I could. It was clear that the museum wasn't doing too well.

It was time, I'd decided, to write the Carmichael Park tennis story for Neighbors. So the next time I went there I cornered "Mayor" Maurice: and did an interview, getting him to tell me everything he knew about all the park regulars.. I started the piece with: "Early-morning motorists on Fair Oaks Boulevard may wonder about those people playing every day on the Carmichael Park tennis courts. What they are seeing are members of the unofficial old-timers

Carmichael Park tennis club. These are about two dozen retirees, ranging in age from the early sixties (for the youngsters) to the eighties, who have played regularly there for the past 25 or so years."

That took care of Neighbors for the time being. Karl had come up with another Sacramento Press story for me, this one about a natural foods store, another one of his interests. The store, like the car museum, was in south Sacramento, on Freeport Boulevard. The people who'd opened the store were, I suppose, pioneer environmentalists and animal rights activists. They didn't carry eggs because of the conditions on "factory farms." where chickens are crammed into cages. The store also carried no meat or dairy products because the large amount of water needed to maintain herds of cows was harmful to the environment. I ended the story by writing: "If you are completely unfamiliar with the area, the Natural Foods place is located directly across the street from another food establishment whose name I forget now but which is readily identified by its golden arches. So, when driving along Freeport Boulevard, look for those arches but if you want to test out natural foods be sure to turn in on the other side of the street."

Steve had officially graduated from our community college, much to our relief. He'd gotten a job working in a neighborhood pet store and had become very interested in salt water fish. He'd already gotten a tank and was constantly fiddling around with it. Well, it was less likely to get him in trouble than fiddling around with his computer. Jack was still in Chico. Although the term had ended, he'd gotten a job doing maintenance, but that would end in July and he'd be coming back home then. Something to look forward to.

My appointment with Dr. Volkman, finally, was in the third week of June. I had to wait even longer than usual before he came into the little cubicle where I was nervously waiting. He was a big man, in his fifties, I'd say, with a square jaw and graying hair in a crewcut. He somehow looked as if he belonged in the military. I observed his hands to see if they looked like those of a surgeon. He didn't have long, slender fingers but, like my father's, they looked strong and capable. Like my own doctor, he gave me the digital test and told me I had a large prostate. Then he led me into another room, where, stripped down to my shorts, I lay down on a table, feeling like a sacrifice on an alter. I felt even more so after what followed,.but, without going into the gory details, let's just say that he was able to examine my bladder. The report he gave me was that it was already slightly scarred. This didn't sound good.

After we left what I now thought of as the torture chamber and was back in his cubicle and I was at least dressed again the doctor gave me his opinion that I needed surgery, not too surprising as he was a surgeon.. This was in the dark ages before Google, but I had done some research on prostates, in medical books in the library. I asked him if perhaps we could go the "watchful waiting" route; "watchful waiting" had a nice ring to me. He said that wasn't an option, reminding me of the scarred bladder. I asked him about the medications I'd read about that were supposed to shrink prostates. He dismissed them with a shake of his head; none of these medications was a proven success. Surgery would do the trick; he had an opening the next week.

This was too fast for me. No, that was too soon, I told him. I wanted to think it over for a few days. Also, if I did have surgery I'd have to clear my calendar. I told him about my writing for two newspapers. I had to get my outstanding stories in. He handed me a pamphlet, which, he said, would tell me all about the surgical procedure. We left it that I'd call his department the following week with my decision. I left the cubicle, went down the hall, then I remembered. I rushed back to the cubicle. He was still there, making notes on a form.

What about cancer? I asked. Did I have prostate cancer? He looked at me as if I had just said something outlandish. No, of course not, he said. I don't know what I said; maybe, Good. The next thing I knew I was in my car in the HMO parking lot. I might have to undergo surgery, but I didn't have cancer.

When I got home I told Sally about the HMO visit. I then read the pamphlet. The surgical procedure was called transurethral resection of the prostate,. TURP for short. To those who'd had it, it was also commonly known as the "rotor rooter." The surgery itself seemed pretty straightforward and, as this was an HMO, you'd stay in the hospital just overnight before they kicked you out. However, there was a list of possible after-affects, which included painful urination and blood in urine, that didn't sound pleasant. There was also a list of possible complications, such as incontinence and impotence, which sounded even worse. Retired, incontinent and impotent. What a prospect. At least the possible complications didn't include death.

After dinner, which I ate without much appetite, I called Dr F—— at home and luckily got him. I told him about the proposed surgery and asked him what he thought. He was careful to say he couldn't give a definitive opinion because he hadn't seen my medical charts but he seemed to be in favor of the surgery, which he said was a standard procedure, and he had nothing but good things to say about Dr. Volkman. So I slept on it, then called Dr. Volkman's office the next morning and said I was ready to go. The girl I talked to said the doctor's schedule was pretty full and that it probably wouldn't be for a month or two. I suspected that when

Dr. Volkman had said "next week" he wasn't really being serious. So I was committed, unless I changed my mind.

I don't know if it was because of my sterling work on the gay heroes story, but Karl assigned me to do a story on a lesbian book store downtown. The store was called Lioness Books and I asked if he was throwing me into the lioness's den, which did not elicit a smile from him. Although I entered the book store with some trepidation, expecting to find it crowded with belligerent women who'd glare at me because I was a man invading their premises, it went off okay. I wrote: "Lioness Books … is a reflection of owner T—- C—- in more ways than one. C—, who has taught Women's Studies at Sacramento State for 20 years, views the feminist bookstore as an extension of her efforts to bring a greater awareness of feminist writing to the larger community.. The store is also, like C—- herself, pleasant and interesting to get acquainted with."

C— was indeed a pleasant person, not at all forbidding or contentious, and we had a nice conversation in the back room over a cup of tea. I learned that we had something in common; her mother had also recently broken her hip in a fall. She'd also written two books and adopted cats.

When I turned in my story I told Karl I wouldn't be in the next Monday. That weekend, the last one in June, Sally and I drove down to San Francisco. It was a spur-of-the-moment trip. I was retired, so I could do things like that. We stayed at a motel on Van Ness, walked down to Union Square and strolled around downtown, visiting a couple of art galleries. On Sunday we drove to the ocean and had lunch and Ramos fizzes at the Cliff House, listening to the seals barking off shore. It was, except for the driving back and forth, a relaxing time. I forgot about the Sacramento Press and Neighbors, about Jack and Steve, and I tried to forget about my upcoming surgery. I did have one depressing thought: just when my tennis elbow was finally gone and my game was coming around, I'd have to take a break and start all over again.

JULY

On our return to Sacramento, I realized how pleasant it had been in San Francisco, where it had been refreshingly cool. Sacramento is always hot in the summer and this one was no exception. On July 3d, the temperature went to a record 109 degrees. We seriously debated calling off our club's annual July 4th tennis tournament, but in the end decided to go ahead with it as we had all the entry fees, had bought the trophies and arranged for food and drinks. We hoped that nobody would succumb to heat stroke.

We did change the schedule so that the tournament started at 7:30 in the morning instead of the usual nine. This of course created a lot of confusion as some members either didn't get the message of the changed time or forgot about it. In any case, we finally got underway around eight. Everyone was to play five sets of doubles, two of which were mixed doubles. I've mentioned that I'd done pretty well in club tournaments and I must admit that, facing an enforced break from playing after my upcoming surgery, whenever that would be, I wanted to do well in this one.. I wouldn't mind winning another trophy.

After four sets, in which I'd made more errors than usual but also hit more winners, I was in pretty good shape, tied for the lead in most points. Then I found that my partner in the last set, mixed doubles, would be a woman new to the club. As nobody knew how she played she'd been put in my bracket, which was the mid-level one. It didn't take more than two or three points to realize that she belonged in the novice bracket. She swung hard and hit the ball all over the place, rarely in the court. Worse, as I'd found to be true with most players of her type, she wasn't content to just play her side of the court but ran all over the place. I tried as gently as I could to tell her to stay on her own side and to let me take any balls in the middle. I think she made an effort but it didn't work. We were slaughtered 6-1 (I held serve once). Damn, I thought after the set, there goes the trophy. She came over and apologized, saying she'd never played in a tournament before. I told her that it was okay, but I'm afraid I said it through gritted teeth.

I didn't have much time to brood over this tennis fiasco because I found myself busy writing, both for the Sacramento Press and Neighbors. The next Monday I went to the Press office, handed in my column and did some editing. Karl wanted me to do a story on an art gallery which was next door, run by two young women. The gallery was going to have an exhibit of paintings about fishing. He also gave me a book to review, something about fighting censorship. After I finished my editing, I looked in next door, and introduced myself to the two women owners. They were both young and attractive. They'd be happy to have a story about their gallery, which I guessed was struggling a bit.. I looked at the paintings they'd received so far received for the exhibit. They were by local artists. All were different, but each had a fish of some kind in it. I told them it was interesting, even though I didn't know one fish from another. Then I drove down to my old office building to have lunch with Art Chang. He said things weren't looking any better for my old agency and that he was still trying to transfer to a different department, so far with no luck.

As for our family, Steve liked his job in the pet store, although he was spending all of his pay on fish for his new salt water tank. We had no recent word from Jack, who was due to come home later in the month after his maintenance job ended. He'd probably just show up one day. I hoped he didn't arrive late at night and have to come through our window again. My mother seemed to have recovered from the broken hip, but she was still having "spells," according to my sister. She was going to drag her to see a doctor about them. Sally was talking about having our kitchen remodeled; all of our neighbors, she said, were doing this.

At around mid-July, my fan and Sacramento Press supporter, Norma Eisenstein, invited me to come to a school downtown which housed a senior citizen's television station. The station had a program interviewing a Japanese lady, an economist, who was one of an International Visitors Group that Norma was hostingThe interviewer was a gray-haired gentleman who, I was told, was 75-years old. The other people working there were similarly old. I thought it might make a good story for Neighbors. After the program was over, I talked to several people and made notes. Norma then took the Japanese lady and myself to lunch at a nearby restaurant.

I'd done my book review for the Sacramento Press and when I looked at the issue in which it appeared I noticed that I'd been promoted. On the masthead I was listed, not merely as a contributing writer, but as an associate editor. I wondered if Norma had anything to do with this. Meanwhile, I had my art gallery story to do. Since their exhibit was devoted to fishing, I tried to get into the swing by starting my story with:: "OK everybody, art-lovers, outdoors people and just plain folks, y'all come on down to L Street between 17th and 18th, the fishing's fine. No, the river hasn't been diverted and the sewers haven't burst, it's the first annual 'Gone Fishin' exhibit at the A—— Framing Gallery." I then went on with: "For the exhibit, gallery co-owners D—- O—— and S—— W—— have thrown their nets wide and hauled in a fine catch of artists, many from other local galleries. (Sorry, but this kind of writing just naturally seems to happen with a story like this.)" The story must have not been too "fishy" for Sacramento Press readers because the gallery owners told me afterwards that they had a big crowd at the exhibit opening, much bigger than expected.

Lois Bremmer liked the idea of a story about a television station run by seniors and gave me a go-ahead on it so I had another Neighbors story to do. I'd received a $50 check for the antique car story so the money was pouring in.. I started the TV station story with: "Senior citizens are doing almost anything nowadays but I didn't know they were putting on their own television programs in Sacramento. That is, I didn't know until I went to Cable Channel 17's studio at the Coloma Community Center to watch a talk show whose guest was a foreign visitor I'd been invited to meet afterward. I thought the people in the control room and manning the cameras were on the elderly side. The talk show was an offering of 'We Seniors Present,' a program operated entirely by senior citizens (who are all volunteers) and designed primarily, but not exclusively, for senior viewers."

It turned out to be a longish story, as I then went on to tell how the project got started (it was through an agreement with Sacramento Cable to provide community access cable channels), give some background on the senior personnel who operated the station and gave a lot of facts and figures about what they'd done so far, over 200 shows. I'm not sure how the people I talked to reacted to being described as being "on the elderly side," but they must not have been offended because a year or so later I was invited to be on one of their programs.

Near the end of the month I had a phone call from my friend Ralph Foxx, the sculptor I'd written about, which resulted in another Neighbors story.. For the past few years, Ralph had done one of the county exhibits at the State Fair and he was calling from the Fair, where he was at the County building in the process of putting together the exhibit for this year. He suggested I come on down to see what was going on and maybe do a story about it. I wasn't doing anything else so I drove to the Fair, found the County building, and, sure enough, there was Ralph, along with a bunch of other artisans, busily creating their exhibits. I spent an hour or so there, talking to various people amid a lot of noise and took my usual notes. When I got home I made my usual call to Lois Bremmer and as usual she was receptive and told me to go ahead. I realized that I couldn't have found a better editor than Lois. She was always receptive and encouraging and after a story appeared I not only received a check but Lois sent me a copy of that Neighbors issue, usually with a nice note written on it.

I began the county exhibit story with "Those county exhibits at the California State Fair, year in and year out possibly its most popular attraction, how do they get put together, and who does it? Most fair-goers, if they're like myself, probably don't give this much thought while enjoying the exhibits, some of them with elaborate moving parts, all of them interesting and colorful."

I found the people who constructed the exhibits interesting and colorful, too. Many of them (not my friend Ralph) went all over the state, from fair to fair, during the year. The dean of what I called "artists/designers/technicians" in my article was a fellow who taught puppetry at Sac State and whose displays, not surprisingly, featured puppet-like figures. There were two family operations that had been doing fairs for years, an art instructor and a retired high school football coach. I concluded my piece by writing: "At the time of my visit, about two weeks before the opening of theState Fair, the county building seemed big and empty. The beginnings of a few displays were in evidence and that was all. Ralph was high up on a ladder painting in a background. At the next-door display, a cardboard cowboy was about to fall off a cardboard bucking bronco. In another display, a big Raggedy Ann doll was sitting in a large rocking chair. The sound of a power drill mixed with that of a crane lifting somebody up to the roof. Somehow, I knew, by opening day all of the county exhibits would as always be up and ready for our viewing. And at least some of the exhibitors would be making ready to go to Los Angeles a d do it all over again."

I also had to write my Adventures in the City column for the Sacramento Press. I combined my visits to the Farmer's Market in Plaza Park and the cathedral on 11th and K Streets, the Cathedral of the Blessed Sacrament to produce a fairly long piece.. I started by writing: "Yes, even your dedicated reporter gets tired trudging the streets of Sacramento, but sometimes there are compensations to the City Adventures beat. One such was a recent Wednesday noon visit to Plaza Park. The Farmer's Market was in full swing, with people crowding around the stands to get their fresh fruit and vegetables. The Mariachi Zacatecas band, inaugurating the City Life musical events at the park, was playing to an appreciative audience. Some listeners had brought chairs or blankets to sit on, others just sat on the grass. It reminded me of markets I'd been to in Mexico. And it was happening here in downtown Sacramento."

After giving some details about the Farmer's Market and information about upcoming downtown musical events furnished by my friend Susan, I wrote: "Only a few blocks away but at a far remove from all the activity in Plaza Park is the Cathedral of the Blessed Sacrament … As soon as I passed through the front doors, which are on 11th Street, I had a sense of spaciousness and serenity." I concluded with: "I spent half an hour in the cathedral and found it to be, like my visit to Plaza Park, a welcome respite from trudging the downtown streets".

On the last Monday of July I made my usual pilgrimage to the Sacramento Press office and handed in my column. There was trouble there this morning. While I was editing, the typesetter girl evidently gave Karl her notice because he took her outside and berated her for having no sense of responsibility. She in her turn told him that she could make more money working at a McDonald's. They had quite a heated exchange, lasting 15 minutes, before she left and Karl came back inside. Later, Anna told me that the calendar events girl had quit the last Friday, probably for the same reason. I couldn't get terribly concerned about all this because I'd finally gotten a notice from the HMO that my prostate surgery had been scheduled. It would be done in the first week of August. I told Karl I wouldn't be in for the next few weeks and that I probably wouldn't be able to do my column for the next month. Karl's response was to throw up his hands as if the world was conspiring against him and say he was leaving for lunch. I left shortly after; Anna wished me good luck with my operation.

AUGUST

Having my prostate surgery done wasn't that simple. The HMO had decreed that men over 55 having this procedure first had to have a physical exam, blood work, a chest x-ray and an EKG. For the physical exam I had to see a young doctor who really didn't examine me. He asked me a few questions about my medical history and a few questions about my family and that was it. I told him the only previous surgery I'd had was having my tonsils taken out as a kid. Back in those days almost every kid had his or her tonsils removed; it was standard procedure. I recalled going to the hospital with my sister, who was also having her tonsils taken out, and I remember that afterwards we both had ice cream, also standard procedure at the time. I doubted that the HMO would be serving me ice cream after the prostate surgery.

I told him that my father was 90 and my mother 82. Neither had had cancer and as far as I knew my father had never had any trouble with his prostate. I mentioned that my mother had fallen and broken her hip earlier that year and that it seemed to be taking a long time for the hip to heal. I also mentioned the "spells" my mother had been having. He had no idea what might be causing them. After the "exam," I had the chest x-ray and the EKG, then went to the lab only to be told that the blood work must be done within three days of the surgery and it was now five days before. Typical HMO stuff. This meant that I had to make another trip two days later so that a nurse could stick a needle in my arm. I guess blood is subject to change and my blood might have drastically altered in the last two days.

The surgery was scheduled for the afternoon so I had all morning to worry about it. Sally drove me to the hospital and we went through the usual rigamerol of checking in. I left Sally with all of my valuables (watch and wallet), got into one of those hospital gowns designed to be as embarrassing as possible and went into what I suppose was a pre-op room where I joined a number of other patients laying in beds and waiting. This gave me even more time to worry and as the time slowly passed I began to wonder if this operation was really necessary. I'd been doing pretty well at night the past week; it was like an aching tooth that stopped hurting when you went to the dentist's office.

Finally, just when I'd thought they'd forgotten about me, Dr. Volkman appeared. He asked me how I was doing; I lied that I was doing fine; I was transferred to a gurney and away we went. I'd asked for a general anesthetic as I wanted to have no knowledge of what horrible things were done to my private parts during the surgery. When I came awake, I was back in a bed, in the post-op room, I guess, and Sally was sitting in a chair beside me. She said Dr. Volkman had told her the operation went well, no complications. That was good news.

Somewhere along the line I must have been moved to a two-person room. I recall someone in the bed next to mine, making groaning noises. I don't know if I did the same but I might have. I'd read that in earlier times men having this kind of surgery stayed in the hospital for three days. Nowadays, if you belonged to an HMO, you stayed overnight, then they kicked you out. Theoretically, you might stay longer if circumstances warranted it, but, as I learned later, I was in what was called a "23-hour room," so that the HMO didn't have to pay for anything more than one hospital day. I believe I must have had something to eat, although I can't remember what. Eventually, Sally left, I was given something for the pain (it had started to hurt) and something to make me sleep.

The next morning Sally returned to drive me back home. I headed straight for the lazy-boy chair in our living room. I wouldn't say that I was in great pain, but I felt very uncomfortable. I took one of the Vicodins that had been given to me; Vicodin was the HMO's pain-killer of choice. I had no appetite. I read the morning newspaper, then tried to read a book but eventually gave up and watched one of the cable newscasts. I was supposed to drink a lot of water so I did my best. Mickey came and sat in my lap; Binky sat on the back of the chair. I stroked Mickey, watched television on and off (the Soviet Union was breaking up, I believe), and dozed on and off. Even with Mickey and Binky to comfort me, I felt terrible TURPing was supposed to be a standard kind of surgical procedure. I'd learned that any kind of surgery left you feeling as if you'd been beaten up by a dozen guys with baseball bats.

When my son Steve came home from his pet store job he asked me how I was doing and I told him that I wasn't feeling too bad. In the afternoon, I'd tried sitting at my computer but it hurt too much so it was back to the lazy-boy. In the evening, my son Jack called, which was a little surprising. He'd come down from Chico about two weeks before, declaring that he was through with college once and for all. He hated Chico and would never go back there. We pointed out that he had only one year to go for his degree. I told him that all the studies done showed that people with college degrees did much better in life than those without. This had no effect on him. I told him that I could probably get him a summer job with the State; I'd call some people at my agency. He said he'd never work for the State. One day we had a terrific argument and he'd stormed out, saying that he was going to stay with his girl friend Helen. This was the first we'd ever heard of her. We hadn't heard from him since.

After telling Jack that I was doing okay I asked him where he was. Helen had an apartment downtown. She worked for an insurance agency. What was he doing? Nothing much, hanging out and trying to get his head together. Helen thought she might be able to get him a temp job at her agency. I asked if he needed any money. He said that he still had the money he'd made at his maintenance job and that he was all right. I was feeling tired and it was time for another Vicodin so I left it at that and turned him over to Sally. She found out Helen's full name, her address and phone number so now we at least knew where he was. I went to bed early, taking a couple of sleeping pills, and had an unpleasant night.

In the next few days, Arnie and a few other tennis buddies dropped in to visit and commiserate with me. I also got a card from Lois Bremmer, my Neighbors assignment editor. Anna of the Sacramento Press called to see how I was doing. She asked when I might be able to come down to edit or to write a story again. I told her I'd let her know. I heard nothing from Karl Engel.

The possible after-effects of my surgery, as I think I've noted before, included bleeding, infection, blood clots, impotence and incontinence. This gave me something to think about when I went to bed at night before the combination of the Vicodin and sleeping pills kicked in.It was also common to have blood in your urine and, sure enough, I had some in mine, but not too much, at least I hoped so. In any case, at the end of the week, I had to see Dr. Volkman for a post-op check, Sally driving me down.

We sat in the waiting room for a little over an hour. Sally did the day's crossword puzzle while I tried to read a book. Finally, my name was called and then we had to sit in the usual little cubicle for another half hour. I was about ready to go home when Dr. Volkman bustled into the cubicle, in surgical scrubs. His last operation had taken longer than expected, he said, then asked me how I was doing. I asked him about the blood in the urine and he didn't seem to be too concerned. He gave me a quick look-over and told me I was in good shape. I wasn't sure I agreed with him. I asked him how long before I was back to normal. Six to eight weeks, he said. I'd noticed that no matter what, the HMO doctors always said recovery would be in six to eight weeks. I made an appointment to see him in a month. Then it was back home to my lazy-boy chair, a Vicodin and drinking lots of water.

The next day I tried sitting at my computer again and, lo and behold, I could do it without too much discomfort. I had no articles to write, but I did have my writing class coming up and so I thought I'd try my hand at a few short stories in preparation. Our trip to Miami and now my surgery had caused me to take a serious look at mortality. The first story I tried I actually called "Mortality." I started it by writing: "It's difficult not to think about mortality when you're in Miami Beach. It's especially difficult when you've come there to see your 90-year old father and your 80-year old mother and your mother's in the hospital after falling and breaking her hip." The first sentence of my next paragraph was: "Miami is a city of old people." I wrote a little while longer until I got stuck, then left the story at that. I could see that writing short stories was going to be harder than doing articles for the Sacramento Press and Neighbors.

In the first week after my surgery I had no appetite and lost three or four pounds. After that my appetite returned, I quickly regained the weight I'd lost, and I knew I was getting better. I was ready to resume my journalistic career, but I thought I'd better wait another week or two. So I went back to fiction writing. When I was a kid growing up in the Bronx I was small for my age and not particularly fast. This made me average at best in the street games we played: punch ball, off the wall, curves, touch football, and then, when I got older, the big game, stickball. But when I was ten or eleven I got into a game of handball in the schoolyard and, for some reason, I was good at it. From then on, I'd go to the schoolyard almost every afternoon and play handball. In a short time, I could beat anyone my age.

I graduated to another court where the older kids played and after a while I could beat them, too. One afternoon, Kissel and Lennie, the two best athletes on our block, a couple of years older than me, came to the schoolyard and, to their surprise, I could beat them. They didn't come back to try again. In all other games I was at best average but in handball I was champion of my neighborhood, which gave me a little status.

When I was 12 or so I began going to Crotona Park, which was quite a ways from where I lived, about 20 blocks; that was where the best handball players in my part of the Bronx lived. When I was a kid I guess you could say that handball was a big part of my life. Like many people who play a minor sport, I thought it was the best one going. You had no equipment like a racket or a bat, you hit the ball with your hands, and with both hands, because if you couldn't use your off hand you really couldn't play handball, not beat anyone anyway. What I now wanted to do was write a story about handball. I'd read stories about all the different sports, but I'd never seen one about handball.

I decided I'd write the story in the form of a reminiscence, someone looking back on the days when he was a kid. I started it like this: "Sometimes before I go to sleep I take that walk from our apartment house on Simpson Street in the Bronx to the Crotona Park handball courts, the walk I took so many times with my older brother Jake during the summer of 1953. Jake was just back from the Army then (this was Korea)and he was again playing in the money games at the park; I was twelve years old and Jake's biggest rooter when I wasn't playing myself."

Later on, my writing teacher, Seymour Kahn, would ask me if this was a memoir and if I really had an older brother Jake. No, I told him, it was all fiction; I'd made up Jake for the story. I took his question to mean that the story was believable, I called it "The Happiest Time," because, looking back, I thought that in those days when you were twelve that was before the two greatest complications of life set in: sex and money. When I described the walk to the park I wrote: "The handball courts …were reached by climbing up a flight of concrete steps. Whenever I climbed those steps I felt my legs being lifted by some unseen force, propelled by excitement and expectation." That was my attempt to recapture the feeling I'd had as a kid. If I was a better writer, a John Updike, say, I'm sure I could have found a better way of expressing this.

In my story, I had Jake, the returning Korean War veteran, kind of bumming around, not looking for a job, but making more at the big money handball games on weekends than he could have by working. Finally, though, after a family wedding, at which all the relatives tut-tut at Jake's not having a job, he does get one, in the office at his uncle's business. The uncle was known in the family as "Al, the button king." So Jake no longer goes to Crotona Park every day. A while later, he brings a girl to dinner at the apartment, then he moves out, over his mother's protests, to his own place, then he marries the girl, stops playing handball and takes up, of all things, golf. So, in a way, Jake was prolonging his childhood when he first returned, playing handball and doing not much else. Eventually, he had to enter the adult world, the job, the girl, the wife.

The younger brother, who's telling the story also has to leave the childhood world. The next summer, when he's thirteen, he also gets a job in Al, the button king's business, as a stock and delivery boy. And a cousin of one of his friends, a girl, starts coming to the handball courts. She's a tomboy but she's a girl (she has breasts) and he finds himself thinking about her. Of course, nowadays 13-year old kids have known all about sex for years. I wrote: "These were innocent times, before kindergarten kids knew all about sex, so usually I'd think about funny things I might have said to make her laugh or imagine she was in some kind of danger and I came to the rescue. But still sometimes I had other thoughts." So money and sex had come into his life.

I ended the story when, some years later, the younger brother tells Jake, who'd just gotten divorced, that their last summer going to Crotona Park together was the happiest time in his life." Jake replies: "That's funny. I don't remember being happy that summer. There was going to work and trying to figure out what to do about Laurel. I was miserable." I ended the story with: "So sometimes before I go to sleep I still take that magic walk to the Crotona Park handball courts that Jake and I took that summer of 1953 and I still see Buddy Wolfe (actually one of the top players in the Bronx then) and Manny the Bookmaker and the other guys and every now and then I'll still remember the feeling I had going up those steps, a feeling I'll never have again." Not a very upbeat story, but when you're still recovering from surgery you don't feel too upbeat.

Toward the end of the month I was feeling pretty good and ready to resume normal activities, except for playing tennis. I had a phone call from Lois Bremmer. Neighbors had a story for me; she wanted to know if I was ready to get back to writing.. I told her I thought I was. I'd done a story about a natural foods store for the Sacramento Press, mentioning the MacDonald's across the road. Now Neighbors wanted me to do a story about a MacDonald's. This one was in midtown Sacramento and it was trying to be something different, a 1950's-looking MacDonald's.

Shortly after that, I was surprised to get a call from none other than Karl Engle himself. Without any preliminaries, he told me he wanted to do a story on our big local utility company and what, if anything, it was doing to aid the environment. Karl anticipated Al Gore in his concern that people were polluting the world and would soon destroy it. The head of the utility, D— F— was a genuinely important guy in Sacramento. In fact, he was known nationally, having run one of the federal agencies. Somehow, Karl had managed to get him to agree to give an interview to the little weekly Sacramento Press. Karl wanted to know how soon I could meet with D— F—. I told him I'd call the utility and see if I could set up an interview the next week. Karl didn't ask me how I was getting along and I hadn't expected him to. He was a one-interest man, and that interest was his newspaper. When I hung up the phone, I thought, Well, at least I'm in demand.

There was good news, of a kind, that same week. My sister called and told me my mother's latest doctor had decided the cause of her "spells" was a medicine she'd been taken, Halcyon. Since she'd stopped taking it she'd been feeling much better and no more "spells." The name of that medication rang a bell. I thought I'd recently read an article about it in some magazine. I rummaged through the pile of old magazines I hadn't thrown away yet and there it was. It said Halcyon was the most popular drug prescribed for sleeplessness. After a lot of complaints had surfaced, it had been identified as having dangerous side-affects. In Europe, it had been taken off the market. No wonder my mother had been having problems. I hoped that they'd now ended.

There was even more good news on the last weekend of the month. Jack had called, saying he wanted us to meet his girl friend Helen. Sally asked them over for dinner. I wondered what she would look like. I imagined a girl with dirty hair, her nose pierced, a bellybutton ring, who knew what else. When she came in with Jack she turned out to be a perfectly normal looking girl, not really pretty but pleasant-looking, dark-haired with lustrous brown eyes, dressed in a white blouse and blue slacks. Jack himself looked different. The long hair down to his shoulders was gone and his beard was trimmed. He looked a lot more like the son we knew before his "rebellion."

We found out that Helen was from Salinas. She'd graduated from a community college there and had been in Sacramento for three years, working in an insurance office. She'd met Jack at a "club" somewhere downtown; so that's where he'd been going when he went out at night. We had a nice meal. Helen asked me how I was feeling after my surgery and Jack said, you'll be back on the tennis courts pretty soon, Dad. Helen complemented Sally on her cooking and then helped her collect the dishes and put them in the dishwasher. While they did this I confined my conversation with Jack to sports. That was something, maybe the only thing recently, we could talk about without getting into an argument. But when we went into the living room to have coffee, Jack had another surprise for us. He'd decided he was going back to Chico State after all and get his degree. Helen said that he was going to take some business courses as he wanted to get a job in Sacramento after graduating. He definitely didn't want to teach. All we could do was agree that this was a sensible course. Maybe the rebellion, after Jack had met Helen, had run its course.

I told Jack that he wouldn't be the only one going back to school next month. Of course, Steve would be starting at UC Berkeley. And I, the old man, would be going to their old community college to take a course in writing.

SEPTEMBER

My class was on Tuesday morning so on the first Tuesday of September I drove to the community college, found a parking space at the very end of the lot and hiked to the designated building. Having taken my Shakespeare course there in the spring, I had a pretty good idea of the college's layout so I found the building and the classroom without too much trouble. I'd say there were about 30 people in the classroom. As was the case in my Shakespeare class, I was the oldest one there. Some were of college age, most were in their late 20's, 30's and forties, all, I was sure, would-be writers like myself.

Our teacher, Seymour Kahn, told us he grew up in the wheat lands of Nebraska and he looked a little bit like a farmer, tall and lanky, with big hands and feet. His face was long too, lantern-jawed, with keen gray eyes under black eyebrows. For such a big man, he spoke in a soft voice and we had to lean forward to hear him. He'd evidently gone to Southern California from Nebraska as a young man and worked in television because he mentioned being nominated for an Emmy award.

In that first session, he said that writers (and would-be writers) would do well to keep a daily journal and he wanted us to start doing this. I found this interesting as I'd started keeping a kind of journal while working for the State. I did this originally because I had a supervisor (one of those worst managers in State service I mentioned at the start of this memoir) who give out assignments and then, after you'd done them, claim that he'd asked you to do something else. So I kept notes of everything he'd assign me as a self-protective device. These notes eventually evolved into a daily journal I tried to keep up, even after I'd moved on to other jobs and saner supervisors and didn't have to protect myself. So here I'd been doing what a writer was supposed to do all along.

Seymour Kahn assigned a couple of books for us to buy and told us that, in addition to the journal, we'd start out by reading and writing poetry. I was a little disappointed. I didn't know anything about writing poetry. But he did say that after the poetry we'd go on to short stories. I was anxious for him to look at the stories I'd written so far and see what he thought of them.

Meanwhile, I had my journalistic assignments to get to. After making several calls to our local utility company and speaking to D— F—'s secretary I finally was granted 15 minutes of the great man's time. I was given to understand that this was a rare privilege and that it was between meetings so I'd better be prepared to dash in, write quickly, and dash out. It reminded me of times I'd been allowed to meet with State legislators, who wanted some kind of information, immediately, of course; their underlings always acted as if this was doing me, a lowly State analyst, a great favor.

When I did get to see D—— F——, I found him to be a genial man in his fifties, white-haired, very tanned, with a square, handsome face and shining white teeth. He didn't seem to be in a rush to get me out of his office and even asked me one or two questions about myself; how did I, as senior citizen, get to be a reporter for a newspaper like the Sacramento Press. The utility had been in the local news for a long time because it ran a nuclear plant that had provided half of its power. F——'s main job now was to come up with a plan to replace the nuclear plant and he provided me with loads of written material detailing such a plan, which included (I'm quoting from the article I wrote) "solar energy, wind, geothermal, hydroelectric and fuel cell power." : One thing he was clear about was that the utility would no longer rely on nuclear power. He told me he'd visited Chernobyl earlier in the year and that seeing was believing; the damage was immense and he was no longer reluctant to say he was scared of atomic power.

The interview ran well over half an hour before he said he had a meeting to go to, stood up, shook hands, and told me to call if I had any questions about the written material. He'd confirmed what I'd always thought, that the higher-up an executive the more gracious he (or she) was; it was the low-level bureaucrats (and the State had many) who always acted as if they were too busy with their important duties to give you a second of their time. When I returned home I plowed through the utility's plans and even made notes before writing the article. It was a long one, about 1,500 words, and when it ran it took up almost the entire issue. I regret to say that I don't know if all the things in the plan came about. I do know that Sacramento doesn't have a nuclear power plant any more.

Then I turned my attention to the McDonald's story for Neighbors. This proved to even harder to set up then the utility story. It seemed that I couldn't visit this McDonald's unless the Operations Manager was there and the Operations Manager was always out of town. Finally, I pinned him down to a date in the second week of the month. I drove downtown, entered the McDonald's with my trusty notebook and there was the Operations Manager, plus two persons, a man and a woman, from a public relations agency, and, improbably, a man from McDonald's Paris office. There was a lot of introducing and handshaking while the customers, munching on their Big Macs and fries, were, I'm sure, wondering what was going on.

This McDonald's, which was supposed to remind you of the 1950's, was a little unusual. For one thing, there was a large plastic dinosaur in the center; I was told his name was Elvis.

There was also a large jukebox, which played 1950's and 1960's songs, and on the walls a lot of old movie posters, magazine covers and ads, all dating from the 1950's. I managed to tear myself away from all of the McDonald's operatives and walked around, making my usual notes. I can't remember if I ate anything there.

I started my story with: "Elvis has been seen in Sacramento; no, not Elvis Presley, but Elvisaurus, the eight-foot tall dinosaur figure, green, with a purple shirt, complete with microphone and guitar, who sets the theme for this unique McDonald's at A—— and H—. When McDonald's had the opportunity last year to obtain this prime location, according to J—— R——, McDonald's Operations Manager …, the corporation decided it didn't want just the standard building, it wanted a landmark both for itself and for Sacramento."

I went on to describe the rest of the McDonald's, which included a Jaws-size shark, crunching an orange surfboard between its teeth. The jukebox had songs which took you down memory lane: "Are You Lonesome Tonight?", Heartbreak Hotel," "All Shook Up" (sung by Elvis), "Everyday" and "Good Golly, Miss Molly." Among the old movie posters were such classics as "Because They're Young," "Muscle Beach Party" and "Twist All Night." I wrote that the old ads also brought back memories. One was for Bond bread with Hopalong Cassidy, that is, William Boyd. Another, for Bufferin, had Arthur Godfrey. Another, before cigarettes were a health hazard, had Lucille Ball and Desi Arnez. I ended the story by noting the first year's anniversary of this McDonald's would be October 15, that a week's activities were planned and that "if Elvis Presley is seen in Sacramento it may well be at this time, having his Big Mac, fries and shake at a table next to his namesake, Elvisaurus."

The next Monday I went to the Sacramento Press office and delivered my big utility story. Karl observed that it was pretty long and said that he'd have to go over it and maybe edit it down. As I've said, when the story appeared it took up almost the entire issue although Karl had taken out a few of my remarks about D— F——. This was another time when I was asked to go over to the coffee shop across the street to get coffee for the office. I exchanged a significant look with Anna but went, telling myself I was making my contribution to the smooth running of the office.

After doing my usual editing, I drove to the State building housing my old agency.. I hadn't visited there for a while and had arranged to have lunch with my friend Al Chang. But when I went into the agency's outer office a young girl I hadn't seen before told me that Al had left a message for me, He had to go to a meeting and wouldn't be able to make lunch. I asked her if Rochelle, my old assistant, was in. At first, she didn't seem to know who Rochelle was, then her eyes lit up and she said, Oh, Rochelle had transferred to another agency last month, she didn't know which one. What? Rochelle was no longer there; it didn't seem possible. I asked about Dr. George. Yes, she was still there, but she was in San Francisco at a conference. What about Dr. Denny Morgan, the Assistant Director? He'd taken early retirement. I thanked the girl and went over to the cafeteria by myself, where I had a tasteless sandwich and muddy coffee for lunch. I noticed that even Tina wasn't there. I wondered if she'd also transferred somewhere.

Driving back home, I decided that it was time to cut my ties with the old office; or, maybe it was more accurate to say it was time to acknowledge that any ties I had to my old office had been cut. I'd try to have lunch with Al Chang sometimes but no more dropping into the old stomping grounds. It had completely changed. During my recovery period, besides thinking about mortality, I'd also done some thinking about my work career. I wasn't sure why I'd kept my relationship to my old job for so long. Maybe it was because I wasn't satisfied with what I'd done during my two years in it. I knew I wished I'd been able to do more.

I supposed that the same thing was true about my 27 years with the State; in fact, I wrote this at the start of this memoir. I also wrote that I wasn't exactly ecstatic about my State career. After reaching what I'd call a mid-level position I found that I was stuck. By that time, although some written exams were still given, as everyone knew, including the State employee associations, they were meaningless. As in the business world, advancement was a matter of playing office politics. I'd never been very good at that game, one reason why I knew I'd never get very far in advertising.

One of the things I've learned in life is that people don't just sit there when something is done to them; they take some kind of action. There's a principle of physics which says that for every action there's an equal and opposite reaction. The reaction that people have may not be equal or opposite but they'll do something. I'd noticed that in the case of fellow employees of the State, when they realized they'd gone as far as they could go, some branched out into other fields, such as real estate or insurance (while still keeping their State jobs); some got into hobbies like coin collecting or music; a few, like Bab, simply stopped working (while staying on their jobs) and spent most of their time calculating how soon they could retire.

In my case, since I was stuck at my current pay level, I started to pay more attention to money matters than before. A friend of mine had introduced me to his broker at a stock agency downtown and often during lunch we'd stop there to see how the markets were doing. I started off very small by purchasing a mutual fund (before there were millions of them) and, through the broker, some stock in a local utility, the same one which D—- F— now headed. When I'd seen him I mentioned I had some stock in his company and hoped he'd improve its earnings. I'm by nature conservative so when, in the 1980's, interest rates reached new highs, I took advantage of this by buying bonds, through the broker, and again stocks of the two largest local utilities. More recently, as interest rates became more volatile and those bonds came due, I shifted money into the safest of all investments, treasury bonds.

This had another effect. The State had something called "deferred compensation," which was like an early 401K. This was one of the few programs in which the State actually helped it's regular work force (as opposed to high-level appointees and legislators); it matched the employee's contribution. The opportunity was obvious: take advantage of it by putting as much money as possible into your deferred comp. As I had interest money coming in from the bonds I'd bought, I was able to contribute the maximum. I also put money into an IRA every year, at the same time reducing my taxes and storing up money for retirement.

Well, enough of money but money is a vital part of retirement, so maybe a little more later. I'd let go of my State connection but still had my writing jobs. I'd finally been able to get hold of Joanne Johnson, the older woman writer, she was 79, whose name I'd gotten after the writers' lunch honoring her. A few days later I drove downtown once again to interview her for a Neighbors story. She lived in a small but comfortable house which she told me, she and her husband had built. It was full of collectible items, one of the things she wrote about. It also had what she called her "workroom," containing 24 file drawers of all the published stories and articles she'd written, plus the ones that weren't published. There were also stacks of books around on animals, the Old West, old autos, antiques and Oriental rugs.

It was an interview but I'd say it was more like a visit. She brought out tea and we talked for at least two hours. By this time, I'd learned that Mrs. Johnson was a bit of a legend as a writer and teacher in Sacramento literary circles. When I wrote my story, I started with: "Long-time Sacramento writer/teacher Joanne Johnson may be slowing down. Her current activities merely include writing columns for three separate publications, a magazine article on old slot machines and a Western for juveniles." I went on to write: "In a writing career that has now spanned over 50 years, Johnson has had over 30 published books, not to mention hundreds of magazine stories and articles. Her first short story, 'Ballerina,' was published in 1936. When she had two small daughters she wrote her first book, 'From One Mother to Another,' (a pre-Spock Spock, she says), which went into five printings, selling in the old Woolworth stores."

I found Mrs. Johnson to be a remarkable woman. With her husband, who'd worked for the State as a highway maintenance engineer, she'd traveled all over the world to get background for her fiction. This included trips to Australia, Japan, and Canada to stay with the Cree Indians. She'd also had tragedies in her long life. She lost two of her three daughters to cancer and her husband of 51 years died after a senseless attack by two thugs. She told me that after that attack she lost her voice and even now she had a hard time speaking, although I could understand her with no trouble.

I asked her what advice she had for beginning writers. She said, "Have faith in yourself. Writing is a profession like medicine or law; you have to learn the basics. A writer must have aptitude with words. Think of your typewriter keys as having different colors. When you write, put those colors in your work. Writing is re-writing. Your job is to bring enjoyment to your readers, If you've provided an hour's release from your readers' worries, you've done your job." I told her that I myself was a beginning writer and ask if I might send some of the stories I'd been writing to her. She said she'd be happy to read them. I could have stayed there longer but could see she was getting tired. I thanked her and left.

I still had my monthly City Adventures column to do for the Sacramento Press. Somebody had told me about a photographic exhibit called "Chernobyl" at a downtown art gallery. The photos were all taken in the aftermath of the Chernobyl nuclear explosion and included one of people fleeing with all their possessions, people putting up a sign warning that Chernobyl was a danger zone and a busload of volunteers dressed in surgical masks and gowns. The exhibition, I wrote, was a "grim one" but also powerful. There was no charge but visitors could donate to a 250-bed hospital in Kiev dedicated to treating victims of the blast, especially children. I talked a little with the gallery's owner. His name was Zeke X——; he was a youngish guy, Greek and pretty interesting. I gathered he was operating the gallery on a shoestring, similar to what Karl Engle was doing with the Sacramento Press. In fact, he was an advertiser in the Press and owed Karl some money for his ads.

This was the first item of my column. I followed it with an item on my old staple, a farmer's market, this one in Roosevelt Park. I hadn't known there was such a thing until someone had told me about it, and I noticed many of the same vendors as in Plaza Park. My next item was a listing of the latest Downtown Plaza events as given to me by Susan, the marketing person.. One of these was a "honey roll." What was this? The lucky winner of some radio, or maybe TV station, contest got to roll around in a wading pool filled with honey which also had dollar bills in it and to keep any bills that stuck. Finally, I got in a plug for my old friends at the antique car museum, which was not, strictly speaking, downtown but could be reached from there. In any case, I wrote, I wanted to mention the museum because of its somewhat remote location.

I was pretty well running out of things to write about for my City Adventures column, but at least that took care of it for another month.

On the home front, both of our sons were now safely off to their respective colleges. Jack had called us once from Chico. He and a group of friends had rented a house off-campus and he seemed to be satisfied with that. He was taking three English and two business courses, a lot of work, he said, but he didn't say anything about wanting to drop out. It was hard for us to believe, but maybe he'd actually finish college the next spring and get his degree.

Sally and I drove Steve down to Berkeley to get him moved into his quarters. He was staying in a dorm, which was not like anything I knew from my old college days, admittedly was back in the Dark Ages. His room, which he shared with another student, was small and pretty shabby, looking as if it hadn't been painted or even touched for many years. Not too good, I thought, considering the money we were paying for Steve's room and board. But the dorm was co-ed and there were girls running around all over the place. This would have been unheard of in my day. I was cautious going into the restroom, which was unisex, making sure the coast was clear. After installing Steve, we found a place nearby to have lunch, then walked a few blocks along Telegraph Avenue. . There were still some left-over hippies, or beatniks, or whatever they were, all, it seemed, with huge mangy-looking dogs. When we left Steve and drove back, I said to Sally, Well, he's going to have an interesting time. I hope he'll be okay, said Sally. He will, I assured her, keeping my fingers crossed.

In the last week of the month, a special issue of the Carmichael Neighbors came out and in it were three of my stories. The first was the one about the Carmichael Park old guy tennis players, with a picture on the front page of the "Mayor" and the "Judge" standing on either side of a tennis net. I thought I knew who'd arranged for that. The second was my story about our neighbor and drug-fighter Myra Lake, with a nice picture of her in the middle of the page. The third was a smaller piece, one I'd written after a lot of phone calls made while I was recovering from my surgery, on the League of Carmichael Artists.

I started the tennis piece with: "Early-morning motorists on Fair Oaks Boulevard may wonder about those people playing every day on the Carmichael Park tennis courts. What they are seeing are members of the unofficial old-timers Carmichael Park tennis club. These are about two dozen retirees, ranging in age from the early sixties (for the youngsters) to the eighties, who have played regularly there for the past 25 or so years." I gave some information on a few of the individual players, which I'd garnered from Maurice, then concluded with: "These old-timers may not cover as much ground as formerly. Several wear knee braces and others wear devices for tennis elbow. One brings liniment to rub on his arthritic legs. One has been somewhat slowed down by recent cancer surgery. G—, the oldest player at age 85, is temporarily sidelined because of a fall. Despite all this, play (as I can personally testify) is spirited and competitive. Every March there is a tournament, dubbed the "Old Farts Tournament," by the participants. It's round-robin doubles and the winners get trophies. In fairness, all of these retirees deserve awards. Each one is a testimony to the spirit that refuses to allow age and its associated infirmities deter people from what they want and like to do. Long may they play at Carmichael Park."

When I went out to get my Sacramento Bee that morning I found a note from Arnie stuck in the rubber band: Congratulations. You are the Bard of Carmichael. I was glad that these stories had finally made it into print. I'd also be glad when I received my check for them $150. Who said there wasn't big bucks in writing? Re-reading my tennis article, I thought it was time for me to get out on the tennis courts again. I'd go to Carmichael Park sometime the next week.

OCTOBER

If I wasn't famous in all of Sacramento after having three stories in one issue of Neighbors I was at least well-known in Carmichael Park. "Mayor" Maurice and Jeff tthe Judge were especially pleased with having their pictures on the front page of Neighbors. A few of the other players I hadn't mentioned wanted to know why I hadn't included them in my story. I told them I couldn't name everybody. If I ever did a sequel I'd see to it that they were in. This seemed to satisfy most of them.

I wasn't ready to actually play yet so, after I'd had my brief moment of fame, I went over to an unoccupied court and hit a couple of baskets of balls over the net, practicing my serve. I'm one of those players who needs to play regularly to have a decent game. After being idle for about two months, my first serves barely reached the net. By the second basket though I was doing better, then my shoulder, unaccustomed to the exercise, began to hurt. I decided that was enough for a start. I'd take a break and hit some more baskets in a few days. Once again, I regretted that I'd finally shaken off my tennis elbow and was playing fairly well before my enforced sidelining.

In my writing class, we'd had two weeks of composing poems. Seymour Kahn liked to separate his class into small groups and have each member of a group critique the others. I was in a group with three ladies, two of college age and one slightly older named Arlene. She was about 30 and very pretty.. I'd managed to put together some poems, using plain ordinary language while throwing in a simile and metaphor or two. I had no idea if the meter was right. But evidently when writing poetry nowadays you didn't have to worry too much about such things. The ladies liked my poems..

I'd written a few more short stories. They were about the adventures, or misadventures, of a young man who'd come out from New York to San Francisco.He wanted to escape from the path his life was supposed to take—get a job, marry a nice girl (as he was Jewish, although I didn't dwell on this, a nice Jewish girl), start a family— to a life where he was on his own. As he was a young man in San Francisco his misadventures usually had something to do with the girls he met. In one, he falls into an affair with the wife of someone he knows (and likes), knowing it will lead to nothing but trouble. In another, he's about to jump into bed with a woman at a party only to discover she's his boss's wife. (The story was supposed to be funny). In still another, he dates a girl for a while but she's on her way up in the San Francisco social world and he's soon left behind. I used some of my own experiences in writing these stories, but my actual life was far tamer than that of my young man.

I'd had a couple of meetings with Seymour Kahn, who thought my stories not bad, if not actually too good.. I'd gotten to know him pretty well by then. He'd gone as a young man from Nebraska, not to San Francisco, but to Hollywood, where he roomed with a couple of friends and they tried to get into the screenwriting business. Through some relative of one of the friends they'd started writing for a television quiz show and I suppose he was successful at it, hence the Emmy award nomination. I wasn't quite sure why he'd left that job and why he was now teaching writing at a community college. He lived in Auburn, which he said both he and his wife liked. I thought he was working on a novel and maybe the teaching job paid the bills while not taking up too much of his time. He was also the advisor to the college's literary magazine, which I was told was a prize-winning one.

I asked his advice on possibly getting my stories published. No, he didn't say he'd send them to his agent. (I'm not sure if he had one). He did tell me about a book that gave the names of the smaller literary magazines and suggested I look at it, then try some of those. I guess he didn't think I was ready for the New Yorker. He knew by this time that I did stories for the Sacramento Press and Neighbors. I broached the idea of doing a profile of him for Neighbors. He said okay but not now, maybe after the term. I said I'd remind him when the time came.

Meanwhile, I had a couple of other writer stories to do for Neighbors. The guy who wrote most of their articles for the Yolo County Neighbors was on vacation and they needed stories for that area. I'd tracked down two writers who lived in Davis, which is in Yolo County, and who happened to know each other. They were also both going to be much more well-known in the future. I drove to Davis, the farthest I'd gone for a story (but Neighbors paid for gas mileage) to see the first one, a woman. She turned out to be attractive, about 40 years old I guessed, soft-voiced and unassuming, married with two children. She'd started by writing science-fiction, or speculative, stories and was going to have a novel published shortly. She gave me a copy of one of her books, a collection of sci-fi stories, and after reading it I tried, in my profile of her, to contrast her appearance of an ordinary Davis housewife, with her fiction, which was pretty wild.

The next week I again drove out to Davis, this time even a little further, found the writer's house, this was a man, but nobody was home. The Neighbors photographer arrived about ten minutes later and we waited outside the house for half an hour, while he told me something about his life and struggles. He was barely making it in his job with Neighbors and hoped to get a job with the Bee eventually. We then decided the writer wasn't going to come, so left, and I drove back to Carmichael. I called the writer, he called back later, and he couldn't have been more apologetic. He'd simply forgotten about the appointment. His books were already selling pretty well, and I guessed an interview with Neighbors wasn't a big thing in his career. He told me that he could come over to my place and do the interview. Davis was a long trip so I said, Sure.

When he arrived, he, like his fellow Davis writer, was about 40, a pleasant, athletic-looking guy. The first thing he did was to apologize again but I told him it was okay and thanked him for driving over; I didn't think too many writers, or anyone else, would have done that. I started my piece on him with: "What if the attempt to rescue the hostages in Iran had succeeded instead of being a disaster? Carter would have been re-elected president and the losing candidate … who was he anyway, some ex-actor or somebody? This is the kind of historical speculation that Davis science-fiction writer K— S— R— explores in his novels and short stories. R— does not ignore future technology, which he attempts to make as realistic as possible, but his work concentrates on social and political concerns (with emphasis on the environment), issues of war and peace, and possibilities for international cooperation."

R— told me, and I wrote, that he had an ambitious project, a trilogy about the colonization of Mars 200 to 300 years in the future. He also revealed that he was interested in backpacking and mountain-climbing. This accounted for his looking so fit. He and his wife had been to the Himalayas and had climbed to within three miles of the top of Mount Everest. That was impressive. When he left, R— gave me a signed copy of one of his books (so my trips to Davis had netted me two books).

Without revealing their names, I can say that K— S— R—'s novel was well-received, that one of her later novels was even more successful and was made into a movie (not too good a one, I thought). K— S— R— did go on to write his Martian trilogy and these too were very well-received. I saw them in the library and on a trip to London his books were prominently displayed in a bookstore we visited. So, besides getting to meet and interview the celebrated D— F—, my journalistic career had given me an introduction to two well-known writers. This wasn't as good perhaps as the perk from a story on Christmas goodies I later wrote, a box of truffles sent to me by a Grass Valley candy maker, but it was something.

By this time, my chief interest was in doing Neighbors stories (they paid $50 each) but Karl had given me another assignment, this one to write about something called the "men's consciousness movement." I hadn't been aware that there even was such a thing, but there was and it seemed to be pretty widespread. It turned out that Tim Moore, the Press's book editor, actually belonged to a men's group that met weekly. Tim invited me to attend one of these meetings; I politely declined. I was never much for movements of any kind.

My research found that stories about the men's movement had started to appear in magazines like Time and Newsweek and that there was an episode on the then popular sitcom, Murphy Brown, about it. And comics were making jokes about it, which indicated something was going on. One of the movement's founders (or maybe the founder) was a poet named Robert Bly who'd written a book, Iron John, about men recovering their masculinity. The book made the best-seller lists and, I read, it was estimated that over 100,000 men had participated in Bly's "Gathering of Men" workshops.

Instead of going to one of Tim Moore's meetings, I called someone, Frank Hooper, whose name Tim had given me and who was the founder and director of Men's Rights, Inc., which, as I discovered (and wrote), "was a Sacramento non-profit organization dedicated to raising public awareness about the male position in custody and property, military and health issues." I'd assumed that this men's movement was a response to the feminist movement, which everyone knew about, and Frank agreed with me. He told me that feminism had "destroyed the balance between the sexes with negative messages about men" and that this balance must now be restored. In talking to Frank I learned that he was a fellow Bronxite and, I'm not sure how this came up, also a fellow tennis player. I invited him to come over to my house, bringing his tennis racket. I'd interview him and then we'd hit some tennis balls. I was still tentatively feeling my way back into playing and I thought this would be good practice for me.

I'd sent Joanne Johnson my handball story and one of my San Francisco stories, the one in which my hero was about to jump into bed with his boss's wife. She'd returned them with a lot of my deathless prose lined out and a note to tighten them up and not let my narration get in the way of the action. I thought it was good advice. I put the handball story away for a while; I was going to follow another piece of her advice and rewrite, rewrite. I did one rewrite of the San Francisco story, making the hero a young guy who'd defied his Jewish mother to leave New York for San Francisco and who then went against all of her admonitions to him with disastrous results. He gambled and lost, bought a used car which broke down, got entangled with a strange woman (the boss's wife) and, maybe worst of all, went out into the rain without his rubbers and caught a terrible cold. At the end, I took mercy on him and had a neighbor, a gorgeous blonde girl who happened to be a nurse, come over to take care of his cold. But she turned out to be a nice Jewish girl, also from New York, so his mother had won after all. .

When I took the San Francisco story to my next class, my group, three young guys, thought it was pretty funny. Theirs were pretty grim, with themes of suicide, drug-taking and general misery, but maybe that's the way young guys have always seen the world. As a change from writing about a young guy in San Francisco, I'd written a story about a middle-aged man, he worked for a State agency, who's awakened at night by a dog barking next door. After telling the reader about all the disappointments in his life that have made him bitter, I had him get out of bed, take a gun from his bedside table and go out into the night. His wife hears four shots and she fears the worst. When he returns she asks him if he shot the dog. He replies, Of course not. Nobody was home and the dog obviously hadn't been fed or given water. He'd filled a dish with water from a garden hose, then shot out the tires of the flashy car of the owner, a real estate agent, in which she liked to speed around in. She deserved it, he tells his wife. I sent this story to one of the little literary magazines Mr. Kahn had told me about. Why not? I thought.

The next week a good many people in my neighborhood had reason to feel disgruntled, not about barking dogs, but about something even worse. Let me go back to the previous month or two. Our swim and tennis club had a new member, a man named George Franklin. He was a big guy in his forties, blonde, good-looking, with a flashing smile and a smooth line of patter. Franklin was a salesman; he was selling shares in some company which was supposed to pay a high rate of return while at the same time protecting the investor from taxes. Franklin had approached me once about his scheme, but, as I've said, I'm very conservative when it comes to money and I told him I'd pass.

According to the headline in the Bee that morning, a number of our neighbors hadn't passed. The story came out when Franklin was arrested in his palatial Lake Tahoe home. His company had of course been a Ponzi scheme. He'd done well for himself out of it, buying the home, several cars, a boat and similar trappings of wealth. Of all the money he'd collected, there was almost nothing left. I was amazed at how many of our neighbors, all members of the club, had bought into his company and at the amount of money, in the hundreds of thousands, that three or four of them had given him. It hadn't occurred to me that anyone would be taken in by this smooth talker. But at that time many people had done pretty well in the stock market and who wanted to give back their money in taxes to the government, which would squander it anyway? Needless to say, the "big scam," as I thought of it, was all the talk the next time I went to the club. I'm happy to say that none of my tennis buddies had been taken in. Charley was all for stringing the guy up. Arnie thought that at most he'd get a year of two in jail for a white-collar crime. Mike said that guys like that gave the finance business a bad name. We played our usual three sets. I was doing better, but by the end of the second set I was pretty well beat.

As I've said, I'd planned to retire when I was 59, at which time I'd get a fair retirement from the State. I'd also have the money coming in from my investments, by this time mostly Treasury and utility company bonds and a mutual stock fund, plus the money I'd take out from my deferred comp and my social security payments, which I'd elected to start taking at age 62 instead of waiting until I was 65. I'd thought the total of all this would be enough to live on. Since I'd worked another two years, I now had a little more coming in than I'd projected.

The millions of books written about retirement all have their advice about getting enough money to last you for the rest of your life. Some have elaborate calculations of the "nest egg" you'll need and of how much money you can take out monthly so it doesn't run out. I too thought I had it all figured out. What I learned in my first year in retirement is that you could never really figure out how much money you'd need. I knew that our ancient house would need repairs as long as we continued to live there. I didn't know that all of our appliances— dishwasher, garbage disposal, water heater— would need replacing. I knew it would be expensive to have both of our sons in a four-year college at the same time. I hadn't counted on Steve going to Berkeley, which was a lot more costly than a state college. The $50 a story I received from Neighbors wasn't much, but every dollar helped.

In the last week of the month, Sally and I drove to Folsom. I was going to do a story for Neighbors on a group of five artists, all women, who worked in a building on Sutter Street, the main street of "historical" Folsom, then we were going to have lunch. I started my story with: "'Oh, it's like a little Carmel.' This is a typical visitor's comment when coming upon the group of artist studio-galleries at 705 Sutter Street in Folsom. Joan and Bill B—, owners of the building the past 25 years and both artists themselves (he does the roadside signs telling you how far you are from the Nut Tree), have traditionally reserved five spaces for local artists. The artists actually do their work there, as attested to be easels, paints, brushes in coffee cans and works-in-progress. The spaces also give them the opportunity to display their completed works and, not of least importance, sell them."

After going through all five spaces and talking to all five artists, which took up just about all morning, Sally and I found a place to have lunch. Sally had taken art lessons many years ago and now she said she might want to take lessons again. As it happened, we had a neighbor, Anne C—-, a member of our club, who was an artist and who taught art. Sally said she'd call Anne and see if she could get into one of her classes. I told her that was a good idea. If I ever wrote a book she could do the illustrations for it. She then asked me if I thought I was doing too much writing for the Press and Neighbors. I asked her what she meant. Well, she said, you seem to be running around all over—downtown, Davis, now Folsom, chasing after stories. You're supposed to be retired. Aren't you overdoing it a little? I said I enjoyed meeting new people and writing about them. She said, All right, as long as I liked what I was doing. I said I'd think about it.

As we'd arranged, Frank Hooper, the Men's Rights, Inc. guy, came to our house. He was young, or youngish, in his thirties, tall, with dark wavy hair and sharp features. He told me he'd gone to an Ivy League school, then had obtained a law degree. I wasn't clear about how he'd gotten into the men's thing, but he seemed to be pretty avid about it. He'd been on a local TV show the night before espousing his cause and he was flying to New York that weekend to appear on a national talk show. So I'd met still another celebrity, at least a semi-celebrity. After I'd interviewed him for the story and we'd exchanged tales of growing up in the Bronx (he never played handball) we went over to the club. He was a pretty fair player. We hit for a while, then played a set, which I won 6-4. He wanted to play another, but I told him that was enough for me. I was just getting back into playing and didn't want to overdo it. He said he'd call me when he got back from New York and we'd have another tennis session.

My "City Adventures" column for the month was called "Fall Art Frenzy." I described the exhibits, current and coming, of several downtown art galleries, one of them the Matrix Gallery, which I'd written about before. Veering off from art, I went on to write about a place in the Downtown Plaza called The Joy of Cookies, "where at lunchtime dozens of downtown workers and shoppers line up to get their chocolate chip cookie fix." To fill out the column, I had an item about the central library, which was in a temporary location, but which still had books and CDs to loan out and what they claimed to be the "best reference service in Sacramento." .

I called my folks that week. My father had turned 91. Sally and I sang "Happy Birthday" to him over the phone. He said he felt fine and asked about the "boys." I was happy that we were able to tell him they were both doing okay. We spoke to my mother. She was feeling much better since she'd stopped taking the Halcyon. So all seemed well on that front.

At the end of the month, we learned that one of our neighbors, an older woman, had lost $400,000 in the "big scam." She wasn't the first senior citizen I knew of to be taken in by such a scheme, and she wouldn't be the last. She remained secluded in her house. Sally and others took food over to her. Then her son arrived from somewhere in the East and shortly after that a "For Sale" sign appeared on her lawn. After the house was sold, no one heard from her again. Her life had been completely changed. Charlie was right; the guy should be strung up.

NOVEMBER

In the first week of November, Sally and I drove to Chico to see Jack. The house he was sharing with three other seniors wasn't too bad. The tables and chairs looked as if they'd come from a thrift store but they had a TV and a hi-fi set. We went to downtown Chico and had a nice lunch, then walked around the campus. As I've said, we'd always liked Chico; the college sort of blended into the town and you could walk, or bicycle, everywhere. Jack's dislike of Chico seemed to have abated. He told us Helen had come up to visit him the weekend before and I wondered that if having a girl friend made living there more bearable. We told Jack that we hoped to see him and Helen at Thanksgiving.

My last column for the Sacramento Press had been called "Fall Art Frenzy." Now I seemed to be involved in a lot of art stories. Karl wanted me to do a story about a group called Los Co-Madres, six Chicano female painters whose works were being shown, not in a gallery, but at Luna's Café on 16th Street. I walked over there and found a few of the women. Co-Madres, I learned, referred to women selected to be godmothers of a friend's child. The name was chosen to signify the close relationship of the women painters.

The group had a formal mission statement: "Women coming together to inspire and encourage each other to create art. Los Co-Madres was conceived from the mutual need to bring women's art to the forefront of the male-dominated art world. Co-Madres are alive and well and together. Our voices will be heard and our art force will shine! AVELANTE!" Two of the women worked for the State. One was a member of another artists group known as the RCAF, the Royal Chicano Air Force. (I was learning a lot in this interview). I wrote something about each of the women and ended up with a longish piece that Karl put on the front page of the Press.

Neighbors also had an art story for me. There was a gallery just off the main street of Fair Oaks called the Art Works which had been there for almost 20 years and which, I was told, had always been considered one of the outstanding galleries in the Sacramento area. It was currently owned by an Oriental gentleman named Makepeace T— and the focus of my story would be that a group of Fair Oaks artists was negotiating to buy it and operate it as a cooperative. I drove out to Fair Oaks and found the gallery, which was a large place in a kind of vacant lot that had chickens strutting around in front of it. Mr. T—, who was an interesting interviewee. He was, he told me, a painter, a sculptor and a photographer. He was born in Shanghai, left there at age 19, received a doctor's degree in chemistry from the University of Michigan and had lived in Davis since 1967. He was chairman of the board for the non-profit

Davis Art Center and said he took over operation of the Art Works to experience the working of a commercial gallery. He gave me a tour of the gallery and one of the exhibitors was my friend Ralph Foxx, so I was able to mention his name in my story.

T— summed up what he'd learned from his commercial art gallery experience in two words: "It's tough," and this was his message to the prospective buyers. He pointed out that a number of Sacramento art galleries had closed during the year and said there was a direct relationship between the current recession and art sales. The leader of the artists who wanted to take over the Art Works was a lady named Norma M—, who told me she wanted it to be a venue for local artists to exhibit and serve as meeting place for exchanging ideas. At the time I wrote my article, the sale of the Art Works was up in the air, but, as I wrote, Mrs. M— and her fellow artists were determined, and some time later the deal was made.

I was also busy with writing for my class. We were supposed to write a play so I took one of my San Francisco stories called "The Last Drink" and converted it into a play. There were only three characters and it took place in a San Francisco bar. The characters were essentially the guy and the girl, plus Jim, the bartender. The guy and the girl were meeting for a last drink before she went back to the Midwest to tend to her father, who'd suffered a heart attack. Things were strained between the guy and girl because, being a guy, he had a problem with commitment. But, needless to say, he was unhappy about her leaving.

In the dialogue of the play, which, I admit, owed a lot to Ernest Hemingway, the guy asks the girl not to leave, even promising to think about getting married; the girl says she has to go. The guy asks if she's coming back; she's non-commital, but when he tries to embrace her she pulls back and when he volunteers to drive her to the airport she says she'll take a taxicab. When the girl leaves, the guy says to the bartender, "She's not coming back, is she?" and orders another drink.

Seymour Kahn must have liked my little play. At any rate, he picked it to be acted out in class. I was to be the guy; Arlene , who, as I've said, was very pretty, was the girl. I had a good time pretending that Arlene was my girl friend, even though she was about to leave me. The class seemed to like the play. After class, I went to the Rush Haven coffee shop to pick up some artist material Tilly was leaving for me. I was having a latte and looking at the latest pictures on the walls when my classmate Dick Allen walked in. I found out that he worked at Rush Haven and was going on in half an hour. I bought him a latte and, by now being an experienced inter-viewer, found out that Dick wasn't quite as young as I'd thought, he was 28, that he wanted to be writer and that he was writing a novel. He earned $500 a month working at the coffee shop and tried to keep his expenses down by eating only two meals a day. Even so, he wasn't making it and was looking for a higher-paying job as a bartender.

My conversation with Dick gave me food for thought. I'd learned from Tilly how hard it was to be a full-time artist. Makepeace T— had told me how tough it was to run an art gallery. Dick was an example of how equally hard it was to be a writer. I was glad that I hadn't tried to be a writer when I was young. I'd liked to write but never considered trying to make a career of it, although if somebody had offered I'd have given it a try. As I've said, I also had a certain knack with numbers so fell naturally into becoming a research analyst. It was a lot easier being a writer now when I had my State retirement and other income to count on.

Having become an occasional visitor to Rush Haven, I'd become aware of coffee houses and, as I drove around Sacramento in pursuit of stories, I'd seen that Rush Haven wasn't the only one. Every little shopping area seemed to be getting a coffee house. Although he wasn't too enthusiastic, I convinced Karl that coffee houses in Sacramento would make a good story. I talked to the owner of Rush Haven, then drove to the others I'd seen, which seemed to extend in a straight line from Carmichael to Fair Oaks. My story started with: "Coffee houses have come to the suburbs. The Sacramento suburbs? you ask. That arid landscape we all know, tract houses, congested surface streets, fast-food joints and tacky strip malls. Yes, it's true. Coffees houses, long centers of downtown social activity, have not only spread to the suburbs but are springing up there faster than crabgrass in a tract house lawn."

The coffee house proprietors themselves had varying explanations for this phenomenon. A couple told me they thought people were drinking less and that coffee houses were replacing bars as places people could meet, socialize, and also stay sober. A couple thought that it was the coffee itself, that people were getting educated in what quality coffee was and wanted to experience it. One thing the proprietors had in common was that they all liked good coffee and each thought his or hers was the best. (This was years before Starbuck's moved in and theirs was only that brand to have).

Each coffee house, as I wrote, had its own individual character. "Rush Haven 's customers include children from a neighboring day care center (hot chocolate and cookies), exercisers from a nearby aerobic center (nonfat mocha and low fat muffins), mothers waiting to pick up their offspring from the dance studio across the way and students who gather in the afternoon to recharge with double expressos."

The owners, a middle-aged couple, of another coffee house said they were trying to create a European-type place, with gift items, candies, pastries and a warm, welcoming atmosphere. "The result is a family clientele, people dropping in after shopping, mothers bringing in children for dessert and coffee, and families coming in on Sunday morning after church."

As a result of my visits to Fair Oaks for art stories, I'd discovered the Fair Oaks Coffee House and Deli, which was the center of that town's social activity and where you wanted to go to find out the latest goings-on there. I wrote: "Every day a regular clientele of local businesspeople and storekeepers as well as doctors, lawyers, bank officers, insurance agents, artists and the firemen from the station around the corner congregate at the coffee house to transact business, exchange gossip and drink the Java City coffees." I was told that the coffee house was involved in an accident two years before, which had become famous throughout Fair Oaks Village; a Cadillac ran through its window, causing a two-months shutdown. The owner told me: "The day we re-opened was a great day. All of friends and neighbors came. They brought flowers, plants, balloons and cards." I wrote that the turnout was a good demonstration of how much a good coffee house meant to its community.

I also wrote that the coffee houses benefit Sacramento's suburban artistic community. Rush Haven always had paintings on its walls, chosen by Tilly. Another place showed paintings of local artists and students. Yet another displayed pictures of local photographers. The Fair Oaks coffee shop, at the time I went there, had an exhibit by an artist who had his studio in the Village (and whom I later did a story about for Neighbors). Now that the Starbuck's tide has swept over Sacramento, and over the world, I'm sure none of these individually-owned coffee shops, is around any more. Like the mom-and-pop video and computer stores, they had their day and have now gone under.

On the home front, I was feeling back to normal. I tried several times but never could get an appointment to see Dr. Volkman again. As none of the dreaded after-effects had occurred, I left a message with his nurse that everything had turned out fine and that if any problem came up I'd call. Sally had started taking art lessons from her friend and neighbor, who gave classes at a nearby framing shop. I told her that she could stop working any time she wanted, but she said she'd stay on until Steve finished Berkeley, which was proving to be pretty expensive. If Jack managed to graduate from Chico next spring that would help. Of course, there'd then be the matter of his finding a job and it was a good bet our recession would still be going on. Well, that was a problem for next year. The latest thing in our house to go was not an appliance this time, it was our VCR. As taping TV shows on the VCR enabled us to fast forward through commercials this was nearly as bad as not having a garbage disposal or a dishwasher. We bought a new one and, with Arnie's help, managed to get it working in only a few hours.

I was still going to the Sacramento Press office to edit movie reviews and such on Mondays. On the second Monday of the month I drove from there to my old State building to have lunch with my friend Al Chang, who'd finally managed to transfer to another safer, he hoped, agency. This time I'd made sure he didn't have any possible meetings to attend. I saw a bunch of State workers milling around and when I met him Al told me it was some kind of work protest as the Governor had announced definitely no pay raises this year. As always in a time of budget crisis, the State had a hiring freeze and there were threats of jobs being cut, although this almost ever happened. Al filled me in on the latest doings of the people we'd worked with at our agency; almost everyone had also transferred out. As we were leaving, Al said, I almost forgot, then he told me that the office tyrant we'd both once worked for had passed away; the news had been posted on a State bulletin board. I told Al I'd call and maybe see him later that month. Driving back home, I thought about the passing of our old boss. I couldn't feel sorry about it as he'd caused so much misery to so many people. Still, that had been a while ago and, at that distance, I didn't feel as happy or as triumphant about his death as I might have in the past. .

I'd written enough San Francisco stories for the time being and I wasn't ready yet to write workplace stories (I'd write quite a few eventually) so I decided to write my first "retirement" story. I set it in the Miami residential hotel where my parents stayed. The hero, who'd been retired for ten years, and his wife have gone to the hotel from New York City every winter in that time. They are among the "senior" members of the senior community there. A new couple moves in and when the wife asks him in to help with something he recognizes the husband as an old boss he'd detested. The old boss is seated in an armchair as if in a throne, ordering his wife around. So he hasn't changed, the hero thinks, and determines that he'll talk to the other members of the community and repay his old boss by giving him and his wife a hard time. Then, when the old boss has to go to the bathroom he has to use a walker that he hero hadn't noticed before and the wife tells him her husband has suffered a stroke. She says it would be a huge favor if the hero could come over every now and then and play some chess with her husband, one of the few things he can still do. When the hero returns to his own apartment, he tells his wife about the new couple, without mentioning that the husband used to be his boss. He says he may be going next door to play chess sometime with the husband and that she should show the wife the ropes around the place. I may well have had my own ex-boss in mind when I wrote the story.

Around the middle of the month I composed my "City Adventures" column. I'd found a store on the way to the Downtown Plaza that sold phonograph records, but it wasn't just any old store, it sold collectibles, out-of-print and rare records. I introduced myself to the owner, Ed H—, who was already at the cash register in blue shirt and red suspenders, trying to locate a record for a collector over the phone. The store was a large one and there were records everywhere, in bins that ran the length of the store, stacked up at the end of the bins, in cartons, in corners, everywhere. The records were of all kinds. I walked up and down the aisles, followed, as I wrote, by Nefra, the store cat, and noted classic, opera, bands, vocalists, folk, jazz, rock, comedy, Broadway shows, movie soundtracks, country, Western, blues.

Some of the individual records I saw were the young Frank Sinatra, the Andrews Sisters, the Beatles (a huge selection, and. I wrote, "for people like myself, who grew up with radio," Jack Benny, George Burns and Gracie Allen, the Aldrich family and The Romance of Helen Trent. Record prices, Ed H— told me, ranged from 50 cents to over $1,000. The most expensive record in the store was the soundtrack from the movie "The Caine Mutiny," worth $10,000 because of its rarity. When I'd finished taking my notes, Ed invited me to take any record for myself. I chose one by the Tiajuana Band. He told me it was worth 50 cents.

I finished out the column with a report on a combined art and poetry exhibit which my friend Tilly had told me about. It was at the Southern Pacific Transportation Warehouse. (These exhibits were likely to be found anywhere downtown). I began with: "In Lak esh, as everyone knows (well, almost everyone), is a Mayan phrase for "I am your other you. You are my other me." This was the name of the show. The project was sponsored by the Sacramento Poetry Center and the art included paintings, sculptures, photographs and videos, with complementary poems hung next to the art pieces or somehow integrated with them. I was happy to have found the record story and the exhibit so I could write another column, which I intended to be my last. It was just too difficult to scrape up enough downtown material to fill up a "City Adventures" column every month.

When I arrived at the Sacramento Press office the next Monday I planned to deliver this news to Karl when I handed in the column, but he wasn't there. Anna told me he was out on his bicycle putting copies of the paper into stands. But my friend Nadia, the Press movie critic and sometimes actress, was there and she had big news for us. She'd just married one of the actors she'd been touring with and was, as she told us, filled with joy. Then Karl came in. He looked around, saw me, and said, How about going over to fill up the coffee urn? I stood up and said, No, I hadn't been coming down to the office to fetch coffee. I hadn't known I was going to say this when I stood up, but I continued, "My last column is on your desk. I resign from that, too," Karl seemed too surprised at my outburst to say anything, but Nadia clapped her hands. "Bravo!" she said. "And I too am resigning. No more movies for me." She grabbed me by the arm and said, "Come, we have some coffee." We went across to the coffee shop and this time she told me all about her happy marriage. Well, it had been an eventful morning for the Sacramento Press..

The weather for the club's annual Thanksgiving tennis tournament was surprisingly good. I also felt pretty good. I'd gotten my game back, finally, after my surgery, and played well in the first three sets of doubles After these, I still felt okay, just a little tired. The fourth set was a tough one; my partner and I managed to pull it out 7-5. So I was among the leaders for a possible trophy (we'd decided not to give a turkey this year, too much trouble) going into the final set.It was mixed doubles. This time, unlike the July 4th tournament, I had a good steady partner, and I played my usual steady game. Our opponents were my friend Mike Snyder and his partner was also one of the club's better women players.

As I've written, Mike was an inconsistent player, able to make amazing shots but usually just as likely to flub on easy shots. But in this match he could do no wrong. We gave them a battle, but the final score was 6-3. After Mike hit his final winner, I went to the net to shake his hand. Great game, I told him. When I'd failed to win a trophy in the previous tournament I'd been pretty upset. Now, reflecting afterward at home, I didn't feel too bothered. Sure, I'd just as soon have won but there'd be other days. Maybe it was the after-effects of the surgery. Maybe I was just getting mellower in my old age. Trophies didn't seem that important anymore. Anyway, I was happy to be back playing tennis and playing well.

We were disappointed, Sally was anyway, that Jack and his girl friend Helen weren't going to be able to come for Thanksgiving. Helen wanted her parents, who lived in Redding, to meet Jack, he told us, so they were going there for Thanksgiving dinner. But Steve had come up from Berkeley and, amazingly, had brought a girl with him. Even more amazingly, the girl was a stunner, with dark hair and eyes, classical features in an oval face, slim enough to be a model. Arnie and his wife Mary were as always at our Thanksgiving dinner; they had no children and for years had been an honorary aunt and uncle in our family.

Sally and Mary, who'd brought over several dishes, as she always did, tended to the turkey and other stuff in the kitchen. Arnie and I watched a football game in the living room. Steve and the girl, whose name was Diana, were in his old room; I didn't want to think too much about what they might be doing. When the turkey was done, I was called upon to do my carving duties. Steve and Diane appeared and finally we were all sitting around the table, passing platters back and forth. Arnie and I were talking about the recent tournament at the club, and

Diane asked if we had any Afro-American members. Arnie sid he didn't think so. Sally said that we had several Asian couples. Diane's look told us that these didn't count.

As we ate, Diane continued her questioning.She wanted to know if we had any Afro-Americans living in our neighborhood. No. What about gay or lesbian couples? Not that we knew of. She'd noticed that we had a fireplace. Did we know that wood fires polluted the environment? Sally said we only had fires a few times during the winter. What about our cars? Did we drive them every day? Were we aware that global warming was the world's biggest problem and that carbon emissions were making it worse? Sally said that we recycled our cans; did that help?

Berkeley was well-known as a bastion of left-leaning thought so it was not surprising that Steve had brought home a girl who asked all these questions. Diane had mentioned somewhere along the way that she didn't eat meat, also not surprising, but evidently she did eat turkey because she asked for a second and then a third helping. I supposed she needed fuel for her world-saving activities. The Iraq, or Gulf, War was over but somehow the conversation got around to this subject and Diane said we shouldn't had invaded; everyone knew our only inter-est was the oil. This led to her saying that she was taking part in a protest in Berkeley the next week against an Army recruiting station that had been set up close to the campus. Arnie asked that if Berkeley was invaded did this mean she didn't want the Army's help in defending it. He was kidding, but Diana answered in all seriousness that she'd rather depend on the common people to repel the enemy. She was a lovely girl, and she may have been intelligent, in her own way, but she certainly had no sense of humor.

After the meal, when Sally and Mary, collected the dishes (Diane made no move to help), I finally had a chance to ask Steve about his classes. They were tough, he said, especially math. I nodded. I'd taken a look at his math book and couldn't make heads or tails of it. Sally began setting out dishes for pumpkin pie, but Diane shot up and said she and Steve were going to a concert and they'd better get moving. The concert, by some rock group, was for the benefit of an animal rights group. I should have known. When they'd left, Arnie looked at me and said, That's quite a girl. She's really a looker though. Mary said, Hmmm. I decided not to say anything.

On Friday morning I was surprised to get a call from Karl Engle. Without preamble, he told me he had a story for me. The subject was a local blues musician named Johnny H——, who was well-known in Sacramento musical circles and who having a concert in two weeks. He didn't mention the column or my not doing any more editing. I'd wondered, after I'd left the Press office that Monday if I was going to be fired, if such a thing could happen to a volunteer. I supposed I still had my unpaid job. When I called, it was evident from his voice that Johnny H— was an African-American. It was also evident from the address he gave me, after I'd arranged to interview him at his home, that he lived in what was not one of the better parts of Sacramento. I wondered if this was why Karl had given me this story, sending me into a possible war zone. .

I'd come across a senior citizen website, I think in the Sunday paper or possibly in a magazine, and when I checked it out found that it had a place for writers to post comments and get in touch with each other. Not only that, it put out an online magazine, run by the lady who more or less shepherded the writers' posts, and if you joined the writers' group you could submit stories to it. The stories would be critiqued by other members of the group and you in your turn had to critique theirs. This seemed to be pretty much what we were doing in my writing class, so I sent "One Last Drink," the story version, to the website and said I'd like to join their writers' group.

DECEMBER

In the first week of December I drove to an unfamiliar part of Sacramento, searching for the house of blues musician Johnny H—. The neighborhood, once I found it, didn't seem to be too bad although I passed a couple of groups of African-American teenagers, who gave me hard looks, I thought, as I drove by. I eventually found Johnny H—'s house, a modest one but a little larger than the rest, got out and rang the bell. A large touch-looking black man opened the door and asked me what I wanted. I told him I was there to do a story on Johnny H— for the Sacramento Press. He looked dubious but let me in and led me to a living room which seemed packed with people. When I got my bearings, I realized that this would be my first (it turned out to be the only one) interview with a celebrity who had an entourage.

Johnny H— was of medium height, stocky, with a large grayish beard.. Among the others in the room was his wife, who was an attractive but nervous-looking white woman, and his 12-year old son. It was an interesting interview because every few minutes or so Johnny H— would interrupt it to command someone in his entourage, all big tough-looking black guys like the one who'd let me in, to do something, go to some ribs place to get him something to eat, go to his office to get him some piece of music he needed, go to the store to get some supplies. I wrote in my article: "Musically, there's not much that H— doesn't do. He plays the piano, keyboard, organ, guitar, bass and flute and, as if these were not enough, is now learning to play the trombone. He's toured with Ray Charles, has played on nearly 300 blues recordings, including three dozen albums, and has put out four solo albums of his own."

In the course of the interview, I asked Johnny H— just what was blues and how was it different from jazz? As I wrote: "He responded by demonstrating the difference on his piano, where it was perfectly clear. Trying to translate it into words, blues has a definite form, a 12 bar round, which makes it more restrictive, while jazz is a freer and more improvisational form. Or, as H— puts it, 'blues is plain meat and potatoes; jazz is more like beef Wellington and potatoes au gratin.'" I spent about an hour there, sharing some of Johnny H—'s ribs, after they'd been delivered. They were pretty good. I then took my leave of him and his entourage, and drove back, passing the same teenagers who gave me the same hard looks, arriving home unscathed and possibly having learned a little something about music.

I couldn't let a month go by without doing an art story. I'd told Lois Bremmer about Zeke X's gallery downtown, run a shoestring. I wanted to do a Neighbors story on the gallery, hoping it might bring in some business and, possibly because the Christmas season was nearing, she finally gave me the go-ahead. I began my story with: "Zeke X moved to the Meadowview area this year because it has affordable housing and finances are important to the 30-year old entrepreneur who is the owner and one-person operator of the L— R— art gallery at 912 12ᵗʰ Street in downtown Sacramento."

I described Zeke's efforts to make his gallery into a viable enterprise. "X— spent his first year making two coast-to-coast auto trips scouting for artists at fairs, in galleries and art communities. Now the L— R— conducts an annual exhibition screening for emerging artists and X— then has exhibits showing works from among thee during the next year. In the previous two years, over 2,000 artists nationwide have entered the exhibition screening, about ten percent of them from the Sacramento area. 'Showing new artists, says X—, 'keeps the gallery and exciting.

"The L— R— Gallery has also offered space to groups of artists who might not have been able to exhibit elsewhere. Past shows have included the works of Latvian and Asian-American women artists, photos of the Chernobyl disaster, and locally-made AIDS memorial quilts. Once a year, X— rents space for a juried theme show which runs for a month."

I mentioned another business enterprise of Zeke X—'s in the article. "Visitors to the L— R— gallery will see displayed, besides paintings and sculptures, a Ben and Jerry ice cream cart. No, this is not a piece of modern art. In exploring other business ventures, X— has become the Sacramento special event representative for Ben and Jerry's as well as for Dreyer's ice cream. He takes his cart to all of the art events in which he participates and his fliers announce, 'Two of life's greatest pleasures, ice cream and art.'"

I ended my article with: "X—'s plans call for finding more installation sites and for having more theme shows …He'd like to expand his ice cream business. He's also getting into the apparel business with artistic tee-shirts and other clothing under the label L— R— Wear. Whatever ups and downs the Sacramento art business experiences in the future, it seems certain that X— will be doing what he advises other entrepreneurs to do, going for it." The article didn't appear until the next month but then it was on the front page of Neighbors with a nice full-color picture of Zeke X— standing in front of his gallery. I hoped it was of some help to him. I lost contact with Zeke after that. I like to think that he's become a big success doing something somewhere.

The weather after Thanksgiving wasn't conducive to much tennis playing. But my friend from the "Men's Movement," Frank Hooper, had returned from New York and we managed to get in a few sets in between rain showers. Frank was facing a crisis of his own. The girl he'd been living with (but wasn't married to) had given birth to a baby girl, and he was in a bitter battle with her over the baby's custody. It seemed a little ironic to me that the girl he'd chosen to live with turned out to have such little regard for a father's rights.

I didn't have much time to ponder this because shortly after Sally and I were ourselves on our way to New York. My sister had called; it wasn't my mother but my father, whom I'd considered indestructible. He'd had a heart attack and was in the hospital. The prognosis was good, the doctors had told her, but she still thought I should come. It was a hassle to get plane tickets on such short notice but eventually we did. My sister met us at the airport and drove us to the Bronx. The best thing, she thought, was for us to stay in my parents' apartment. My mother's first words on seeing us were, "I told him he should take things easy, but he never listens." My sister said, "He had a heart attack, Ma. It wasn't anything he did." I had a hunch she'd said this to my mother many times.

By the time we arrived it was late. My sister stayed over and next morning we all went to the hospital. My father, although he had tubes attached to various parts of his body, was sitting up in bed and looking much better than I'd expected. The first thing he wanted to know was how the "boys" were doing. I told him they were doing fine. After our visit, I talked to one of the doctors. He described my father's heart attack as "mild" and said he had a strong constitution. He said he could go home in a few days and he expected him to make a full recovery. That was good news.

Our stay in the Bronx was in many ways similar to that in Miami. We visited my father every day and then, after he was back home, went shopping to get the things my mother would need. She kept telling my father to take things easy and he kept telling her he never felt better. Just what he needed, he said, a little rest in the hospital. We stayed another few days and, when things seemed to be going well, returned to Sacramento.

On our return, I found that I had a story to do for Neighbors, a Christmas piece. It was to be about a lady who lived in El Dorado Hills and who collected Christmas ornaments. This was to put it mildly. I started my article with: "If there is a category in the Guiness Book of Records for most Christmas ornaments collected by a single person, then K— W— is a prime candidate for that distinction. W—, who has lived in El Dorado Hills for 23 years, is to all appearances a typical suburban wife and mother. Her husband D— is an engineer at Aerojet and an avid golfer. They have four children and three grandchildren. W—, originally a book-keeper, has worked as a store designer …for the last three years. W— also collects Christmas ornaments, but not the way most people do. One of her friends says she has 10,000 of them.

W— says she doesn't know the exact number. She once started to count just the number of Santa Claus ornaments she has and gave up when she reached 500."

This story was easy to write. All I had to do was walk through the house and describe all the ornaments. I wrote: :The kitchen shelves are all filled with Santas and other Christmas ornaments, soldiers, peasant girls, dolls, dogs and snowmen. The shelves below the windows contain Santas, reindeer and sleds … (and so on) Then: "As festive as the kitchen is, the center of W—'s efforts are the living room and the connecting family room. Stockings and a wreath of moving angels are hung above the fireplace. On top of the television set is a Christmas village with lighted houses, trees, a castle, miniature people, a music box set in the center (playing Christmas music) and a Santa Claus on his sleigh flying over everything. (and so on again)."

There was also what was called the "reindeer room," filled, of course, with all kinds of reindeer, stuffed, wooden, clay and ceramic. Then there was the downstairs bathroom. I wrote: "The first thing that catches your eye is the Santa on the shower curtain, washing himself off, possibly after going down all those sooty chimneys, while wearing only a hat and belt but having a strategically placed scrub brush. There is also a Santa bathmat and toilet seat cover, Santa hairbrushes and toothbrushes and Christmas towels." Well, here was a lady who wouldn't have to worry about what to do when she retired. She'd found her calling.

The Sacramento Press also had a story for me to do, but it wasn't a Christmas one. I was to interview a guy who ran an operation called Travel Keys. It put out a monthly newsletter that reviewed travel books of all kinds and also published its own travel books. The interview was memorable in that the publisher, Peter M—, wore a nose ring, not too common at that time. He was a pioneer. Like a number of other people I'd interviewed, Peter M— had been a State employee. He was originally from Southern California who'd gradually moved north, going to UC Santa Cruz and living in Sacramento the last 15 years. He told me his area of expertise was Europe, which he'd visited more times than he could count. I asked him what he'd recommend for an initial tour of Europe if my wife and I wanted to go. He was enthusiastic about Switzerland.

The Sacramento Press didn't have Christmas stories like Neighbors, but it wasn't without Christmas spirit. Sally and I were invited to a Christmas party at the home of Norma Eisenstein. She (and her husband) lived in a Victorian house downtown. The house was large and furnished nicely; it indicated that the Eisensteins had money. There was a large buffet set out on a table in the living room and plenty of drinks. Karl was there, almost unrecognizable in a suit and tie. Anna was there, as well as several of the other people who worked in the Press office and a few other writers. One of these was Nadia, the movie critic, who'd resumed doing her reviews.. As happy as she'd been the last time I saw her, this time she was tragic. She and her new husband had separated. When she'd told me that he was considerably younger, I was afraid this might happen. Well, I suppose Nadia's life was destined to go up and down.

A number of other well-dressed guests were there and I realized after a while that these were the financial backers of the Press. Karl told Sally he was glad to meet my wife and even told her I'd done good work during the year. The coffee urn tiff was, I supposed, a matter of the past. I still didn't intend to resume my editing at the Press office. That was retirement time I wasn't going to use up.

A little before Christmas, I received a present, my story, "Dog Barking," had been accepted by the literary magazine I'd sent it to and would be published, when, in about three months. I was to learn that this wasn't too bad for lit magazines; you were lucky if your story was published within the next year. At my next class, I told Seymour Kahn this important news. He seemed moderately impressed and told me he'd be available after our last class before the Christmas break if I wanted to interview him for the Neighbors story then. I was quick to take him up on this. I learned that he wrote questions and jokes for several quiz shows originating in Hollywood. After doing thousands and thousands of these, he said, he was ready for a career change. He decided the time was right for a return to teaching (he'd previously taught at college for a year), so he enrolled in UC Irvine and received a Master of Fine Arts degree, taught part-time there for a while, then moved north and here he was at our community college.

After the interview it was almost 1 o'clock and Seymour suggested we have lunch at the college's restaurant, which was called the Oak Café. I hadn't known the college had a restaurant; it was staffed by students of the cooking class, which I hadn't known of either. My ignorance was easy to understand because the door to the restaurant had no sign over it. Once in I saw that the place held about two dozen tables, nicely laid out with white cloths and flowers. The servers were students, as were the chefs. I saw that the place was crowded with teachers. We ordered and the food, when it came, was excellent. The lady who was the head of the college's culinary program made the round of tables, talking to the diners. When she came to our table I immediately asked her if she was agreeable to a story about the Oak Café in Neighbors. She said she was. I got her name and number and told her I'd check with my editor but didn't anticipate any problem and I'd call her after the first. So I had my first story of the next year. Naturally, I started it with: "One of the best-kept secrets in Sacramento is … '

The day before Christmas was one of those mild sunny ones Sacramento sometimes gets in between the usual rain and chilly fog of December. I spent most of it in the back yard, raking leaves and otherwise tidying up while Sally bustled around the house, getting things ready for the big day. She didn't want the cats underfoot so Binky and Mickey were out on the patio, watching me and looking up when they heard birds chirping. A smoky smell was in the air; maybe someone had a fire going inside despite the warmth outside. I raked the leaves in a pile and put them into trashcan bags I'd put into a garbage can, remembering how, when they were small, I'd put Jack and then Steve in the can so they could stamp down the leaves. After a while, I took a break, sitting on the patio with the cats and watched the clouds sail by overhead. It was calm, peaceful. I told myself I should have more retirement moments like this.

For Christmas, we didn't have as many ornaments as the lady of my Neighbors Christmas story, but the tree was up, with all the decorations we'd accumulated over the years, including those made by our sons when they were small. .As always, an amazing number of presents was piled on the floor around the tree. It seemed that every year we were going to cut down but somehow never managed to do so. The cats had a good time batting at the ornaments and playing among the presents. This beat any toys we got them.

On Christmas day, Helen was there with Jack, but Steve's girl friend from Thanksgiving, Jenny, wasn't. We asked Steve about her and he said they'd had a fight when he'd failed to attend some kind of protest rally because he had to study for a math exam.. "She's a pretty rigid girl," I said. "Yes, it's kind of a relief not to have her around," said Steve. But she was really good-looking, I thought. Well, it would make Christmas a lot more fun. We wouldn't have to feel guilty exchanging all those gifts while the rest of the world was starving and the ozone layer was being eaten up.

Arnie and Mary were spending this Christmas with his sister in Oregon so we had just our immediate family for Christmas dinner. As we'd had turkey for Thanksgiving, Sally made a beef roast with Yorkshire pudding. For dessert, she made pumpkin and mincemeat pies. Helen helped her with the cooking and, after dinner, with the cleaning up. She seemed to be an old-fashioned girl. Sitting in the living room, she and Jack held hands while she told us she couldn't wait until he graduated next spring so they could be together all the time. Steve told us that after his spring term he planned on getting an internship for the summer. It occurred to me that we wouldn't be having either Jack or Steve around much any more. We'd be "empty nesters." I knew it had to happen sometime, but it seemed to have come about so soon. Hadn't they just been little kids getting us up early Christmas morning so that they could open their presents? When we retired for the night, Helen and Jack went together to his old room as a matter of course. This would have been a problem in the old days, but now, I supposed, it was accepted practice. I wondered if we'd be having a marriage next year. I hoped that Helen was old-fashioned enough to want that traditional ceremony.

My birthday on the 30th, in contrast to the big doings of the year before, was a quiet affair. I didn't want to go out anywhere so Sally cooked me steak with onions for dinner. We watched some television after and then went to bed. The following night, New Year's Eve, we went over to a neighbor's as we did every year and spent most of the evening playing cards while trying to stay awake until midnight. When it came, we watched the ball go down in Times Square on television. I kissed Sally; all the husbands kissed their wives and shortly after, the "party" broke up. Someone asked me how my first year of retirement had been. I said it had overall been fine.

After, lying in bed, I thought again about that question. It had been an interesting year, no question about that. I'd become a writer, a kind of free-lance journalist and I was even being paid, by Neighbors, for what I wrote. People, some anyway, read my articles and maybe some even saw my name under the headline. I was also writing short stories and one of them had even been published. I wasn't sure how many people read that literary magazine, probably not many, but at least the story was out there in print. I'd had surgery, the first since I'd had my tonsils taken out when I was a kid. It hadn't been a pleasant experience but it had seemed to work. I no longer had to get up in the middle of the night to go to the bathroom. Not every night anyway. Between the surgery and the tennis elbow, I hadn't played as much tennis as I thought I would. But I had found some new players at Carmichael Park and a new tennis friend in Frank Hooper . I hadn't been able to win any trophies at the club, but I thought I'd been playing fairly well at the end of the year; maybe next year.

Both my mother and father had had medical emergencies. Both seemed to have survived them. My sister and I had discussed the possibility of their going into an assisted-living place in the Bronx. They said they were going back to Miami for the winter; all of their friends were there. My father said he didn't want to live in an assisted-living place, too many old people there. I supposed we'd wait and see what happened.

As I've said, our trip to Miami after my mother's fall and broken hip had started me thinking about mortality and I'd begun to write a story with that title. My surgery and then my father's heart attack had once again caused me to think about the frailty of life and about the inevitability of death.. In my completed "Mortality" story, I wrote:: "One of the good things about death, I'd always thought, was that it was the great leveler. Sooner or later, everyone died, including the worst of us, the people who clambered to success over others, the arrogant politicians who thought they were above the law, the hypocritical lawyers, the richest rock stars, the smug, the self-satisfied, everyone inevitably came to the same end. I'd remind myself of this occasionally when meeting with a particularly insufferable legislator or pompous agency head."

I also thought about my father and wrote about him: "…he'd always taken care of mother, and of his family, my sister and myself. When I was small, he'd worked on the WPA in New York City during the Depression. He'd also done all the plumbing repairs in our building to help pay the rent.

"When the war, World War II, came, he worked all over the country on defense projects, in Florida, Oklahoma, Wisconsin and at Oak Ridge in Tennessee, which we later learned was making the atomic bomb. His pay checks were always faithfully sent home. After the war, he continued to work on building projects out of town until they finally started building in New York and he could come home." I asked the question: "Wouldn't the goodness of my father, in some sense, persist forever?" I hoped it would. I hoped there was some sense to life.

The next day, New Year's Day, I watched a lot of college football games on television. For dinner, Sally made pork roast with black-eyed peas, a Southern dish which was supposed to bring good luck in the new year.

EPILOGUE

I've said that I'd try to put in this account of my first year after stopping work all the things I'd learned about retirement. Looking back, this wasn't very much. Still, there were some things. I'd advise any about-to-be retiree to devote more thought to what he (or she) would be doing with all that new free time than I did. For most people, life has to have some structure; in retirement, you have to replace the structure given by your working, usually eight hours a day, five days a week. Yes, that daily grind did have some good to it. In my case, I was lucky that, through a series of happy accidents, or maybe it was fated, I became a free-lance writer. In the past year, I'd met a lot of interesting people, seen my stories (and byline) in print and, most of all, had a pretty good time. Running around chasing stories, I didn't have much time to hang around the house, something dreaded by retirees, and even more dreaded by their wives.

If I'd given more thought to my retirement, I don't think I would have done as much running around. I think one of the reasons I did so many stories that first year was that I was afraid of inactivity. Sally had noted that I seemed to be always on the go, and she was right. I gradually cut down on my journalistic activities. Somewhat to my surprise, I continued writing stories for the Sacramento Press for another year. Then the inevitable happened. The bills piled up and Karl Engle ran out of money to pay them. Anna told me that Karl could have kept the paper going if he'd have accepted funding from some of his supporters, like Norma Eisenstadt. But by doing so he would have had to give up sole control, and the Sacramento Press was his baby. He couldn't bring himself to do it.

I kept doing stories for Neighbors until, several years later, it was merged, or rather sub-merged, into the Sacramento Bee and went out of existence as a separate entity. But after a while I stopped looking everywhere for possible stories, except every now and then, when I came across an artist or writer or a gallery or a restaurant or some other business that I thought some publicity would help. My editor, Lois Bremmer, continued to give me assignments and these were sufficient. When Neighbors ceased to exist as such, Lois went on to be a reporter for the Bee. By this time, Sally and I had moved to a retirement community, Sun City Roseville, and I began writing for a monthly newspaper that went to residents there and then to residents of Sun City Lincoln Hills, over 10,000 households in all. I started doing stories about the people and events of both Sun Cities, as well as two features, Favorite Restaurants and Observations. I'd noticed that the retirees of Sun City had two main topics of conversation. One was travel and the other was eating out. Favorite Restaurants grew out of the latter.

Observations started when the editor of Sun Senior News first asked me to contribute something to the paper. I sat down at my computer and wrote "Observations after Two Years in Sun City.," then continued from there. Over the years, Observations has given me a chance to write about a variety of topics: the emigration of Bay Area retirees to the Sacramento; the incredible growth of Roseville and West Placer County; things I don't like (LLA's, or Life's Little Annoyances), things guaranteed to happen (GTH's), usually bad; visits to Las Vegas and to other strange places; cruises; and, not least, the good and bad things about retirement.

In January 1992, the community college literary magazine (prize-winning) came out and I had two stories in it, the one about "The Happiest Time" playing handball in the Bronx and one of my San Francisco stories. I also had a poem in it, one I'd written after our visit to Miami Beach, which I called "Those Miami Jews." It's a short poem so I'm putting it in here:

Those Miami Jews,
Old men with canes,
Old women with walkers.
Talking:
So she says to me,
So I say to her,
So that's the story.
Know what I mean?
Argumentative:
Don't tell me.
What does he know?
That schmuck,
What does he know?
Pushy:
You blind?
I was here first.
You sure this is fresh?
Hey, don't tell me.
Those Miami Jews.
Talking, pushing, exasperating, arguing, admirable.
Survivors.

The story I'd sent in to the senior website, "One Last Drink," was printed in their online magazine. I stayed in the website's critique group for about a year, then decided that having to read and critique at least half a dozen stories every month was taking up too much of my retirement time. So, just as I'd stopped coming in to the Sacramento Press's office every week, I dropped out of the group. In the meantime, I'd discovered there were many online magazines (ezines, for short) on the Web and I began sending my stories to them. No bothering with putting your story in a big envelope with a small self-addressed stamped envelope inside, then going to the post office to mail it. Just e-mail the story, maybe with a short bio, if this was asked for, and that was it. Even better, sooner or later I found, somewhat to my amazement, ezines that would publish my stories. As of now, almost all the stories I've written, about 200 to date, have appeared in ezines Yes, I'm astonished, too.

I'd discovered that as you became older you might have the time to do things, like playing tennis, but you also were subject to the aches and pains, and worse, that come with age. Fortunately, my tennis elbow never returned. I discovered a nearby swim and tennis club that offered membership with no initial fee if you belonged to my HMO. I joined, quit my neighborhood club and stopped going to Carmichael Park to play. Eventually, when they retired, my old tennis buddies joined the new club, which was only a ten-minute drive away. We merged in with a group of other retirees who played there and we had a group of twelve, plus subs, three courts, playing two mornings a week. When I moved to the retirement community, which had half a dozen courts, I joined the tennis club there. I continued to play the two mornings a week, plus once a week at the retirement community. I wanted to play until was 75, and I did. At about that time, I'd been having knee problems (arthritis, degenerative cartilage, etc.) and had slowed down considerably. It was time to cut down, and besides the once 20-minute drive had increased to 40 minutes, so I left the club. I still play casual tennis once in a while, just to keep my hand in. I expect that any time now my aching knees will force me to quit altogether..

A few years ago, I had another surgery, this time for a hernia. I noticed a discomfort in my right hip area but thought at first it was from arthritis, which I knew I had. Then I noticed the suspicious bulge. I had a hernia. I figured years of handball and then tennis playing had caught up with me. When I saw my regular HMO doctor, he told me he didn't think I'd need surgery. This was fine with me; however, being experienced by now, I told him I'd call if it got worse for a referral if it got worse, so I wouldn't have to actually see him again. Sure enough, Sally and I went on a bus tour back East, starting in Boston on July 4th and going through New England and Canada. Two or three days into the trip, I knew something had to be done about the hernia. After barely staggering through the rest of the trip, I called as soon as we returned, got the referral and eventually had the surgery. Like the prostate one, it seems to have been successful One good thing came out of the hernia. I ran into an old tennis buddy from my retirement community. He'd quit tennis because of a bad shoulder and was playing pool. He invited me to play and I now shoot pool (we have four tables in the community's "pool room" three mornings a week. Pool is a lot easier on the knees, and everything else, than tennis.

The year after my first year in retirement Sally and I went to Europe. Following Dr. George's example, we took a bus tour of Switzerland (I'd never consider driving through the Alps). The tour started in Zurich and ended in Lucerne. From Lucerne, we went by train to Paris. If we went to Europe, we couldn't not go to Paris. This was the first of a number of trips to Europe. Recently, we've favored cruises over bus tours, much less tiring. In the last few years, our itinerary had to change as Steve met and married an Irish girl in Silicon Valley and they decided to relocate to Ireland. So now we have an obligatory trip to Ireland every year to see them and our grandson and granddaughter. Like many of our friends, we figure that we'll keep traveling as long as we're able to; we just won't plan on walking as much.

My mother and father eventually did move into an assisted-living place, in the Bronx. Sally and I went back to New York every year, sometimes stopping there on our way to Europe or Ireland. My father passed away when he was 98, almost 99; my mother, when she was 93. I've told you about Steve; he's a "senior software engineer" for a computer company in Galway. Jack is a marketing specialist for a company that provides insurance information on the Web. His wife Helen still works for an insurance company. They have one son to date and I can't help wondering if when he becomes a teenager Jack will see what's it's like to have a rebel on his hands. In any case, as I've learned, no matter how old your kids get you still worry about them and they can still exasperate you. Our cats, Binky and Mickey, both passed away after we moved to the retirement community. After an interval for mourning, a year, Sally and I got two kittens from the local SPCA. Shandyman (means mischievous boy in Irish) and Bun-Bun are now members of our family.

Living in a retirement community, especially as people got older and passed away, made me more than ever aware of mortality. I've thought and read a fair amount about this subject, but as far as I can see nobody has had any earth-shattering illuminations about it. The one thing I've learned as I've aged, not exactly original, is to try to take things in stride (like trying not to get too upset when you fly anywhere nowadays) and to try being more tolerant of other people. The one thing everyone agrees about regarding mortality is that in the end we all go. Until that time, I'll try to keep learning how to make the best of being in retirement.

THE SHORT STORIES

Uncle Pringle and the Stalker
(Hackwriters)

The first inkling I had of the problem was when my friend and fellow science-fiction writer Al Abrams called. "I wonder if I can come over and talk to you," he said.

"Sure. Ellen and I would like to see you. It's been a while."

"I'd like to bring my new girl friend Kathleen."

"I didn't know you had a new girl friend. Sure, we'd love to meet her."

"There is a problem," he said.

"Uh, oh. Don't tell me she's a witch, too." When Al had broken up with his last girl friend she'd turned out to be a witch and had put a curse on him. He'd suffered all kinds of misfortune, until my wife Ellen's Uncle, Claude Pringle, had intervened and brought the curse to an end.

"What? Oh, no, not at all. Kathleen is the furthest thing in the world from being a witch. She's an angel. But there is a problem."

"What have you done now?"

"Well, it's really Kathleen's problem. I thought maybe your Uncle Pringle would be able to help. It's, well, she'll tell you when we come over."

"Okay." We arranged for them to come the next afternoon. I was curious about Al's new girl friend, the angel, and I wondered what her problem was.

*   *   *

We were all sitting in our living room, drinking the coffee and eating the cakes that my wife Ellen had prepared. Al was right, I thought, Kathleen was an angel. She was a lovely girl, in her twenties, with long brown hair framing an oval face and large trusting brown eyes. Her features were almost perfect She spoke in a soft voice that was like water running in a brook. It was clear that Al was gone on her, and I couldn't blame him.

After we'd talked about a number of other things, including Al's latest book, which was doing very well, Ellen finally asked, "So, Kathleen, you have a problem my Uncle Pringle might help you with?"

Kathleen looked down at her slender white hands.. "I hate to bother you," she said.

"That's all right. My Uncle Pringle has a knack for solving people's problems."

"Yes, I know. Al has told me about him. But I don't know if he can help me."

"Kathleen has a stalker," broke in Al. "This guy keeps coming after her and he won't back off."

"That doesn't sound good," I said. "I assume you've gone to the police?'

"Kathleen's done everything," said Al. "Restraining orders, the whole bit. It seems they can't do anything until he actually attacks her and then it'll be too late."

I saw that Kathleen had tears in her eyes. "Look, I can see it's painful for you to talk about your, uh, situation. Why don't we see Uncle Pringle and you can tell him all about it. If anyone can help it's him."

*   *   *

Uncle Pringle had worked in several government agencies, just which ones it was hard to say, but whatever they did was top secret. Now he was, he said, a consultant, although just what he consulted about also wasn't clear. After my last encounter with him, during which time a notorious gangster who'd threatened a friend of ours had been found murdered, I wasn't sure I wanted to know any more. You'd think he'd have an office, but he said he preferred to operate from a bench in one of the city parks. He said it gave him a chance to be outdoors and to observe people.

On the appointed day, all four of us—Kathleen, Al, Ellen and myself—went to the park. Uncle Pringle, as usual, was seated on his bench, feeding the pigeons. He was a small white-haired man who looked remarkably like the old English actor whose first name he shared,

Claude Rains. After greetings and introductions, Kathleen said she had a stalker and she couldn't get rid of him. Uncle Pringle nodded. "Yes, they are notoriously difficult to get rid of. And I suppose the police told you they couldn't do anything unless he committed a crime. May a ask you a few questions?"

Kathleen seemed much more composed; Uncle Pringle had a way of calming people. We found out that her stalker was a man named John Clinton, in his thirties, ordinary-looking, not a person you'd think was a threat. Kathleen had met him through an online dating service. She and a girl friend had tried it on a lark. He'd taken her to dinner, then back to her place and had behaved perfectly. Oddly, he'd hinted at having a top-level but secret government job, possibly in the CIA. He couldn't tell her anything more.

She'd gone on a second date with him, to a symphony concert. This time he brought flowers and when he saw her home he told her he knew she was the girl for him, they were fated to be together. He kissed her, or tried to, and tried to do more until she finally told him he was going too fast for her. Then he drew back and said he understood, he knew she'd come around. He wanted to know when he'd see her again; she said she'd call him.

It so happened that Kathleen's girl friend ran into John Clinton when she brought her automobile in to a car wash. He was one of the workers; she recognized him from the photo on the dating service website. She of course told Kathleen. There went Clinton's tale of being a CIA agent. The rest of Kathleen's story had a familiar ring to it. When she didn't call him, Clinton called her. When she refused to take his calls, he showed up at her apartment. He'd found out where she worked and sent her flowers, candy and other gifts there. Finally, he accosted her after work and tried to push her into his van, but a few of her co-workers came to her assistance and he drove off. That was when she'd gotten the restraining order, but he'd ignored it, calling her at all hours, e-mailing her constantly and lately the calls and e-mails had become more threatening. Here, she lost her composure and said, "I don't know what to do. I'm really frightened."

"That's understandable," said Uncle Pringle. "Let's see. Stalkers are usually insecure young men. That's why he wanted you to think he was possibly in the CIA, to impress you and boost his ego. I think we might be able to work with that."

Here Uncle Pringle's cell phone rang. "Excuse me, my dear," he said. "Oh, hello, Barack. Yes, I see. Well, I wouldn't try bowling again. I might have a few suggestions. In Washington tomorrow then. Good."

"Was that …" I began.

"A young friend of mine," he said. "Now, where were we? Yes. Your stalker. It's clear that he's fixated on you. We must do something to take him out of the picture."

"You can call on one of your, uh, contacts," I said, "and have him, uh, removed."

Uncle Pringle smiled. "You're thinking of our late gangster friend. No, that was an extreme case. I believe there's another way. We must arrange to meet with this Mr. Clinton."

"Oh, no," cried Kathleen. "I couldn't."

"I meant that I would meet with him. And perhaps my nephew-in-law can accompany me; he's familiar with my methods. I want you to invite him to your apartment the next time he contacts you. You won't be there, of course. We'll be there instead."

"He calls and e-mails me all the time," said Kathleen.

"Then it won't be long before you'll have seen the last of him."

*   *   *

Uncle Pringle and I sat in Kathleen's darkened living room. The doorbell rang. "Ah, eight o'clock. He's right on time." He called out, "Come in, the door's open."

John Clinton came into the apartment. As Kathleen had said, he was ordinary-looking, but he also looked fit and able to fight if it came to that. I hoped it wouldn't. "Who are you?" he demanded. "Where's Kathleen?"

"The young lady is fine. She asked us to see you on her behalf."

"Why should I believe you? If you've done anything to her …" He advanced toward Uncle Pringle, his fists clenched.

"I said she's fine. Now sit down." There was something in Uncle Pringle's voice, a hard edge, that was very authoritative. Clinton sat.

"Now," said Uncle Pringle. "Kathleen is an extraordinary young woman, you'll agree."

"She's a jewel," said Clinton. "A princess."

"Yes, a princess. You'll recall that to win a princess's hand a man has to be something special. You tried to pass yourself off as that, but she found out you worked in a car wash."

"That's just temporary. I'll do anything to win her."

"Good. You'll have your chance. Do you remember Osama Ben Laden?"

"Sure. The Al Quada guy."

"Some may have forgotten him. But a special force is still hunting him. Taking part in Osama's capture, that would be special, wouldn't it?"

Clinton's eyes lit up. "Yes, yes."

Uncle Pringle took out a business card and handed it to Clinton. "Call the number on the card. Mention my name, Claude Pringle." He stood up.

Clinton stared at the card as if it contained the answer to all of his problems. "Thank you," he said. "Thank you. Tell Kathleen I'll e-mail her when I can."

"I'm sure you will," murmured Uncle Pringle.

*   *   *

I met Uncle Pringle at his usual bench the next week. "Did Clinton call your friend?" I asked him.

"Oh, yes. He wouldn't miss the chance to win Kathleen."

"Where is he now? Is he actually hunting for Bin Laden?"

"Well, he believes he is. He's with one of the tribes in the mountains of Afghanistan. I don't believe they have e-mail there."

"But if they find Bin Laden?"

"I said he believes he's looking for him. It's very unlikely that they'll find him. A few other men, undesirables, have been dispatched to join with the native tribes there. None has returned. Your friend Kathleen need have no fear."

I called my friend Al Abrams. "Your Uncle Pringle is quite a guy," he said.

"He continues to amaze me."

The next time Al and Kathleen visited, she showed us the engagement ring he'd just given her.

Uncle Pringle and the Bookmaker
(Hackwriters)

I was in a mid-Manhattan coffee house with my friend Bob Cummings drinking lattes. (This was before the recession when we could still afford them). Bob, like myself, was a science-fiction writer, but a far more successful one. He'd conceived of a hero, a mathematician, who'd solved what he called the Universal Theorem, or partially solved it, and this gave him the ability to predict the weather, know what stocks to buy, win at Las Vegas casinos, foresee terrorist attacks, and so on. He'd written several books about this hero, all of which had sold very well. This is why I couldn't understand why Bob now looked so anxious and harassed. I soon found out.

Bob's story was familiar but had a singular twist. He'd become a gambler. The twist was that he'd done so because he thought he could duplicate his hero's powers, using the Universal Theorem, to predict future events, in this case sporting events. The familiar part was that after having some early success the inevitable had happened. He'd lost a good amount of money, then, trying to recoup it, had bet even more and so was over $100,000 in debt. The worst part was that the bookmaker he'd bet with, a man named Manny Roth, was threatening that if he didn't pay up soon Bob would suffer grievous bodily harm or worse.

"I know I've been an idiot," Bob said, "but I was hoping that maybe your Uncle Pringle could help me out."

Uncle Claude Pringle was really my wife Ellen's uncle. He was retired from a government agency whose name I'd never learned and was now, he said, a consultant, although what he consulted about I was never sure. I did know he had a surprising number of contacts of all kinds. He'd helped me out with a sticky work situation several years before and since then had also helped, in various ways, a few friends of mine. In the last instance, a mobster, who'd been threatening a restaurant owner Ellen and I knew, had been found dead in his car, something which had led me to wonder just what kind of connections Uncle Pringle had.

"He might," I told Bob.

"Do you think you could arrange for me to meet him?"

"I can do even better. Since the weather is so nice, I think I know where I can find him. Let's go." It was December, but the day was sunny and unusually warm.

Uncle Pringle didn't have an office. He conducted his business in a midtown park, which wasn't too far away from where Bob and I had been drinking our lattes. Sure enough, as we approached the park, I saw him on his familiar bench, feeding some squirrels. It had always seemed to me that Uncle Pringle resembled the actor Claude Rains who was his namesake. He was a small man with white hair, handsome and always neatly turned out.

Uncle Pringle smiled as he looked up and saw me. He threw a last handful of peanuts to the squirrels and shooed them away. I introduced him to Bob, who once again related his story. "It's my own fault for getting into this situation," Bob concluded, "but I don't look forward to being beaten up by Manny Roth's goons."

"I've read a couple of your books about this fellow and the Universal Theorem," said Uncle Pringle. ""I wouldn't want to see their author come to harm."

"Maybe you can have one of your old CIA buddies visit this bookie," I said.

"I don't believe I ever said I was in the CIA. At any rate, let's see what we can do without resorting to extreme measures. Why don't we pay a visit to Mr. Roth ourselves? I've always wanted to see a bookmaker's establishment."

At this point Uncle Pringle's cell phone rang. "Excuse me," he said. "Yes, Barack, how are you? No, that won't quite do it. I suggest that you stress the theme of change, something like change you can believe in. All right, give it a try."

"Was that …" I began.

"A young friend who needed some advice. Now, where were we? Oh, yes, we were going to beard a bookmaker in his den."

*   *   *

Manny Roth ran his bookmaking operation out of a restaurant near Times Square, one of several legitimate businesses he owned. It was a week later and the weather had turned cold. The New York sky was a grim gray, suitable for our mission as Bob had recently received another warning by phone. We entered the restaurant, which was doing a brisk business, and made our way to the back. A large beefy man stood in front of a door. "Where ya think ya goin'?" he barked out, then he recognized Bob. "It's you. Manny wants to see you all right." He opened the door and we went in.

The room we entered was large, bigger even than the restaurant. The walls were lined with television sets, each showing a different sporting event. A large board showed odds on the week's football, basketball and other games. A diverse lot of people sat at tables, holding pencils and looking at papers, presumably deciding on their bets. We found Manny Roth at a desk in the back. Nearby was still another large goon, who kept his beady eyes on us. "Well, Cummings," Roth said to Bob, "do you have my money?"

"Mr. Cummings is a little short at the moment," said Uncle Pringle. "I'm his, er, representative. I was hoping we could negotiate some mutually agreeable terms."

Roth laughed. "You gotta be kiddin', right."

"Ya want me to take care of these guys?" asked the goon.

"Yeah, I don't have time to waste on small change like a hundred grand. Teach them a good lesson."

The goon advanced on Uncle Pringle and grabbed him by his coat collar. He was drawing back his fist when a large gun appeared as if by magic in Uncle Pringle's hand. "I won't hesitate to use this. I don't think I can miss at this distance."

The goon pulled back. "Hey, where'd that gun come from?"

"Now then," said Uncle Pringle. "Why don't we talk this over?"

"No way" said Roth. "You can't bluff me."

"I wouldn't dream of it," said Uncle Pringle. Then he took aim and fired at on of the TV sets. Bits and pieces flew all over. The occupants of the room scrambled to get out. Uncle Pringle aimed again.

"Okay, okay," said Roth. "What do you want?"

In the end, the agreement was that Bob was to pay off his debt in 60 days. He'd just finished another Universal Theorem book and hoped to get a substantial advance for it. "I knew you were a reasonable man," said Uncle Pringle. "A very interesting business you have here. I may be back to place a bet myself."

"Just don't shoot out any more of my TV's," said Roth.

*   *   *

A few weeks later, Uncle Pringle called me. "How'd you like to accompany me to that bookmaking establishment again?" he asked.

"Why, is there a problem?"

"No, not at all. I have some business there and I also want you to convey some good news to your friend Mr. Cummings."

This time the goon at the door let us into the bookmaking room without question. We went over to Manny Roth's desk. He looked up and when he saw Uncle Pringle he grimaced. "I suppose you've come to collect," he said. "Okay. I still don't know how you did it." He handed Uncle Pringle a large number of banknotes.

"Thank you. Here, this $50,000 will retire half of Mr. Cummings debt. I'll let him pay the other half from the publisher's advance he's just received. He has to learn the folly of gambling."

"Hey," said Roth. "You didn't do too bad."

Uncle Pringle smiled.

When we were out of the restaurant, I asked Uncle Pringle, "What did you beat on?"

"The Super Bowl, of course."

"You mean you bet on the Giants to win. But New England hadn't lost a game and they'd even beaten the Giants in the regular season. They were prohibitive favorites"

"That's why the odds were so good."

"But what made you think the Giants could win?"

"Mr. Cummings' books about the Universal Theorem gave me an idea. I did some research, and …" He shrugged.

"Don't tell me you've solved the Universal Theorem?"

"Oh, I don't think anyone can ever completely solve the Universal Theorem. But it does lead you down some interesting paths."

"So you knew the Giants would win?"

"Nothing is that certain. Let's just say I was lucky. Oh, tell Ellen I won't be coming to dinner next week. I'm making a little trip to Las Vegas."

I shook my head. You never knew with Uncle Pringle.

The Lone Man
(Winamop)

Some years ago, if I remember correctly, there was a series of books about a "Lone Man," that is, about a young guy who had no girl friend and who didn't seem likely to get one. The books, I think, sold pretty well. I want the author to know that long before these books came out I thought of myself as the "Lone Man." Too bad I never wrote any books about being one.

How did I come to be the "Lone Man"? It wasn't hard. I was in my early thirties. I was living in San Francisco, having come there from New York City five years before. My girl had gone back to the Midwest to help care for her father, who'd suffered a heart attack. When she'd left, I had the feeling she wouldn't be coming back, and she didn't. The couple who were probably my best friends got divorced. No more dinners and occasional parties at their place. The couple who were my next best friends had a baby. That was the end of that. I had no family in San Francisco; they were all back in New York. If I was still there, one of my numerous aunts would have fixed me up with a new girl friend, but my aunts were 3,000 miles away.

There were no girls in the office where I worked; none, at any rate that I was interested in, or who might be interested in me. On top of that, I'd moved to an apartment in Sausalito, across the Golden Gate Bridge from San Francisco. This was fine as long as I had a girl friend, who usually came to spend the weekends with me. Without a girl friend, I had no one and San Francisco, the City, might as well have been, like New York, 3,000 miles away. Oh, yes, I'd always liked the wife of my best-friends couple and, after their divorce, had taken her to dinner. At the door of her apartment, I'd made my move and had been gently but firmly rejected.

*   *   *

So, what does a lone man do to fill in the time? After work, I'd drive back to Sausalito and make myself dinner. Ironically, my girl friend had left me half a dozen or so recipes. I alternated these with the TV dinners that were then becoming popular.. Sausalito at that time didn't have many restaurants, and, besides, one of the worst things about being a Lone Man was having to eat by yourself in a restaurant.. .After cleaning up, I'd read, watch my black-and-white television or, most often, look at the view I had of Alcatraz, with the City beyond it. On weekends, I'd walk from my apartment along Bridgeway into town, buy whatever I needed, stop into the little library for books, then walk back and usually do nothing for the rest of the day. Sometimes, to vary my routine, I'd drive back over the Golden Gate Bridge, although it took an effort to do this, and go to Golden Gate Park. Once a week, instead of going straight back to Sausalito after work, I'd drive to the JCC (Jewish Community Center) to play handball (I'd been a pretty good player back in New York). After playing, I'd go to a bar across the street to have a beer, then go home.

What about picking up a girl in the bar; that's the way it's always done in the movies. The bar was pretty much a sports bar and very few women were ever seen there. The one time I did see an attractive girl drinking by herself I moved over to the seat next to her and was cleverly saying, "Can I buy you a . . ." when her boy friend came breezing past me and they kissed enthusiastically while I slunk back to my previous spot.

The thing I remember most about this Lone Man period is that every guy except me seemed to have a girl. When I walked back and forth on Bridgeway I passed couples holding hands while they admired the view. When I went into the market everyone else shopping was one of a pair. When I went into the library guys would be showing the books they'd selected to their girls. On the rare occasions when I ate out I'd be huddled at a table by myself while at all the other tables couples talked and laughed. When I went to Golden Gate Park couples would by sitting on benches or lying on the grass with each other. Even when I was driving in my car all the cars I passed were occupied by couples sitting close together.

I was reminded of all this recently when my oldest son, who happens to live in San Francisco, was divorced and, when my wife and I visited him, was obviously lonely; he was even glad to see us, his parents. Well, I guess I've let the cat out of the bag—no, I didn't stay the Lone Man forever, although at the time it appeared I would. One night after handball at the JCC another player told me of a restaurant two blocks away that had good food, cheap prices and a lot of small tables suitable for guys eating alone. So, after showering and changing I took my gym bag and, instead of going to the sports bar across the street, I found the new restaurant two blocks away. I was seated at one of the small tables, against a wall. The menu looked good. My wife says I deliberately left my gym bag out in the aisle so that she would trip over it. I deny it but this is what happened and so I met my wife-to-be and that was the end of my being The Lone Man.

The Writer and the Devil
(Winamop)

It was a spring day in Paris. I was sitting at an outdoor café, sipping a café latte. A slight breeze rustled through the trees. French pigeons scuttled about, looking for crumbs. Schoolchildren passed by on the sidewalk, speaking perfect French. I'd been drafted after graduating college, during the Korean War, but had been stationed in Germany. I had no desire to return to the States so I took my discharge there, then traveled through Europe, ending up inevitably in Paris, as I wanted to be a writer. In my mind, I was emulating Ernest Hemingway.

I looked up from my latte and gazed hopefully at the young very attractive French girl seated two tables over. She met my gaze, turned down her mouth and looked away. I should have known. Now, if I was Hemingway … The man sitting in the far corner lowered his newspaper, was it? It had to be him: the black hair in a widow's peak, the swarthy angular features, the pointed ears—it had to be.

I approached his table. "Excuse me, sir, " I began. "Are you the …?

"Sit down, Martin," he said, "and don't ask foolish questions."

I sat. I thought I detected a hint of sulfur in the air. "How did you know my name? Oh, a foolish question."

"Yes. How is the writing going?"

"Not good. I'm having a devil of a time …Oh, I'm sorry."

He shook his head. "I've heard it before."

"If only I can write like Hemingway."

"Ah, yes. Ernest. An interesting young man."

"You knew him? Did he…I mean, is that how he became so successful?"

He shook his head again. "Millions of words have been written about Ernest. Do you really want to add to the speculation?"

"No, I suppose not. But I'd give anything to write like Hemingway. I'd sell my ..."

He held up his hand. "That may be, but you must have at least a modicum of talent to begin with. Starting a story with "It was a spring day in Paris." How pedestrian can you get?"

"But I'd be happy to even write like Steinbeck, Sinclair Lewis ..."

"Wait. Ah, yes, that's the man I was waiting for. Do you see that young Asian across the street? When he finishes his studies in Paris, he'll return to his native country, become dictator and slaughter millions in the name of a more perfect society."

"The hell you say! Damnit, I'm sorry. I mean ...".

"Martin, you're hopeless. Go home and get a job. Practice your writing. Perhaps we'll meet again. Now, you'll excuse me, I must catch up with that young man.."

He was gone. I practiced my writing, but I never saw him again. So that's why this story is appearing in winamop instead of the New Yorker.

The Pencil Pushers of Mars
(Bewildering Stories)

"No one would have believed that ,,, this world was watched keenly and closely by intelligences greater than man's and yet as mortal as his own; that as men busied themselves about their various concerns they were scrutinized and studied, perhaps almost as narrowly as a man with a microscope might scrutinize the transient creatures that swarm and multiply in a drop of water," (H.G. Wells, "The War of the Worlds").

"Knight takes bishop," said Spiegel.

"Pawn takes knight," said Lucas.

They were playing four-dimensional chess without a board.

"Bishop threatens Queen."

"Damn, I didn't see that."

"Checkmate."

"Hmmm. You got me. I resign."

Spiegel stretched his long arms, almost like tentacles. "Want to play another one?"

"Nah," said Lucas, also stretching and blinking his large round eyes, which looked like headlights. "I've had enough for today."

"I suppose we should take a last look," said Spiegel.

"Yeah," said Lucas. "Not that anything's changed in the last 62 years."

"You mean when the atomic bombs were dropped?"

"Yeah, that was kind of interesting."

"I suppose so. It's been all downhill ever since."

The two Martians each looked into their telescopes, infinitely more powerful than any produced on Earth. "Nope, nothing new," said Spiegel. "Not even a new Britney sighting."

"Those primary elections in that country, the United States, are still going on, I see,." said Lucas. The Martian telescopes enabled them to see individual Earth inhabitants as well as to see newspapers and television "Hasn't it been a few years now?"

"It just seems that way. Talk about boring. All they do is give those talking heads on television something to blather about. As if a new president will make any difference. They're in a war against what they call terrorists and half of them couldn't care less. They keep talking about an energy program and still don't have one. They keep talking about health insurance for everyone and still can't provide it. They're hapless."

"Yeah. Still, they're supposed to be the most important country on Earth. Do you think they'll ever get out of Iraq?"

"Who knows." Spiegel shrugged his massive shoulders. "Who knows how long we have to keep watching the Earth?" He yawned. "I don't know if I can take any more It's worse than piloting that commute ship back and forth to Venus."

Lucas yawned also.. "The Council wants it."

"So, what are we going to do, invade them or what? You know, the Council is almost as bad as the United States, can't make up their minds what to do."

"Yeah, it's the Reds and the Blues. They Reds want to invade. The Blues want to talk to them. They've been going back and forth for years."

"Meanwhile, it's us Browns that have to keep watch. I've had it."

Lucas could see that Spiegel meant it. "Well, it's a tough call," he said. "We can take over the Earth easily, but once we do that we own it and look what that means."

"Yeah, trying to civilize those so-called humans.. Television, talk radio, rock concerts, politicians, not to mention subprime mortgages and global warming. It would be a nightmare.

Still, I've had enough. I've been analyzing the situation. You know, those atomic bombs did at least get the Council's interest."

"What are you thinking of?"

"Well, what about a real big explosion, like wiping out New York or Los Angeles? Or more, the whole world. No more scrutinizing through those damned telescopes."

"I don't know if the Council would stand for destroying the Earth," said Lucas.

"Okay, let's start small. New York or LA?"

Lucas hesitated, but he knew Spiegel couldn't be dissuaded. "Let's toss a coin," he said.

The Guardian Angel
(Winamop)

It started as a routine crime drama; something like, say, Law and Order. Two young ambitious secretaries at the Ashfeld-Rumsworth advertising agency, coming into the office early to impress their bosses, found the body. The DOA (to use a technical term) was Milton Ashfeld, the senior partner, found slumped over his desk, dead, his head bashed in by a metal statuette, an award from Advertising Age.

The two detectives, Lupo and Green, examined the body. Cause of death was obvious; time, judging from body temperature was sometime late at night. Earl Peebles, one of the building janitors, who was in charge of the two floors in which the advertising agency was housed, said he'd finished cleaning Ashfeld's office by nine PM and the senior partner was still there, so the murder occurred sometime after that. Questioning of agency employees revealed that Ashfeld was brilliant, arrogant, ruthless, bullying, hit on any good-looking girl who worked there, and had a host of enemies in the industry..

One of the good-looking girls Ashfeld had recently hit on was a young copywriter named Marilyn Roberts, who was from the Midwest and had been working there just a few months.. He'd asked her out for drinks, then had her come to his luxurious hotel suite, to discuss some copy ideas, he'd said, kissed her and tried to do worse but, she said, she'd managed to get away from him and ran out the door. That had been a few nights ago. On the night of the murder (around midnight, CSI had determined) she'd been home in her modest apartment; her roommate confirmed this. There were plenty of other suspects to go.

*   *   *

My name is Earl Peebles and I'm a janitor at the Ashfeld-Rumsworth advertising agency. When Marilyn Roberts came to work for the agency I immediately noticed her. She was beautiful, long blonde hair, large innocent blue eyes, lips as red as strawberries. She was not only beautiful, she was intelligent, friendly and charming. I came around one evening when she was working late and, unlike most people, she didn't ignore me. She asked me my name, where I lived, how long I'd been in the city. She told me that coming to New York was like a dream.

When I returned to my small place in Manhattan, affordable because it was rent-controlled, I told my cat Guenevere all about Marilyn. She's like a princess. But she's so trusting and naïve.

She must be protected. Luckily I'm here to do it, Guenevere. I'm going to be her guardian angel. Then, after finishing my supper, I once again read my favorite book, the Morte d'Arthur. Oh, how I wished I lived in those days, when knights protected damsels against villains.

Milton Ashfeld was a villain. I wasn't surprised when he began asking her into his office. The next step was to ask her out for drinks. . I wish I'd been able to follow and protect her, but I had to be at work. The next evening, I started work early and came into her office while she was still there. I could see she was distressed. Her eyes were red and her face pale. I spoke to her gently and she told me what had happened. I was incensed. I told her that there were men like that in the city and that she had to avoid them. But I knew that Ashfeld wouldn't give up after that one setback; he'd keep after her. And he was a powerful man. There was only one thing to do.

I waited a few nights, then came the chance I was waiting for. Ashfeld was still in his office when I came in to clean it. "Working late, sir?" I asked.

He didn't even bother to look up; I was just the janitor. "Yeah, got a big client meeting tomorrow." I left, then came back at midnight. He was still there, still bent over his desk. Again, he didn't look up. I picked up the heavy statuette. He never knew what hit him.

*   *   *

Lupo and Green looked into all of Ashfeld's activities and came up with some interesting discoveries. He'd had an affair with his partner Rumsworth's wife, but Rumsworth had been out the country at the time of the murder. He seemed to have hit on every female employee of the agency and Lupo and Green spent hours interviewing the women, their boy friends and a few husbands. They also found something else. Ashfeld had been systematically skimming off money from the agency. He'd accumulated millions in an offshore account. But before they could investigate further the FBI stepped in, saying they'd been watching Ashfeld for three years as part of an ongoing operation. They couldn't say what it was about but it had to do with national security. Lupo and Green reported this to the DA, who then got into a jurisdictional dispute with the FBI that promised to last forever. Lupo and Green hadn't questioned the janitor, Earl Peebles, since that first day.

*   *   *

It's Earl Peebles again. I'm happy to say that the murder of Milton Ashfeld is still unsolved.

If the police had found someone I'd have to step forward and confess. As it is, I'm still keeping watch over my princess, Marilyn Roberts. She's become a little more sophisticated, but she's still very trusting. Of late, another copywriter. Peter Cheney, has been dropping into her office. He's obviously taken with her. He seems like a nice young man, but I'm keeping my eye on him. If his intentions are anything other than honorable, I'll know what I have to do. I'm her guardian angel.

A Matter of Witchcraft
(Bewildering Stories)

The first time I set eyes on Veronica, at a cocktail party in mid-Manhattan, I was, you might say, bewitched. She was petite but with all the right curves, had blonde hair, sea-green eyes that glinted with mischief and a laugh like music. I won't bore you with all the details but in a short time I had wooed and wed her. About myself, I was 39, came from a good family (my father, John Hamilton, Sr., had been a state senator), was successful (I was a security analyst in a large investment firm), lived in a spacious house in Connecticut, from which I commuted to Wall Street, but seemed to be fated to a life of loneliness. I knew almost nothing about Veronica. She said she didn't like to talk about herself. That didn't matter to me. She had a faint accent of some kind, owned a large black cat and was delightful. That was enough.

The first hint I had that there might be something more to Veronica came at our wedding, a large one . My parents had taken over the arrangements and had gone all out. Veronica's brother George attended; before this, I hadn't known she had a brother. At one point in the reception, George weaved his way over to me and said, "You know you're marrying a witch, don't you?"

"What do you mean?"

"Veronica's a witch. You know, she can make spells, put hexes on people, do magic. All the women in our family are witches. They can be a pain to live with."

This was the year 2008. I was a securities analyst. This man was obviously drunk. "I don't believe in witches," I told him.

He laughed, not pleasantly. "I warned you. Just don't do anything to make her mad at you."

As if I would ever do anything to upset Veronica, I thought. I was madly in love with her.

*   *   *

My marriage, despite George's warning, was everything I could ask for. My parents and all of my friends adored Veronica. When I returned from my office each day I always had a fine dinner prepared for me and I could talk to her about my work. After a while, she became involved in a local election for a city council seat and spent a lot of time on that. Still, I couldn't quite get George's words out of my head. It was remarkable, I thought, how immaculate our home always was, how our fine meals always appeared seemingly without effort on her part, how she still had time for her political campaigning.

Then one day I found out that I was a candidate for head of my department at the investment firm; it came with a substantial raise and the title of vice-president. When I told Veronica, she said, "Do you really want it, John? I know you're good at your job but we have enough money and I've been wondering if you might want to do something else, maybe public life.. Don't forget, your father was a state senator."

"You've been hanging out with those politicians too much. No, I might consider that later but right now I want that promotion.

"Then we'll see that you get it."

"That's what I want to talk to you about. At our wedding, your brother told me that, well, that you had certain powers. I know you want to help me, but I want to win that promotion fair and square. So promise me, no witchcraft or anything like that."

Veronica smiled. "I'll be a good girl."

As always in a firm like mine, there was another candidate for the promotion. . Harvey Smoot was a few years older than I, had been with the firm a little longer, was competent at his job, had gone to all the right schools, had played football in college. What's more, he was a big man, physically-imposing, full of self-confidence. The next weekend the firm's CEO, Alexander Monroe, invited both Harvey and myself to a round of golf at his club. Monroe was very keen on golf. I knew this wasn't just a golf match; it was a test. And Harvey was an excellent golfer. I wasn't too bad myself and thought I could handle it.

At the first hole, Monroe said, "I've always thought golf told you a lot about a man. Shows how you could handle yourself under pressure."Harvey teed off and drove the ball over 200 yards straight down the fairway. My drive wasn't as long and was a little in the rough. Harvey continued to play an excellent game. I had to do some scrambling but when we reached the 18th hole we were all even.

We were both on the green in three strokes. Harvey had a slightly longer putt; he tapped the ball and it went straight in. The pressure was on me. I lined up my putt and hit the ball. I was sure I would make it, but the ball stopped short by a foot. I looked up and saw Harvey making a choking gesture. I don't know if missing the putt was the decisive factor, but the next week Harvey got the promotion. I didn't think I could stay at the firm and keep hearing about my choking on that putt so I resigned. Veronica was supportive. She said, "It's all right, John. That might not be the right place for you. Remember what I told you about public life. I think you'd like it and you can really contribute something."

*   *   *

Veronica's candidate for city council was elected and he offered me a job on his staff. To my surprise, I did like public life and in a short time I was elected to my father's old state senate seat. The reader knows about the financial crisis that gripped the country. Yes, my old investment firm, which was heavily into sub-prime mortgages, went under and I heard that Harvey Smoot lost almost all of his own money.

I'd almost forgotten about Harvey when one day I had a call from him. He had joined a small lobbying firm and wondered if I might be able to help him. I invited him to a round of golf at my club. That night, when I told Veronica about it, I said, "You know, just this one time I'd like to relax my rule. I'd really like to win that golf game." Veronica smiled and I went to bed knowing that this time I wouldn't fail.

At the club, I could tell Harvey had been through some rough times. He'd lost weight but he still had some of his old cockiness. He actually had the lead after nine holes, but I knew I had Veronica's help and eventually I prevailed. At the end I even felt a little sorry for Harvey and said I'd see if I could help him out. When I returned home, I told Veronica about my victory. "It felt good," I said . "Thank you."

"Oh, I didn't do very much. It shows how well you can do when you have confidence."

"Anyway, I was glad to get my revenge. You know, I was thinking, it was a good thing you didn't help me out with that first golf match. If I'd won, I'd have gotten that promotion and gone under with the firm."

"Oh, yes," said Veronica, "that one." She smiled. I knew that smile.

I remembered lining up that last putt and being sure it would go in. "Wait a minute, don't tell me."

"That was so long ago. It's time for dinner. Now, about your running for Governor."

Second Thoughts
(Winamop)

Kyle Johnson, who was getting married the next day, lie in his bed, staring into the dark Earlier, his best man and one of his groomsmen had escorted him back to his apartment. At the requisite bachelor party, Kyle had drunk quite a lot. But now, at three in the morning, he was stone sober, and fear clutched at his heart. What was he about to do? Was he going to ruin the rest of his life?

Kyle had met Meg Richards just four months earlier. It had been one of those "cute" meetings so beloved of Hollywood. He'd been rushing to a momentarily empty table at fast-food lunch place in mid-Manhattan when he'd bumped into her. She'd been aiming for the same table. They'd laughed, taken seats at the table, exchanged names and brief life stories. Kyle, a native New Yorker, had graduated from Columbia University and had been working as a systems analyst for a large bank the last two years. Meg had come to New York from a small town in Nebraska and worked as a secretary in a publishing house. She was a petite blonde with an adorable nose and Kyle immediately fell for her. By the time they'd finished lunch, he had a date with Meg for that weekend.

Things had moved swiftly after that: dinners, movies, plays, a meeting with Kyle's family, who'd also fallen in love with Meg, and almost before he knew it, Kyle had proposed and the wedding was set. Now he was having second thoughts.Meg wasn't a dizzy blonde, but she hadn't finished college. She didn't know anything about computers. The few times he'd tried to talk about his job with her she'd said she was sure he was a genius but it was way over her head. That was fine now, but what about the future?

When they'd gone to movies he'd found out she liked films that "made her feel good," which meant he'd had to sit through romantic comedies that bored him. The same was true of television. She didn't like "Lost." because, she told him, it was too complicated for her. The one time he'd tried to explain it to her she said it didn't make any sense. Her favorite shows were those on Lifetime, the "women's channel."

Then there were her parents, who'd come to New York for the wedding a few days ago. Meg's father was a large, bluff insurance salesman who wanted to know if Kyle was happy working for a bank and said that he himself had never been satisfied working for anyone else.

Her mother kept looking around and saying that she'd never seen anything like New York City before.

The more he thought about it the more convinced Kyle was that he should call off the wedding. Of course, it would be embarrassing, but what was a little temporary embarrassment compared to a lifetime of misery, married to someone who was incredibly cute but who was also entirely unsuited to him. No, he'd made up his mind. He'd tell his parents in the morning. The wedding was off.

*   *   *

Meg Richards lie awake in her bed. She was having second thoughts. Kyle was handsome and smart, no doubt about that, but did she really love him? The proposal had come as a surprise and he'd looked so intense she hadn't wanted to disappoint him. Then she'd been caught up in all the wedding preparations. It had all been so exciting, choosing the wedding dress, selecting a hall, a caterer, a band, the flowers, sending out the invitations, that she hadn't had time to even think about what she'd gotten herself into.

Married? She'd come to New York to have a taste of big-city life. She'd just begun to have a good time when she met Kyle. Why, she hadn't even gone up to the top of the Empire State Building or seen the Statue of Liberty. What would her life be like when she was married? Would Kyle expect her to cook for him? She didn't even know how to boil an egg. And clean. She hated cleaning up. When Kyle came home from work, would he talk about his job. She didn't really understand what he did.

Did she love Kyle enough? Did she love him at all? If she did, why did she keep having thoughts of Bill, her old boy friend in Nebraska? Maybe she wasn't cut out to be a big city girl. Maybe she should go back home. It would be horrible to call off the wedding now, but if she didn't she might be miserable the rest of her life. She'd tell her parents in the morning. They'd understand. She began to cry.

*   *   *

The wedding was a great success; everything went off as planned. Everyone agreed that the bride and groom were a cute couple and seemed made for each other. They'd go off on their honeymoon, return, settle in to married life, and live happily , . . .well, maybe it was a little early to say what would happen. What do you think?

The Marbles King
(Fictionville)

When Arnold grew up in the Bronx there were seasons for the games they played on his block. In the summer, it was punch ball for the younger kids and stick ball for the older ones. In the winter, it was touch football. In the fall, for some reason, it was checkers, played on the sidewalk with bottle caps on a chalked field. In the spring, it was marbles.

On an April day Arnold's mother took him to visit her sister and his cousin Lenny. His cousin was ten, two years older than him, and, Arnold knew, a street-wise kid. Lenny showed him a wooden cream cheese box with three openings he'd made in its bottom. "What's that for?" asked Arnold.

"It's for marbles. You get the other kids to try to roll their marbles into the holes. If they go in, you give them a prize, like five marbles. If they don't go in, you keep the marbles. I made it last year and cleaned up. I'm the marbles king on my block."

"But what of someone gets his marbles in and you lose?"

"Are you kidding? It's almost impossible to roll them in. The sidewalk's too uneven. Let's go out and I'll show you." Lenny was right. No matter how carefully Arnold aimed he couldn't get one marble in.

"Boy, I wish I had one of those boxes," said Arnold.

"You could make one. It's easy. Or, hey, you can take this one. The guys on my block are wise to it now."

"Okay. Boy, thanks."

The next day was a Saturday. After breakfast, Arnold took his box down to the street. As usual, there was a lot of activity. Some girls were playing rope. A couple of the bigger kids were playing catch with a baseball.. A few kids were playing hit-the-penny. A bunch of his friends were shooting marbles. He went over to them. "What's that?" asked the oldest one, Kissel, pointing to the box. Arnold explained it to them. "Ah, I bet I can get a marble in there," said Kissel. "What do I win?"

"Five marbles."

"Make it ten."

Arnold hesitated but then said "Okay." He set the box up against the building. Kissel stood about six feet, or two boxes, away. He knelt down and rolled a marble. It went straight in the middle opening. "Hah," said Kissel. "I told ya."

Arnold gulped. He had taken all the marbles he had with him, 25. He might be wiped out. But that first try had been a fluke. Kissel couldn't get one in again. A few of the other kids tried, but they couldn't get any in either. "Ah," said Kissel. "The marbles always go crooked. Forget it."

Kissel and the other kids went away. All except one, Harold. He was a big blubbery kid. He was almost 12 years old but he played with the younger kids. He was supposed to be slow. "I think I can do it, just like Kissel did the first time. I got a lot of marbles. Can I go get them?"

"Sure," said Arnold.

Harold was back in a few minutes with a large bag. "I got them for Christmas," he said. He started to roll them. Some marbles just missed. "Almost got that one," said Harold. "Next one will be good." But none went in. Harold started sweating but kept trying. Finally, Arnold said, "You can move in closer, one box."

"Okay." The next marble veered off path but went in one of the side holes. "I knew I could do it," shouted Harold. Arnold gave him ten of his marbles back. In the next half hour, two more marbles went in but at the end Harold had lost everything he'd brought in his bag.

Harold started to go away, looking sad, then he said, "Hey, I just remembered, I have some more marbles upstairs, another bagful. Can I go get them?"

"Not now," said Arnold. :Maybe tomorrow.".

When Arnold got back to his apartment, he counted the marbles he had. Almost 100. He was the marbles king of his block. The next week Arnold's aunt and his cousin Lenny came for a visit. "So how'd ya make out with that cheese box I gave ya?" Lenny asked.

"Okay," said Arnold. "Do you want it back?"

"Nah, ;I told ya, the guys on my block are wise to it now."

"Yeah, the guys on my block, too. I won't use it again."

Slim
(Fictionville)

Danny started going to the McCombs Dam handball courts the fall he started high school. He'd beaten everyone in his neighborhood schoolyard and everyone knew the best handball players in the Bronx played at McCombs Dam. He first noticed Slim when some big guy challenged everyone to a money game and Slim said he'd take him on. Slim was a black man, tall and thin with long arms and large hands. Danny couldn't say how old he was but he looked pretty old, maybe 30. He had a crooked nose and a couple of missing teeth. He always wore a white t-shirt and raggedy-looking pants. He didn't look like much.

The big guy hit the ball pretty good warming up and he got off to a big lead. Then Slim began getting to balls he couldn't seem to reach earlier and started to put some balls away. He hit with lots of wrist and his shots really zinged. The game was close but Slim won 21-19. The big guy said Slim was lucky and challenged him to another game. The same thing happened. Slim fell behind, then picked up his game and won again. By this time Danny could see that Slim was hustling the big guy. But the big guy still thought it was luck and challenged Slim to a third game. Slim played all out this time and won 21-6. The big guy was furious. "You hustled me," he said and refused to pay up. He swung at Slim, who easily moved out of the way and hit the big guy once, in the solar plexus. The big guy went down. Slim bent over, took his money from the big guy's pocket and calmly walked away.

After seeing Slim beat the big guy, Danny hung out near the court where Slim and his buddies, George, Eddie Lemon and Gene, played. He heard that Slim had been a boxer. Somebody said that he worked in the garment district. Someone else said he ran numbers in Harlem. At the courts you didn't wonder too much about what people did when they weren't playing handball. Danny knew that one of the men who sometimes played with Slim and his crowd was the film critic for the New York Post. Other players were doctors and lawyers and one was supposed to be a judge. Others looked as if they might be appearing in the judge's court. All that mattered was how they played.

One day when somebody didn't show up, Slim looked over Danny's way and said, "Come on, kid, I need a partner." At first Danny was so nervous he played like a stiff.

"Take it easy, kid," Slim told him.

"It's hard to see the ball," said Danny. "The sun's right in my eyes."

"The sun? Well, just ignore it."

Danny played better and in the end they won the game, 21-20. Danny was elated. Slim winked at him and said, "We had it all the way, right, kid?" From that time on, Danny hung around Slim and was his partner when he needed one. Slim showed him how to use his wrist to hit the ball hard. He showed Danny how to move so the other guys wouldn't block him out. He told Danny to always shove back when somebody shoved him and showed him a few boxing moves to use if he needed them.

When winter came, nobody at McCombs Dam said good-bye or arranged to meet again in the spring. It was understood that when the weather was good again they'd all be back. That winter was a long one. There was a lot of snow. Danny went to the courts a couple of times but they were icy and you couldn't play on them. Finally, in March when it was still cold but the sun was shining Danny tried again and this time the old gang was back. He saw George and Eddie Lemon and Gene. "Where's Slim?" he asked.

"Dincha hear?" said George. "He got shot over the winter."

"Shot? Is he okay?"

"Are you kidding? He's dead."

Danny sat down on the bench next to George. He watched the game being played but didn't really see it. After a while, he heard George saying,, "C'mon, we're up. You gonna play?"

"What? Oh, sure." Danny got up and stepped onto the court. Another handball season had begun.

The Innocent Man
(Clever Magazine)

I'm my younger brother Bobby's best friend, lawyer and, at least I try to be, protector. Bobby's an innocent. He thinks all those other people out there in the world are basically good, no matter what the evidence to the contrary. He's kind of like those people who say terrorists are just misguided and if we could only sit down and talk with them they'd see they have no reason to hate us. Right.

Anyway, when we were growing up in New York City, I had my share of fights with schoolyard bullies who picked on Bobby, not that they'd have to threaten him to get his lunch money, if they'd have given him a sob story he'd have gladly handed it over. Then, when we got to college, Bobby turned out to be not only an innocent but a genius. He got into computers early, made a pile of money, retired at 40 and decided to devote the rest of his life to, what else, helping those less fortunate.

I set up a foundation for him, hired an efficient secretary, Miss Ward, and scrutinized all the appeals for money that were sent in. It was amazing how many of them were phony. Anyway, I pretty well kept Bobby on the right track until the time I had to go overseas for some tricky legal business and that, as I found out when I got back, was when Bobby met Marlene.

It happened at one of those charity dinners to which Bobby was always being invited. Somehow, he'd bumped into her and made her spill her wine. There were the usual apologies, the futile attempts to sponge off the wine, then, at Marlene's suggestion, an invitation to dinner to make things right. Marlene was young and beautiful. She told Bobby what a nice man he was, how noble he was to give his money to the needy, how she was from a once-wealthy family that had fallen on hard times and that she was forced to work as a saleslady, albeit in an upscale shop, how lucky she felt that Bobby liked little old her. Bobby was hooked.

Of course, the first thing I did when I returned and heard all this was arrange to meet the wonderful Marlene. It was at the foundation's office. My immediate thought was that this girl was a phony. She was young, although maybe not as young as she made herself out to be, she was blonde (dyed, I thought) and she was a knockout. Bobby looked like a nerd; in fact, a little like Bill Gates, his idol, before Gates had his makeover. Girls like Marlene didn't immediately fall for guys like Bobby unless it was for his money. And Bobby was a little clumsy, but I'd bet that bump at the charity dinner had been of Marlene's doing.

When Bobby introduced Marlene to me, she came forward, her little hand extended, and in a little breathless voice told me she was so glad to meet me, she'd heard so much about Bobby's big brother. She was wearing a tight-fitting dress, a jacket and she carried, Lord help me, one of those little dogs that women like her seem to come equipped with from birth. I put out my hand and the dog growled at me. "Hush, Sadie," said Marlene, giving the dog a playful slap.

Anyway, we all sat down and, okay, I gave Marlene a little grilling. I'd already done a background check and she indeed was working as a salesgirl, or had been; she'd quit a week ago, to be with Bobby full-time, I guess. I have to admit that Marlene gave all the right answers: she was a vegetarian; she loved animals (like Sadie); she wanted to save the whales, dolphins and baby seals; she thought we had to fight to the death against global warming. After half an hour, she looked at her wristwatch and said, "Oh, we must go. I'm taking Bobby to lunch. Would you believe he's never been to the Four Seasons?" She swept him away. Miss Ward, sitting at her desk in the outer office, gave me a sympathetic look and shrugged.

The next few weeks went by like a whirlwind. Marlene wanted to marry Bobby as soon as possible. I urged a waiting period, but Bobby wouldn't hear of it. I told him to at least have a prenuptial agreement. Bobby said he'd already talked to Marlene and she had no objection, proving how sincere she was, and that a prenup wasn't needed as he trusted her completely. The wedding was a small one and the newlyweds went off the next day to some remote place in Mexico that Marlene had found. "We want to have time just for ourselves," Marlene declared.

Well, I'd tried. I was in the foundation's office the next morning to look over the records when Miss Ward came in. "You have a phone call. He says it's urgent."What now, I thought. The caller identified himself as a private investigator. He wanted to know if it was true that my brother Bobby had married a Marlene Wolfe. When I told him he had, he said, "Your brother is in danger. You have to warn him at once." I asked him what this was all about.

"Marlene Wolfe was married to (he named a prominent industrialist). He hired me when he suspected she was seeing another man. Then I found out she was planning to kill him."

"What? I did a background check. There was nothing about all this."
"Her husband was afraid of the scandal. It was all hushed up and made to go away."

So that's why she had to go to work as a saleslady, I thought. "You think my brother is in danger."

"I wouldn't take any chances."

"Why didn't you contact me sooner?"

"I was in Mexico, on a case. I just happened to see in a Mexican paper that a famous American computer whiz and his new wife were honeymooning at some resort on the coast here."

I thanked him and hung up. "Miss Ward," I called out. "Do you know where that honeymoon place is?"

The efficient Miss Ward did and I told her to book the next available flight. She asked if she could come with me and, seeing the look of concern on her face, I said she could. A few hours later we were in a rent-a-car speeding up the Mexican coast, the Mexican Riviera, as it was called. Miss Ward studied her map. "I think that's it," she said, pointing to a large building up ahead. I pulled in and we ran to the desk. Yes, said the clerk, the American and his senorita were indeed staying there. No, they were not in their suite. They'd gone for a walk along the cliffs behind the resort.

Miss Ward and I ran behind the hotel and followed the path leading to the cliffs. "There they are," she said. Bobby and Marlene were standing at the edge, then there was a scene that might have been choreographed out of a Laurel and Hardy movie. Marlene was behind Bobby. She rushed forward, her arms extended. She was going to push him over. Bobby bent down. He was picking up a dog that seemed about to go over the cliff. Yes, it was Sadie. As he bent over, Marlene flew over him and disappeared. Miss Ward and I watched, both stunned.

In a minute, we recovered and ran to Bobby, who was standing stock still, looking out over the cliff's edge, still holding Sadie. "Marlene must have slipped," said Bobby. "She went over and down into the ocean. She disappeared."

Eventually, Marlene's body was found. We all returned to New York. After a decent interval, I told Bobby about what we'd found out about her. He decided that he'd put almost his entire fortune into his foundation, following the example of his idol Bill Gates, and he promoted Miss Ward to be the foundation's manager. I had a feeling she'd soon be more than that and that Bobby wouldn't be needing my protection too much longer..

The Rational Man
(Clever Magazine)

My older brother Jonas prides himself on being a rational man. I suppose that's why he's been so successful. On the other hand, I tend to act on impulse, which is probably why I'm, if not a complete failure, certainly not a success.

Jonas and I both had artistic inclinations, from our mother, I'd say. But he knew that only a handful of artists and writers ever earned a good living so at an early age he immersed himself in the then new field of computers. Upon graduating with the highest marks in computer science he went to work for Microsoft at a very good salary. I decided to become a painter and went to Paris to study.

After a few years, Jonas, after carefully weighing all the pros and cons, left Microsoft, taking his stock options, and started his own company. With his careful planning, the company steadily grew. Earlier, Jonas had almost become engaged to a fellow worker at his original employer. She was smart and attractive. She loved Jonas and I'm sure he loved her. But she was from a working-class family with a slatternly mother and an alcoholic father. Jonas weighed the possible outcome of a marriage to her and in the end broke off their relationship.

When he became president of his own company, Jonas married the daughter of a wealthy family. Emily was the perfect company president's wife, arranging parties and dinners for influential people. She was also a dull woman and I'm sure Jonas was bored with her. They had no children, then Emily did the one unconventional thing in her life, she died in an automobile accident.

What about myself? I failed as a painter, spent a number of dissolute years drifting around Europe and then, what else, took, or was given, a job with Jonas's company. It was in the personnel department, mostly paperwork, so I couldn't do too much harm. I suppose Jonas thought it was the rational thing to "save" his younger brother before I brought scandal upon the family name.

Jonas met Sharon as a result of another auto accident, or near-accident. He was in the back seat studying company reports when he heard a thump at the front of his Mercedes-Benz. The chauffeur, driving in a heavy rain, had hit a woman who'd suddenly appeared out of nowhere. Fortunately, the woman wasn't badly hurt, only shaken up. She was also extraordinarily attractive, young, no more than 25, blonde, with an oval face, blue eyes like gems and, as was revealed after Jonas had taken her back to his mansion and she'd taken off her coat, a truly lush figure.

Jonas may have been a rational man, but he was still a man and after this he started taking Sharon to the dinners, fund-raisers and charity balls that, as a rich and influential company president, he was compelled to attend. When I asked him about this he told me not to worry, having a beautiful young woman on his arm only added to his prestige. And Sharon, he added, was not a bimbo; she was an art dealer, quite knowledgeable in the field. Quite a coincidence, I thought, as Jonas had become an avid collector of modern paintings.

I had my suspicions of Sharon but knew that nothing I could say would sway Jonas. It was as if, after being the rational man all of his life, his emotions had taken over. Keeping my own counsel, I hired a top-flight private investigator I'd come across in my personnel department work. He had no difficulty gaining access to the luxurious apartment in which Jonas had installed Sharon and planting "bugs," which provided both visual and audio tapes. I'm afraid that the tapes confirmed my suspicions. Sharon had a boy friend and their plan was to defraud Jonas with a fake painting, supposedly a masterpiece worth millions of dollars.. Jonas's hitting Sharon with his car hadn't really been an accident.

When I showed Jonas the tapes, he acted as if he wasn't surprised. He told me he knew it wasn't rational that a beautiful young girl like Sharon would be attracted to an old fellow like himself. It was of course all about his money. He would immediately break it off, although he wouldn't pursue Sharon about her intended crime. He seemed very sad as he said this.

I was also a little sad. I hadn't shown Jonas the last tape, on which Sharon told her boy friend that she'd really fallen in love with the old guy, who hadn't had much fun in his life, and that their plan to defraud him would have to be abandoned. After all, even if she thought it would work out I knew their differences were too great and would eventually lead to grief for my brother. Besides, as Jonas's younger brother, I was heir to all of his wealth. It just wouldn't have been rational to show him that last tape.

The Getaway
(Hackwriters)

My wife Sally and I were pleasantly surprised when our youngest son Steve dropped in on us. It was a pleasant spring weekend. He'd driven up from Sunnyvale, south of San Francisco, where he had an apartment, to the retirement community just outside of Sacramento where we'd moved a few years before. In fact, we'd moved shortly after Steve had graduated from UC Berkeley and gotten his job as a computer engineer in Silicon Valley.

We had two other sons, Jack and Ken. Jack, the oldest, was in Los Angeles, trying to be a screen writer. As far as we knew, he was working as kind of a gofer for one of the studios. Ken, the middle son, was still, as he'd told us, trying to find himself. At the moment, he had a temp job in Sacramento, which was at least better than being unemployed. Steve had become interested in computers when he was ten years old. By the time he was in high school, he could put together a computer from scratch and write his own programs. After getting his degree in computer science he was immediately offered a job, with a $2,000 signing bonus.In the three years since then, he'd been promoted and had received nice raises. We were happy that we had one son who'd always known what he wanted and was doing very well at it.

Steve had arrived in the late afternoon. Sally told him that if she'd known he was coming she'd have prepared one of the meals he liked, but she really didn't have much in the house. That's all right, he assured her, he wanted to take us out to dinner. Wasn't there that French restaurant we liked nearby? Before we left, I asked Steve if he'd talked to his grandparents, my mother and father, lately. He hadn't, no surprise there. My parents lived in New York. My father was approaching 90 and my mother 80. They couldn't travel to California any more; I called them every weekend. I went to the phone and my mother answered. I told her to put my father on the other phone and that her grandson Steve wanted to say hello to them. Steve talked to them for about 15 minutes. I could imagine them telling all of their friends they'd had a nice conversation with their grandson in California, the computer genius.

*   *   *

We were lucky in that the restaurant wasn't too crowded that night. We were seated at a nice table with a view of an open area with trees and a little creek. Before we ordered, Steve said, "Don't forget, this is my treat. Go wild."

"All right," I said. I ordered the steak. After the waiter left, I said, "Okay, what's going on?"

"What do you mean?" asked Steve.

"You pop up here, then take us out to dinner. Did you get a big promotion? Are you planning to be married?"

Steve laughed. "No, nothing like that. But I do have something to tell you."

I glanced at Sally. "What?" I asked.

"I'm planning to take a year off and go backpacking through Europe."

The word "flabbergasted" best describes how I felt at this announcement. "Why?"

"Well, you asked if I was planning to be married. I do have a girl friend, Alice, the one I told you about. We're pretty serious."

"Then why are you going to Europe?"

"Well, it's my last chance for a getaway. If we do get married, then we'll buy a house, start a family, all of that, you know."

Yes, I knew. A house, a family, your life will be over.

"Have you discussed this with Alice?" asked Sally.

"Oh, sure. She's all for it."

"How about your boss?"

"I asked if I could have a leave of absence. He said he couldn't hold my job open but I'd have a pretty good chance of getting re-hired when I came back."

A pretty good chance but no guarantee. I grew up in the 1930's. Giving up a perfectly good job to go gallivanting around for a year was inconceivable to me. "Can you afford to take a year off?'

"I saved up some money. And I'll be backpacking, staying at hostels, not at fancy hotels. Don't worry, I'll be okay."

"You say you'll be backpacking. Do you know exactly how you'll get around and where you'll be going?" Since my retirement, Sally and I had been to Europe several times. I tried to imagine Steve arriving in Paris at night, then wondering where to stay.

"Not really. I haven't done any research yet, but I'll manage."

I could see I was getting nowhere. "Don't you think you'll be hurting your career?"

He shrugged. "I'm pretty burnt out, Dad," he said. "I need a break, a long break."

The waiter brought our dinners. My steak was very good, but I'd have enjoyed it a lot more under different circumstances..

*   *   *

We talked some more about Steve's plan through dinner, of course, and I thought of a few other good reasons for him not to throw up everything and go to Europe, but he was determined to go through with it. When we returned to our house, he called one of his old Sacramento friends and told us he was going out to a club; we shouldn't wait up for him.

Sally and I sat down in our living room chairs. "Well?" I said.

"I can understand why he feels burnt out," said Sally. "He worked awfully hard getting through Berkeley, then he went to work right after and he hasn't really had a break since then."

I shook my head. "I don't understand it," I said. "What if he doesn't get his job back? Things are slowing down in Silicon Valley."

"He's always been resourceful. Besides, I've been thinking, is what he wants to do any different than when you up and left New York when you were about his age and came out to California?"

"That was different. I didn't have a great job. I couldn't even afford to get my own place to live."

"But your parents didn't think going to California was such a great idea."

No, they hadn't. I remembered my mother crying when I'd left for the airport. I suppose that's what parents were for, to be left behind by their kids. At least Steve would be coming back to California. He wouldn't want to stay in Europe, would he? No, not with his girl friend Alice waiting for him.

"I'm going to dig out all that stuff we have on Europe," I said. "If he's going over there, he should know something about it."

Starting Out
(Hackwriters)

"So you're leaving us?" the Colonel said.

"Yes, sir," I said.

"Think you're ready to be a civilian again? No more free room and board. No more Army to take care of you?"

"I'll manage," I said.

We were in the Colonel's office. He was Ordnance Officer for the Seventh Army in Stuttgart, Germany. I'd been drafted during the Korean War and was a corporal. For the last sixteen months I'd been more or less the Colonel's secretary. We had a curious relationship. I wouldn't say he'd been my mentor (I don't know if anyone even used the word "mentor" way back then) but I knew he considered me a hopeless college kid and he took a certain amusement in instructing me on how to survive Army life.

"That remains to be seen," the Colonel said. He lit a cigarette. He was a man in his forties, ruggedly built, handsome, with jet-black hair, a square jaw and piercing blue eyes. He used a cigarette holder, and I emulated him, not on base but when I went on leave, although I knew that instead of looking sophisticated and all-knowing like him I probably looked foolish puffing on my holder. "Do you have any plans?" he asked..

"To sleep for two weeks." Whatever our relationship, I could say things like this to the Colonel.

"And after that?"

"I guess I'll have to look for a job.".

"I hope you'll remember some of the things I told you."

"I remember them all. Don't be impulsive. Weigh all my options. Regard strangers as potential enemies, not friends. And don't be a wise-ass."

The Colonel smiled. "Well, maybe you'll stand a chance after all."

The next day I shipped out, going by train from Stuttgart to Hamburg, then boarding a troopship back to the States and my future.

*   *   *

I stood by the ship's rail, gazing out at the blue Atlantic, waves glistening in the sun. I didn't know it then but at times of crisis in the future I'd make a habit of looking at large bodies of water. Perhaps subconsciously, the sight of something which had been there long before and would be there long after put whatever problems I had in perspective.

I'd just been talking with a group of soldiers, New Yorkers like myself, also on their way back to be discharged. They were what we now call African-Africans, and they vied with each other in their stories of the cushy jobs they'd secured in the Army; outwitting The Man, I suppose they'd say. I wondered what kind of future awaited them back in Harlem. As for myself, I'd return to my parents' apartment in the Bronx, commandeering my old bedroom, then, as I'd told the Colonel, I'd look for a job, one, I hoped, that would enable me to move out to my own place. The thought of wandering around the towers of Manhattan looking for work filled me with both excitement and anxiety. I wondered what kind of future awaited me.

The next day the weather turned stormy and we were all seasick until we reached harbor in New York.

*   *   *

I was sitting in a small conference room, wearing the civilian suit I'd bought when I'd returned. I was interviewing for a job. The alumni office of my college had sent me a slip of paper with nothing on it but a company name and a phone number to call. When I stepped off the elevator in one of those glass and metal buildings springing up all over midtown Manhattan I'd found myself in a large reception room with a sofa and some armchairs and glass cases filled with plates and ceramics. I'd thought at first that maybe the company manufactured dishes. It was only when I was being interviewed that I realized the company was an advertising agency and that one of its clients was a major cigarette maker.

I was on one side of a table and three men were on the other side, which I felt was a bit excessive for someone like me interviewing for an entry-level job. One of the three, I knew, was the Personnel man, his name was Jerry, red-haired and freckled, barely older than I was. Another was a chubby, harassed-looking man in his thirties, Jack Goodman, head of the agency's research department. The third man looked like a matinee idol, handsome, with chiseled features and lacquered hair.

Jerry started by asking me a lot of questions as to why, as I'd been a liberal arts major, I wanted to work in advertising, implying that I should have been going back to school to study something useful, and what I thought I could contribute to the agency, his tone indicating he thought it was nothing much. Remembering what the Colonel had told me, I tried to mask my dislike of this buffoon and answered all of his questions in an even, courteous tone. It wasn't easy.

Jack Goodman then asked me questions about finding out who used certain products and if I thought advertising in magazines was better than on radio. The matinee idol was silent until the end when he asked me how I'd increase the sales of their cigarette client. The only thing I could think of was to hand out sample packs to people, as had been done in the Army, and which in fact was what had started me smoking. I don't know if I was responsible for the pretty girls who'd appear on the streets of Manhattan in the fifties, giving out cigarettes; I doubt it, as I'm sure somebody else had thought of this before. At any rate, after I mentioned having been in the Army, they asked me questions about where I'd been stationed and what I'd done and I tried to make my job as the Colonel's secretary (I didn't use the word "secretary," of course) sound as important as possible. No one seemed too impressed and I was prepared to be dismissed, when the matinee idol, who was smoking a cigarette, said, "Well, we should give a returning vet a chance," and so I was hired. The matinee idol, I found out later, was Philip Mason, head account executive for the cigarette company. I was pretty excited about getting the job on my first interview until I went with Jerry to the Personnel Department to fill out papers and discovered that my salary would be $75 a week, not nearly enough for me to get my own apartment in New York City.

*   *   *

The agency's research department, to which I'd been assigned, was working late. The cigarette company, whose sales had been slipping, was going to launch a new campaign. The government had released some reports that cigarette smoking was bad for you and that may have been one reason for the slippage, although all the cigarette makers vigorously denied the reports. In any case, I was just as glad I'd stopped smoking upon getting out of the Army. There'd also been rumors that our cigarette client might be looking for a new agency so everyone was on edge.

I'd learned that such rumors were common in the advertising industry and that under all the activity and bonding with the clients (every in our agency smoked our company's cigarettes), ran an undercurrent of fear.

The room in which we worked was like a big classroom, each one of us at our own desk out in the open, except for Jack Goodman, who had his own little office. The cigarette company wanted all sorts of sales and advertising information. Everyone was busy adding up figures on the big metal calculating machines we had at that time. At the next desk, Al Zimmerman, Zee as he was known, glanced at me and shrugged his shoulders as if to say, Is all of this any use? I didn't know but I knew that Jack Goodman was frantic to get everything we could dig up. Every so often, he'd dash out of his office and ask someone if he had that data yet.

I'd been working at the agency for three months. Every weekday morning I'd take the subway from the Bronx down to Grand Central, then walk the few blocks to the office. There, following the Colonel's strictures, I tried to be friendly to everyone, even Jerry the Personnel guy, who I knew didn't like me, but not too friendly. I read the industry's bible, Advertising Age, to keep up with what was going on (Advertising Age reported the rumors that the cigarette company was looking around), listened, observed and kept quiet. Despite the Colonel's cautionary advice, I'd become friendly with Zee. He'd been drafted also and, although a college graduate, had actually been sent to Korea and seen some fighting there, which I thought was something to respect.

The figures I was adding were starting to swim before my eyes when I became aware that Jack Goodman had come out of his office again and was standing over my desk. "Where's that share-of-market data you were supposed to get?" he demanded.

"I have them," I said. "I gave them to Zee to graph them. I thought that'd make them easier for the account execs to understand." I was pretty good with numbers: Zee was a whiz at graphics.

"Oh," said Jack. "Okay. That's a good idea. As soon as Zee's through, bring them into me."

When Jack had gone back into his office, Zee gave me the high sign. We worked another two hours, to nine. We weren't getting paid for this overtime but they'd given us some money to pay for dinners. I took the long subway ride back to the Bronx and went to bed, wondering what my future in the advertising world would be, if I had any.

*　　*　　*

Olga Simonette's apartment wasn't too long a drive from the theater so I'd splurged on a taxi. Now we were in the back seat, doing what was known in those days as "making out." Olga was a short, dark girl, very sexy, I thought, and professionally she was ahead of me; she'd been a production assistant (whatever that was) at a television station for two years (those two years I'd lost to the Army). I'd been given her phone number by one of my numerous aunts, all eager to "fix me up" with a nice girl. This was our fifth date. The first time I'd met her for a drink after work. The next two times I'd taken her to dinner, then it had been a movie and dinner. We'd just seen a popular Broadway musical; the agency, which hadn't paid for overtime work but had given us dinner money had also given some of us theater tickets.

I was feeling pretty good about the agency. The cigarette company hadn't left us. The new ad campaign was said to be going well and sales were picking up. Along with all the data I'd given Jack Goodman I'd sent him a memo saying I'd noticed our company, which was an old and rather staid one, wasn't doing as well with younger smokers as a few other cigarette makers whose ads were considerably jazzier. I had no idea if this memo had gone anywhere but once in the men's room Philip Mason had seemed to know my name and had told me to keep up the good work. I'd just stopped myself from saluting and saying, "Yes, sir."

When we reached Olga's building I kissed her (and fondled her breasts) outside her door. Inside, I knew, were her two roommates, so that this was as far as I was going to go. It was very frustrating, but, as the Colonel said, premature attacks were self-defeating, and you should plan for the long-run battle. My plan was to have my own place in Manhattan. Eventually, we broke our clinch and I walked to the subway station. It was once again back to the Bronx.

*　　*　　*

The party was in full swing. The apartment was filled with young people, most from our agency, some friends, some people we knew, some we didn't know at all. Zee and I had moved in a couple of weeks before, right after my promotion and my raise in salary to a lordly $100 a week. It was in Yorkville in Upper Manhattan, in a tacky building; it wasn't big; it needed painting; nothing in it worked very well, but it was all our own.

Naturally, Olga Simonette was there. I'd had only two or three drinks but this was enough to make me almost drunk. Around midnight I managed to drag her away and into my room. It was hurried and I was afraid that at any moment someone would barge in but it was also good. We went back to the party and I think she said something about my meeting her parents but I was drinking again and wasn't paying too much attention. Shortly after that, I must have passed out.

I woke up back in my bed. I had a blanket over me but still felt cold. I looked at my watch. It was three in the morning. I remembered what Olga had said. This was the 1950's and sex hadn't yet become as casual as eating and drinking. Meet her parents? Did our going to bed together mean that I'd more or less proposed? I liked Olga but I certainly wasn't ready to marry her, or anyone else. And, it suddenly came to me, I wasn't ready, despite my promotion, to become a full-fledged adman. Did I really want to be in a business persuading people, especially young people like myself, to smoke cigarettes that might kill them? Thanks to my following the Colonel's precepts, my co-workers at the agency thought I was mature and confident, knowing exactly what I wanted. But I knew now that I hadn't the least idea of what I wanted and had no idea of where I was going. After all the noise of the party, the apartment seemed strangely quiet. I shivered and drew the blanket around me. Well, tomorrow, as the Colonel would say, I'd re-consider my position and try to think of some new strategy.

Coming of Age in San Francisco
(Hackwriters)

It was ten o'clock on a July weekday in San Francisco. Outside, the typical fog still hung over the city. In his small office, Paul Lerner was preparing a report on the latest monthly West Coast beer sales. The largest client of the advertising agency for which he worked was a local brewer. Their client's sales were down slightly from the same month last year, something the beer company's president, Oscar Fiegelman, wasn't going to like. As it happened, a meeting with Fiegelman was going on right now in the agency's conference room.

Paul's phone rang. It was his boss, the Research Director, Bob Prosser. "Paul, bring the latest sales figures to the conference room, please."

"I haven't finished my report yet."

"That's all right. Bring whatever you have." Bob's voice sounded urgent.

When Paul opened the conference room door, a hoarse voice was saying, "All that money I'm spending and we're still only third in California. Shit, maybe I'd be better off finding some other agency." The speaker was a short, frog-like man at the head of the table who Paul knew was Oscar Fiegelman.

"But we do have a larger share of market and I'm sure our new campaign will …" This speaker was Steve Selig, the ad agency's head, a handsome man in his forties, who normally looked like a matinee star but who was now pale and sweating.

"The new campaign stinks," interrupted Fiegelman.

Paul went over to where Bob Prosser was sitting, at the foot of the table, and gave him the report.

"Who the hell is that?" growled Fiegelman.

"This is Paul Lerner, our new research assistant. He's from New York."

"Hah!" said Fiegelman, indicating he wasn't impressed.

Paul briefly wondered what the Colonel, his mentor while in the Army (he'd been drafted during Korea), would have made of Fiegelman. He thought he knew: a bully who liked to use his power to cow people. He deliberately smiled and said, "It's nice to meet you, sir,." Then he turned and quickly left. One of the Colonel axioms was to keep the enemy off balance.

Although he'd been introduced as the new research assistant, Paul had been with the agency for six months. One of the reasons he'd left New York City for San Francisco, after two years in a much larger ad agency, was that he'd wanted to get out of the industry. In that agency it had been a cigarette company which rumors had said might depart. He'd hated the current of fear that ran through all ad agencies, fear of a client leaving. But in San Francisco, although a research firm had shown some interest in him, only this agency had offered him a job. He'd known that the beer company was by far its largest client, but he hadn't known that the company president was a tyrant. So now he was in a worse situation than before. If the cigarette maker had left, the New York agency would have had to cut back but it would have survived. If the brewer left, as Fiegelman had just threatened, his current agency would undoubtedly go under

On his way back to his office, he stopped at the desk of Mara Kovaks, the research department's secretary and all-purpose assistant. "How was the meeting going?" she asked.

"Not too good." Paul told her about Fiegelman's threat.

"Poor Bob. That man should be taken out and shot." Mara was a woman in her forties, dark, attractive and tremendously competent. She and her husband had come to the States from Yugoslavia several years ago. Paul knew she'd been some kind of company executive there and her husband, who now drove a delivery truck, had been an engineer. "Here, let me get you a cup of coffee." This was the 1950's and women did not yet consider getting coffee for men to be demeaning.

"Has it always been so bad?" Paul asked.

"Not always. Fiegelman senior died last year; since his son Oscar took over it hasn't been good."

They talked a little more, then Bob came in. Both Paul and Mara looked at him questioningly. "Fiegelman wants more data," Bob said. "We'll probably be working late nights. Is that okay with you guys?"

They said it was. Paul remembered that when the cigarette company in New York was rumored to be leaving they had to work late nights. Some things didn't change.

*　　*　　*

It was a Friday evening. Paul had once again worked late, had a quick bite to eat, then had come to this party, which was in a large apartment on Pacific Heights with a view of the Bay. He'd been told of the party by Bill Morrow, a media buyer at his agency, also a New Yorker, with whom he had a casual friendship; they sometimes played tennis in Golden Gate Park on weekends. When he'd arrived at the party, Paul had talked a little with Bill about the agency. Bill had told him not to worry too much about the beer account leaving. "He enjoys terrifying the agency execs too much; Selig's scared to death of him. Besides, I don't know if any of the other agencies in town would take him. His reputation has spread around." Bill had then seen a girl he knew and had gone over to speak with her.

Paul had been at the party for about two hours now. There were a few attractive girls but they were all surrounded by other guys. Besides, remembering the disastrous outcome of his relationship with a girl in New York, who'd assumed that he'd wanted to marry her after they'd spent one night together, he was in no hurry to start anything. He was tired from his nights of working overtime and was ready to go home when he saw a girl by herself looking out the window at the lights on the Golden Gate Bridge. She wasn't bad-looking, he thought, and started walk in her direction. He was only a few feet away and she must have sensed his approach because she turned and he saw she had a large port wine birthmark on her right cheek. It was too late to retreat so he introduced himself to her and learned her name was Caroline, that she was from the Midwest and that she worked in a bank downtown.

When she found out he worked in an ad agency she asked him a lot of questions about it and said she'd always thought it was a glamorous business, unlike, say, banking. Paul laughed and said it wasn't so glamorous. He told her about the agency's problems with its beer account, trying to make it sound more humorous than he really thought it was. "Oh," she said. "Then why does anyone put up with it?"

Paul tried to explain the nature of the advertising world, how every agency, even the big ones, was deathly afraid of losing a major account. He realized that he was talking a lot and that it was because Caroline was easy to talk to. It was time to leave, he thought. He looked at his watch, then said, "Uh, you'll have to excuse me. I have to talk to someone over there." He found Bill and they made a date to play tennis on Sunday. Paul was on his way out when he thought, What the hell! He turned around and went back to Caroline, who was still standing alone by the window, got her phone number and said he'd call her.

*   *   *

The conference room was filled to capacity. The agency was presenting its revised campaign to Fiegelman, who, as before, sat at the head of the table, looking more frog-like than ever in what seemed to be a green suit. Bob Prosser was again seated at the foot of the table. The others included account executives and copywriters. Tom Selig, the agency head, was himself making the presentation, standing at an easel with a pointer. Paul was seated alongside the wall. This was the first time he'd attended this kind of meeting. Bob had told him he might be needed if Fiegelman had questions about the details of the marketing data they'd be reviewing. Paul remembered the Colonel's admonition. Listen and observe. Don't commit yourself. Hold your fire..

The new campaign focused on their client's being a local company; it's slogan was "A California Beer for Californians." Paul thought the ads put up were pretty good. The latest ad featured a blonde model in a bikini offering a bottle of beer to a tanned, muscular young man with the Golden Gate Bridge in the background. Fiegelman interrupted. "I'd like to meet that blonde," he said, then cackled. The two minions seated on either side of him obediently cackled also.

"That can be arranged," said Selig. He put up the next ad. Paul could see that he was sweating. After the last ad, Selig said, "Now we have some interesting market data. We think we've found a new demographic for your product." He looked at Bob, who stood, put a large graph up on the easel and began to discourse on facts and figures. He was just getting into his presentation when Fiegelman croaked out. "I don't give a shit about demographics and all that crap. Let me meet that blonde and I might consider the campaign. Go on, sit down. And you might do something useful. How about getting me some coffee?"

Bob went to the phone at the end of the room and made a call. In a few minutes, Mara came in with a cup of coffee, which she placed in front of Fiegelman. He took a sip, then said, "This takes like piss. Who the hell made it?"

"I did," said Mara.

"Then I want you fired." He glared at Selig. "Fire this bitch right now or I pull the plug," he said. .

Selig started to say something but Paul had already stood up. In a loud voice, he said, "Actually, I made that coffee, this morning when I came in. And you don't have to fire me. I quit." There was a time when you couldn't hold your fire any longer. With everyone staring at him. he left the room.

*   *   *

Paul stood looking out over the Pacific Ocean. After leaving the meeting, he'd walked back to his apartment, taken his car and driven out to the spot where tourists usually went, by the Cliff House where you could sometimes see and hear the seals on the rocks. The morning fog had burnt off and the sun glistened on the waves rolling in. He recalled that not too long ago he'd been standing like this on the deck of a troopship coming back from Europe, looking at the Atlantic Ocean and wondering what was in store for him. He could never have imagined that he'd now be here 3,000 miles away.

Well, he'd done it. It was, contrary to the Colonel's philosophy, not exactly a well-thought out move, quitting like that. Still, it had felt good, and it still felt good. Somehow, although he'd left his home, his parents, had his own place, his own life, until now he hadn't felt like a real adult. Everything depended on a job that he'd known he couldn't stay in. By leaving it, maybe he'd come of age.

Of course, his quitting hadn't been an entirely spontaneous action. The Colonel had always said to leave a line of retreat open, and he'd talked to the research firm that had shown some interest in him when he arrived in San Francisco and found out they had an opening. Also, there were two or three other possibilities, with local companies, not ad agencies. Advertising was something he was never going back to. He suddenly felt hungry. There was a coffee shop in the amusement park that was then on the other side of the highway by the ocean. He'd get a bite to eat, go back to his apartment, call the research firm, then call Caroline.

A Day at the Office
(Magnus)

The appearance of our Division chief, Glenda Chetwitch, in my tiny office was an unwelcome sight at any time. It was even more so when I'd just come in that morning, glanced at my calendar to make sure I didn't have an early appointment and there she stood in the doorway, one hand clutching a file folder. "You're looking good today, Glenda," I said insincerely. I always tried to greet Glenda with a complement, knowing that she was not used to this and hoping that it might throw her off balance. Glenda was not at attractive woman. She was of average height, with dyed blonde hair, a face like a cauliflower, and a figure that was flat in front and wide below. Glenda flushed slightly, then holding out the file folder, said, "We have a request for information from State Senator Maxine Peters. Marcus just called me. It's top priority." I said to myself: Here we go. Another day at the office.

I doubt if the ambition of many kids growing up is to spend most of their lives working in an office. Yet this is what often happens, an example being our oldest son, who was an accountant.. It's even more unlikely that anyone envisions a career working in a government agency office. Yet this too does happen, as evidenced by all those many civil service workers, and it's what eventually happened to me. When I was growing up in the Bronx I was a fervent Yankee fan, Yankee Stadium being only 20 minutes away. My dream was to play baseball for the Yankees. My ambition was modest. Knowing that I'd never grow up to be tall, husky and athletic, I didn't want to become a great hitter like DiMaggio or a great pitcher like Ruffing. I'd be a relief pitcher, coming into the ninth inning with men on base and, with my well-placed pitches (I had pinpoint control to compensate for my lack of a good fastball) get the final out.

When I was 13, the earliest age at which I could get a work permit, I had a summer job as a stock and delivery boy in Manhattan's Garment District. During summers in high school I hitch-hiked to Idaho and worked in the Forestry Service. After college and two years in the Army during Korea, I went to work for an ad agency. For various reasons, I went West to California and got a job with a marketing research firm in San Francisco. When the firm went under I caught on as a research analyst with the State of California.. As most State offices were in Sacramento, this is where, with Sally, my newly acquired wife, I'd moved and started a family. I was now, some 25 years later, head of the Health Demographics Section, HDS, consisting of myself and four people, three analysts and a clerk, in the Statistics and Date Division (SADD) of the State's giant Health Department.

The Marcus that Glenda referred to was our Department Director, Marcus Aurelius Gonzales. When a State Senator like Maxine Peters wanted information of any kind, she of course didn't contact a lowly State section head, she (or more likely an aide) called the Department Director, who then called a Division Chief like Glenda, who then came running down to see me with a file folder marked Top Priority. I looked into the folder. The State Senator was going to speak at an Oakland high school and wanted information on teenage birth rates for the past ten years.. "Do you think you can get it to her today?" asked Glenda.

"I'm afraid not," I said firmly. "It means running two files and then doing the calculations to get rates and I assume she'd like to have the data by race." Maxine Peters was Afro-American.

"How soon can you get it done? By tomorrow?"

"I'll do my best." I hoped I sounded sincere.

"Marcus will be on me."

That was hard to envision. "I'll do the job myself," I said.

"All right. Keep me informed."

"I will." I knew Glenda would be calling me during the day; that was her management style.

As soon as Glenda was safely out of the way, I turned on my little transistor radio to get the latest stock market report; in those ancient days, you couldn't just go to your computer. Good grief, the Dow Jones was down over 200 points; what was going on? I put aside the Top Priority file folder. The State Senator's information request was important only in our little government bureaucracy world. This was the real world. I immediately called my broker. We discussed the situation and decided this was a buy opportunity. I put in a couple of orders, for IBM and for Hewlett-Packard. Just about all the State's data processing was done on IBM mainframes and the State had begun to buy H-P copiers.

That done, I called our clerk, Rachel Montoya, into my office. As soon as she came in, she said, "Sorry I couldn't alert you that Glenda the Witch was coming; she was past me before I could pick up the phone."

"That's okay, but be on the alert. Everything else okay?"

"You have a meeting tomorrow morning, Dr. Sanderson."

"Oh, yeah. How are those tables you're doing for him?"

"Almost done. My spies saw Glenda and her husband huddling together in the cafeteria yesterday. They might be plotting something."

To the surprise of most people who knew her, Glenda was actually married. Her husband, Harold Chetwitch, was also a Division Manager, in the Department of Mental Health. They mercifully had no children, possibly because all of their time was spent in scheming to advance their careers. They were like an early version of Bill and Hillary Clinton. "Okay, keep your eyes and ears open and keep me informed." Rachel was a tiny woman who'd been with the State for years and had all sorts of contacts. If you wanted to know what was going on, really going on, Rachel was the person to ask. "Send George in, please."

"Right, Chief," said Rachel, giving me a mock-salute.

I gave her a look back and leaned back in my chair, waiting for George Rozier, who came in a moment later. "Sit down, George," I said, and he did, carefully. George was big, about six feet tall, and more impressively, about 300 pounds. He was, I knew from his personnel file, 53 years old and had been with the State for 20 years. He was a UC Berkeley graduate and had taught college for several years, then there was a blank in his resume before he had his first State job. George was an irascible fellow and I assume he'd had some kind of personality conflict that ended his teaching career. He was probably the best statistician in the Department and I always assigned him the toughest jobs. He'd been stuck as a journeyman analyst because, aside from his weight and rumpled suits and tendency to sweat a lot, he had no social graces, was blunt, loud and antagonized people with what they thought was a superior attitude. Glenda Chetworth hated him for his boorishness and he despised her for her lack of competence as a researcher.

"How's the AIDS project coming along?" I asked. AIDS had recently raised its ugly head in the health community and, at the request of Marcus Aurelius Gonzales, I was trying to extract some information on the deaths it had caused from our computer tapes. Or, I should, say I'd assigned George the task of doing this. Needless to say, AIDS had no specific identifying code, but the Feds has issued a list of "AIDS-related" diseases and George was working with that.

"It's slow," said George. "A lot of those old tapes are in bad shape and the fields vary all over the place."

"I see. Well, keep plugging. Marcus would consider it a feather in his cap if we can give him anything." I paused, then I asked, "How's your wife?" George, as unlikely a candidate as Glenda, was also married. His wife had also worked for the State, but she was now on disability with some kind of cancer.

"About the same.".

"Well, hang in there. I'm still working on your promotion." Getting George, who, I know, could use the extra money, a promotion was my long-term project. I'd tried once a couple of years ago and failed, but the State had a new classification called Research Specialist that was at an in-between level, that I thought I could fit George in.

"I don't have a chance," said George.

"We'll see," I said. I made a mental note to talk to Marcus again the next time I caught him in a good mood.

The rest of the morning was uneventful and I used it to review my finances. What, doing personal stuff on State time? Didn't I feel guilty about this? No. If I still hoped to move George up a notch, I knew my chances of any kind of promotion were zero. I don't want to get into a long explanation of this. Let's just say that I tried to provide honest data, not fudge it; that I was outspoken (not to the same extent as George); that I was not obsequious enough for some department managers and legislative aides. From the point of view of the managers and aides, I was probably a rebel and a maverick. At any rate, I was going nowhere.

I'd learned a few things about work and one of these things, of which management was blissfully unaware, is that people don't just sit and take what is being done to them, they react in some way. So how do State employees who know they won't be promoted react? I'd seen them do so in various ways. Of course, one way was to retire early; that is, not to do any work at all. I knew someone who did a profitable real estate business on the side. Another guy I knew played in a band at night. In my own case, I managed my money.

It started, I think, when one of Sally's uncles left her a small inheritance. With this, I ventured into buying a few conservative stocks, then a couple of mutual funds, then some individual stocks. When interest rates soared, I had enough money to put into high-grade bonds. Who could argue with 12 or 13 percent and safety? In one of the few things the State did for ordinary employees, it had what was known as Deferred Compensation, a kid of 401K, to which it matched your contribution. I tried to put in the maximum. I also had the maximum IRA every year. This reduced my taxes. It also reduced my take-home income, but the interest from the bonds made up for that. My goal was to accumulate a quarter of million dollars, in those days a substantial amount, and then retire. As life would have it, when I reached this goal I had, against all odds, received a promotion and so continued to work for a few more years. But that's, as they say, another story.

I had lunch in the building cafeteria with a friend, Al Cheng, a systems analyst in the Department. Al was one of those early computer geniuses. He had also gone as far as he could with the State. He hated office politics and was happiest constructing or untangling intricate computer programs. Al was a neighbor and a fellow member of our local swim and tennis club. We played tennis together after work once or twice a week. I told Al about my latest stock purchases. We discussed our respective jobs and our respective bosses, who were, we agreed, complete incompetents. Al asked if I could get away a little early for tennis. I said I thought I could; I'd call him.

About an hour after lunch, one of my analysts, Priscella King, came into my office, somewhat breathlessly telling me about a call she'd just had from a local television station. "Sit down, Pris," I told her. Priss was an attractive girl in her late twenties, far too attractive for a State employee, I thought. She was bright but a little scatter-brained. I'd given her the job of handling requests for information from the media. Surprisingly, we had quite a few.

Priss sat and crossed her long, shapely legs, always a highlight of my day. "So, what do they want?" I asked.

The TV station wanted information about kids who drowned. This wasn't surprising as there'd been two or three such incidents in recent weeks. I told Priss where to quickly find the information and said to call the station back. "Just give me a little memo of what you send them." Priss smiled and rustled out. I thought that if the TV station knew how she looked they'd ask her to come down and give the information in person.

As soon as Priss left, my phone rang. "It's your favorite, Glenda the Witch," said Rachel.

"Put her through," I said. As I'd expected, Glenda wanted to know if I was getting the birth rate information for State Senator Maxine Peters. I told her I was working on it. She was clearly not satisfied with this, but, as she knew almost nothing about data processing, there wasn't much she could do about it.

It was time to get out of the office. I strolled through my little section, asking everyone how they were doing with their various tasks. I stopped and had a few words with my newest analyst, a young guy named Harvey Weiss, who'd recently come in from another section. I'd put him to work on a report we put out periodically, the ten leading causes of death in the State. He said that so far he'd had no problems. Harvey was engaged to be married soon, he'd told me so, and he'd already asked me about chances of promotion. He'd told me he was ready to work overtime and would undertake any job I gave me. He was young and still under the impression that getting promoted in the State had something to do with working hard. Well, he'd learn soon enough. I said some encouraging words to Harvey and returned to my office.

I thought about Harvey. He was on his way. First marriage, then the kids, then the house, the lawn, the crabgrass, the mortgage, the repairs, the whole works, then he'd be a State employee for life.. Once we'd settled in Sacramento, I put out a few feelers for jobs in the private sector, but evidently once you became a civil servant you were disqualified from being anything else. I'm not sure when I passed the point of no return. It was probably when our youngest son became a teenager. The State provided a good, if not great, pension. There was Deferred Comp. The State health insurance plans were as good as any. The boys must be put through college, then I wanted to retire. I'd stay put..

I read through the usual memos I'd received that day. State managers were always sending memos; it gave them some justification for their jobs. I sent a few memos of my own. State agencies were also always having meetings. I checked my calendar; yes, the meeting with Dr. Sanderson tomorrow. I called Rachel; the tables for the good doctor were ready. Good. I spent a few moments thinking of what I'd do when I retired. Play tennis every day? Definitely, no memos and no meetings.

I called my wife Sally. She gave me the latest news of our sons and of the state of our aged house. Our youngest son's car might need a brake check; they were squealing.. One of our fences was sagging. A faucet was leaking. Not too bad. My phone rang; it was none other than Marcus Aurelius Gonzales. He wanted to know how I was coming with that birth rate data for our State Senator. So Glenda, after she'd called me, had called him. I told him I was on it and she'd get it in time. He said that was good. We chatted a little more; he wanted to know about the AIDS project and I told him we'd have something soon. When we did, I'd bring up the matter of George Rozier's promotion.

After this call, I looked at my watch. I got the teenage birth rate tables from the desk drawer where I kept computer printouts and other such data for which I knew there'd always be requests. (It helped to have a friend like Al Cheng in Data Processing to get all those computer printouts). I looked at the tables; better have Rachel put the data in a graph as well; that way even a State Senator might understand it. I wrote a short covering memo pointing out the things the Senator should tell her high school audience. Yes, I could have provided the information right away, but you didn't want to do this with anyone connected with the Legislature. The same was true of Department heads and certainly of the Governor's Office. This would spoil them. The next time they'd expect an instantaneous response. I straightened out my desk, a little, called Al Cheng, then left my office, tossed the tables and memo onto Rachel's desk, told her to make the graph and to have everything ready for tomorrow morning, then said I was leaving a little early. Another day at the office.

The Test Results
(Winamop)

Paul Lerner had lived, with his wife Sally, in a Northern Californian retirement community, for the last ten years. When you've been a retiree for that length of time you develop certain routines. Paul's last action before going to bed was always, unless, as sometimes happened, he forgot, to check his computer for any late e-mails, then close it down for the night. In his retirement, Paul had become a kind of writer, doing a monthly column for a senior newspaper and writing short stories for a number of online magazines, whose editors did sometimes send him e-mails that arrived late at night.

On this night, after going through his usual routine (there were no e-mails), Paul looked at the letter on his computer desk. It was from his health plan and, he was sure, contained the results of some tests he'd recently taken. Normally, he'd have opened the envelope as soon as it arrived and looked at the results. Why hadn't he done so this time? He supposed it was because he'd had such a good day and didn't want to take a chance on spoiling it. The test results could wait another day; they wouldn't change.

Paul considered that if he was writing this as a short story (called, say, "The Test Results"), starting it before just before going to bed would be unusual. It was common for authors to start a story when the main character first awakened. This allowed the author to set the stage for the action to come. *Sam turned the alarm clock off and buried his head beneath the pillows. He didn't really want to get up and face going to work that day.* Or: *Suzie leapt out of bed. He was coming home today, after two years in Iraq; but would he remember her?* It also gave the author a chance to describe his character as he or she looked into the bathroom mirror. *Sam saw an anxious face with bloodshot eyes and a stubble of beard. Suzie saw a teenager with blonde hair and sparkling blue eyes.* How would he describe himself in the mirror? An elderly gentleman with sparse hair, age spots, and many lines from … from what? A lifetime of care? No, not really.

After getting into bed, Paul kissed Sally and told her that he loved her, another customary routine. Then, as usual, he went over in his mind the events of the day. It had begun when he turned on his computer, as he always did first thing in the morning, and found an e-mail from one of his editors saying that Paul's story would be featured in the next issue of his online magazine. Paul had been fond of that story, and the editor had turned down the two previous stories he'd sent, so that was good news indeed.

After breakfast, he'd done the day's crossword puzzle, not easy on a Saturday, sometimes harder than the Sunday one. At his weekly pool game that morning, after losing the first two games and seemingly on his way to defeat in the third, he'd made a miraculous two-cushion shot, then had sunk the eight ball with another difficult shot. At his weekly bridge game that afternoon, he'd held good cards in almost every game and had ended with the most points after three rubbers. Very satisfying.

It was satisfying also that he and Sally had enough money to live comfortably in retirement. And they'd both been fairly healthy, even though he'd had a surgery last year. One of the drawbacks of living in a retirement community was that as everyone became older, friends and acquaintances began to get sick or pass away. When you were in your seventies, approaching 80, Paul had found that it was difficult to avoid thinking of your own mortality, thoughts that usually came just about this time, before falling asleep. He repeatedly told himself to just take life one day at a time, a cliché but not that easy to do. Well, this day was over and he'd look at those test results tomorrow.

Paul slept until almost nine the next morning. After breakfast, he tackled the Sunday crossword puzzle (good for the aging mind, the experts said) and, with the help of his computer (you could Google nearly everything nowadays) finished it. Then he opened the envelope containing his test results. If he was writing this as a story, he thought, he could end it right here and leave the reader in suspense. The creator of the TV show, "The Sopranos," had recently done something like that, ending with a scene that went black, and the critics had thought this was a stroke of genius. This was the way life was, they'd said, no neat endings; it just went on.

But he didn't think this would be fair. You couldn't string your reader along and then leave your story up in the air. He looked at the test results. Damn! They were inconclusive. His doctor had scrawled a note on them; he wanted Paul to take the tests again in three months. Well, at his age three months was a considerable time. He'd try to take the three months one day at a time. He went to tell Sally the news.

.

Just Another Afternoon
(Pink Chameleon)

Sam Mitchell got back to his home in a Northern California retirement community around noon. He was well-satisfied with himself. He's shot a pretty good round of golf, nothing spectacular, but good enough. There was a note on the kitchen table from his wife Connie, reminding him that she was going out to lunch "with the girls";: she'd left him a sandwich in the fridge. He took an unhurried shower, changed, found the sandwich, egg salad, which Connie knew he liked, and had lunch while reading the paper. The news was the usual: the war in Iraq; the mess in Washington; a missing child; some movie star going into rehab.

After eating, Mitchell washed up and looked for a book to read. He started one, some kind of medical thriller, but it was so poorly-written he put it down after a few pages. He remembered a book of short stories by John Cheever he'd bought at a garage sale and had been meaning to read. Taking it down from the bookcase, he accidentally displaced one of the photo albums that Connie meticulously kept; the heavy album came down on his shoulder before landing on the floor. Mitchell picked it up and saw that the pictures were of the time they'd moved into their first house some 40 years before, before the kids, before the grandkids, before Connie's breast cancer, before his heart surgery.

Mitchell took the album into the living room, sat in his armchair and started looking through it. There was a picture of him and Connie standing in front of the house; a neighbor must have taken it. God, they both looked so young, and so slim. He was grinning, presumably with the pleasure of having become a home owner. There was a picture of Connie in their then immaculate kitchen, pretending to be drying a plate and a picture of him behind a lawnmower. He kept thumbing through the album. A picture of him holding a tennis racket; he'd played two or three times a week then, before his knees went to hell. A picture of him standing on a ladder, painting the front of the house. Had he once done that? .

Mitchell leaned back in the chair. He'd looked so happy back then. Now look at him. The kids, two boys, had grown up and were out of the house; they had their own lives. He and Connie were lucky to see their grandchildren a few times a year. He often wondered how many more years he had left. And what did he have to fill them? Playing golf a few mornings a week. Reading, half-dozing, during the afternoons. More dozing in front of the TV at night. . Eventually, maybe not so far in the future, his heart would give out. He felt suddenly tired, all the energy going out of him, like air from a leaking tire.

The doorbell rang. Who could that be? He wasn't expecting anyone. He opened the door and a fresh-faced young man in a suit and tie handed him a pamphlet saying, The End is Near. The young man said, "If I could have a moment of your …"

"No," said Mitchell. "I don't have that much time left." He closed the door firmly and went back into the living room. The end may be near, he thought, but I'm not going out without a fight. He picked up the Cheever book and read about suburbanites like himself, drinking and divorcing, but still alive to the beauty in life. When Connie came home, he surprised her by getting up and hugging her.

"What's that for?"

"I don't know. I missed you."

"You look a little funny. What have you been doing all afternoon?"

"Nothing much. Just another afternoon. Let's go out to dinner tonight."

She laughed. "I just went out to lunch."

"Okay. Tomorrow night then?"

"All right. You're sure you're okay? Nothing happened?"

"I'm sure. I told you, just another afternoon."

Lest We Forget
(Winamop)

Paul Lerner looked forward to his quarterly dental check-up with the same enthusiasm, he thought, as going to, well, as going to the dentist. But at his age, late seventies, fighting a rearguard action against receding gums (as well as against a host of other calamities), he supposed his teeth had to be examined every few months no matter how he felt.

On this visit, he had a new dental hygienist. Her name, he saw by the badge on her white uniform, was Ruth. She was young, not that most people didn't seem young to him nowadays, but she couldn't have been any more than 20 or 21. Ruth. That had been the name of Paul's secretary when he worked. And, like that Ruth, this one had blonde hair worn in what he supposed was a pageboy and was very pretty. Paul had lost touch with his secretary after he'd retired, then somebody else who'd worked in their office had called to tell him that she was in the hospital and he'd gone to see her. He'd known that Ruth had diabetes and now she had some rare related disease.

Paul had been saddened to see how puffed-up Ruth's face had become. Her voice was also very weak. He'd stayed for an hour, trying his best to make conversation. He went to see her again and this time she seemed a little better, but then he'd gotten a phone call from Ruth's sister, telling him that she'd suddenly passed away. Ruth had been about 15 years younger than him and Paul had been shocked and then saddened.

Ruth, the dental hygienist, installed Paul in the dentist's chair and asked him if there'd been any change in his health since his last visit. "No," answered Paul. "Just keep on getting older and more decrepit."

"Oh, you don't look decrepit," she said. She asked him if he still lived at the same address, Sun City Roseville, which was a retirement community just outside of Sacramento, the capital of California.

He asked her if she lived in Roseville and she told him she'd just moved there. "How do you like it?"

"Oh, it's great, I found a great apartment and there's so many things to do."

Paul wondered what there was to do in Roseville, not much of a place for young people, he'd have thought,, although its population had soared in recent years. He would have asked, but it was time for the cleaning and he had to sit there, his mouth open, while she scraped away at his gums, something he'd always hated.

He thought back; his secretary Ruth's death had been about five years ago and he realized he hadn't really thought about her since that time. God, how quickly people forget. During his time at the retirement community, any number of residents he'd known had passed away, guys he'd played golf with, persons who'd organized clubs, those who'd served on committees with him. Now he played golf with different people; the clubs and the committees went on with different members.

He was thinking more and more about his own mortality lately and wondered how many people would remember him after he was gone. His wife, his sons, maybe his grandchildren for a while. His friends at the retirement community? They'd come to his memorial service and then, after a short while, he'd have faded away with all the others.

If he didn't show up for his next check-up, how would this Ruth remember him? As a set of not especially good teeth? That is, if she remembered him at all. What could he do to make her remember him. He could tell her how pretty he thought she was and ...

"Don't you dare, Mr. Lerner."

"What?"

"I said we're all through here. Did you doze off?"

"No, I was just thinking about something."

"Well, you seem to be holding your own. Keep flossing. I'll see you in three months.'

"Three months. Right."

*   *   *

The way back to Sun City passed Roseville's mall, the Galleria, and since it was only mid-morning Paul stopped there. He went into Border's, the book store, got a latte in their coffee shop and went to a table by the window. Outside, the sun shone brightly. It was the kind of day that when he was younger would have made him wish he was on the tennis courts. Now he managed to play golf once a week. He raised his latte and said to himself, "Here's to you, Ruth. I'll try not to forget you again." He drank and put down his cup. He'd try, at least every now and then, to also remember the others who'd passed on. He'd never told the dental hygienist how pretty he thought she was. And he'd never really completed the image in his mind of how he'd follow up on this. He smiled to himself. What he'd half-imagined would really make her remember him. It would also get him a slap in the face and he'd have to find a new dentist. Well, the prospect of seeing pretty Ruth again gave him an incentive to hang on for another three months

Saying Good-bye
(Fictionville)

Paul knocked softly on the door. Jack's wife Myra opened it. "Is it okay if I come in?" asked Paul.

"He's on the back patio," she said. "He likes to sit out there and watch the sun set."

"How are you holding up?"

"Not bad." Myra's face looked strained and there were dark circles under her eyes. "How was Ireland?"

Paul and his wife Sally had been to Ireland to visit their youngest son and his family. "We had a good visit. The grandkids are cute. I brought some Irish truffles for Jack." Since Jack had been sick, Paul had brought back something for him whenever they'd gone anywhere. Jack had a sweet tooth.

"Thanks," said Myra, taking the small box tied with a ribbon, "but he hasn't been eating much."

"Oh. Can I see him?"

"Yes, but he might be asleep."

Paul went out on the patio. Jack was sitting in one of the rocking chairs. He had a blanket over his lap and a wool hat on his head, although it was late September and still warm. The hat, Paul knew, was because Jack's hair had fallen out during the chemo Paul couldn't tell if Jack was sleeping. He sat down on the other rocking chair. Someone had recently mowed the back lawn and he could smell the grass. A few small birds twittered around the feeder, hung on a tree. The sky was turning pink. It waa funny, their Northern California retirement community sometimes had beautiful sunsets..

"How was your trip?"

It took Paul a minute to realize Jack had spoken. "It was good. We had a nice visit."

"Kids okay."

"Yeah, getting bigger."

"Good." After a silence, Jack said, "I like it out here."

"It's nice," Paul said. There was silence again. Jack looked shrunken since Paul had last seen him. His face was puffy; maybe that was also from the chemo. Jack still had a way of talking out of the side of his mouth in a way that made what he said sound sardonic. Jack and Myra had moved in at about the same time as Paul and Sally. They'd gone out to meals together and played bridge together. Paul had found out that Jack was also a tennis player, a much better player than him.. The other top players in the retirement community formed a clique and played only with one another, but Paul had become Jack's tennis partner. They were a pretty good team. Once, in a tournament, they'd made it to the finals against two guys who were only in their forties. "Let's beat these young whippersnappers," Jack had said out of the side of his mouth, and thanks to Jack's playing they had.

As if he'd known what Paul was thinking about, Jack said, "Still playing tennis?"

"A little," said Paul. "The knees are going."

"Yeah, I know how it is. Everything goes." Jack took out a pack of cigarettes from underneath his blanket and lit one. Paul knew Myra had tried to get Jack to quit smoking. He guessed that now it didn't make any difference.

"How was your trip?' asked Jack once again.

"It was good. The grandkids are getting bigger."

Jack coughed. "That's good," he said. He coughed again. He put out the cigarette and closed his eyes. The sun went down, the clouds turned from pink to gray and it became cooler. Somewhere Paul could hear quails calling, then a pigeon cooing. He got up, put his hand on Jack's for a moment, then went inside, said good-bye to Myra and went home.

Life's Little Annoyances
(Hackwriters)

Paul Lerner wrote a monthly column called "Observations" for the senior newspaper that went to his Northern California retirement community. After eight years, he sometimes found it difficult to come up with a subject to have observations about. Usually, when this happened, he fell back on what he called LLA's, or "Life's Little Annoyances." There was an endless supply of these: the car that zipped in front of you to take the last space in the parking lot; the lady at the supermarket check-out who had to write a check for her purchases and took hours doing so; the daily mail with its load of credit card offers; the phone calls at dinner from people wanting you to donate to their cause; and so on and so forth.

Nothing was so annoying first thing in the morning, thought Paul, than not to have your newspaper there when you went out to get it. It was one of those things you couldn't quite believe, like not finding your keys in your pocket after locking the door of your house. Of course, it was also a rainy morning. He ventured out to see if maybe the paper was in the driveway, but all this accomplished was to get him wet and more annoyed. He went back inside and told his wife Sally, "No newspaper today." He found the newspaper's number in the phone book, called and was put on hold. He held on for almost ten minutes while an automated voice kept assuring him that his call was important. Finally, he banged the phone down with a curse. "Can't even get through to a human being any more," he told Sally. "I don't have all morning to wait."

"Go ahead and have your breakfast," said Sally. "I'll call them later."

"Good luck," grumbled Paul..

This was the morning that Paul played pool with Sid Kaplan, another retirement community resident. The pool room, which held six tables, was in a building called the Lodge, the center of most of the community's activities. Sid was an acerbic guy, who had all kinds of rules about playing pool. If you scratched when sinking a ball, not only did that ball have to come out but another one as a penalty; if you were snookered and couldn't hit your ball you were penalized a ball. This resulted in their having very long games. Sid was very competitive and when he was losing he complained that Paul was playing too slowly and sometimes he claimed that Paul hadn't hit the proper ball when Paul was sure he had. All of this was annoying, but

Sid had introduced Paul to the game when Paul was recovering from a surgery, so Paul didn't think he could complain. He just kept on getting more and more annoyed.

In their first game that morning, Paul was shooting well, then with only the eight and one other ball left he kept getting snookered because Sid had so many of his balls left on his table. After a while, Paul had almost all of the balls he'd sunk back up on the table. Paul eventually won in one of their usual long, drawn-out games. Then at the end of their next long game, when Paul tried to just tip the eight ball and missed it by a hair Sid claimed that meant he'd lost the game, although Paul could have sworn the same thing had happened a few weeks ago with Sid and he'd only penalized himself by putting up one of his balls. At any rate, Paul said, "Okay," and when Sid suggested a third game, he said he had some errands to run. Paul left the pool room even more annoyed with Sid than usual.

Paul did have an errand to run; he had to go to the bank to deposit the monthly check he received for writing his "Observations" column. Going to the bank was invariably an annoying experience and this time proved to be no exception. There wasn't the usual long lunchtime line (the bank seemed to be able to provide only two tellers even at the busiest times), but each of the tellers had a woman customer whose transactions, whatever they were, seemed to go on forever. Finally, one of the women took a considerable amount of cash and managed, after a struggle, to get it stuffed into her purse.

Paul stepped forward and handed the teller, a young man who looked barely out of high school, his check and deposit slip. The teller looked at these, then said, with a bright insincere smile, "How're you doing today, Paul?"

Paul? Had he met this youngster before? No. Paul was tempted to say something, but he was of a polite generation, unlike the current one, so he just replied, "I'm fine. I'd like to deposit the check."

The teller examined the check, then said, "Do you know your PIN number?"

"Why? I just want to put some money in, not take it out." Now Paul was getting really annoyed.

"If you'll just enter your PIN."

Paul almost asked what would happen if he had forgotten his PIN; did this mean he couldn't put money in his own account.? But, still polite, he entered his number and, after a time, the slip with his deposit amount came out. "There you are," said the teller. "Anything else we can do for you today?" Another big insincere smile.

"Just don't lose my money," Paul muttered as he left.

When Paul returned home, Sally told him they'd gotten their newspaper. They had a new carrier on their route and he'd missed a number of homes. "Great," said Paul. "I hope he doesn't mess up tomorrow, too."

"Steve called," said Sally. Steve was their youngest son, who lived only a few miles away. "They want to bring the kids over Sunday afternoon. There's some kind of concert they want to go to."

The kids were their two grandsons, Mark, age four, and Eric, age two. "You mean we'll be baby-sitting? For how long?

"I don't know; all afternoon, I suppose. Isn't that all right?"

As far as Paul was concerned, that wasn't all right. Sunday was his day of relaxation. He liked to have a leisurely breakfast, then do the Sunday crossword puzzle, and this Sunday there was a football game he was looking forward to watch."You know I watch football Sunday afternoons. When are they going to find a baby-sitter? Besides us?" Steve and his wife Jane had moved to their new house two years ago and ever since Paul and Sally had been doing a lot of baby-sitting. Sally would never refuse and it seemed to Paul that his son and daughter-in-law were taking advantage of her. And if Sally baby-sat that meant Paul would also have to do so.

"Don't you want to see your grandsons?"

"Yes, but I don't want to be on call all the time. Next time can you please ask me first before you say we'll baby-sit?"

"You weren't here."

"All right, we'll baby sit, but next time ask me." God, Sally could be annoying at times. Paul grabbed the newspaper and went into the bedroom to finally read it.

After lunch, Paul went to his computer to compose his "Observations" for the month. When he'd finished a draft he turned on his printer so that he could print it out and show it to Sally as usual. But as soon as the printer was on it began to spit out paper, one page after another. Paul turned off the printer as quickly as he could. He went into the living room and asked Sally if shed used the printer that morning.. She said she had but something had gone wrong. "Well, you've messed up my printer again," he told her.

Paul went back to his computer and saw that, sure enough, there was an uncompleted printing job. Sally appeared in the doorway. "I was going to tell you," she said, but then Steve called and I forgot. Can I do anything?"

"Yes, just go away and let me alone." This had happened before and he went through the steps to delete the job to clear the printer. He didn't always remember the correct sequence of steps and this time it took him almost half an hour before he was successful. Damnit, Paul thought, this was turning out to be a miserable day. When he printed out his "Observations," he left them on his desk. He didn't want to see Sally just then.

Paul and Sally ate their dinner mostly in silence. Afterward, Sally watched her usual television programs; Paul again went back to his bedroom chair and read. The young hero of the novel he was reading had decided that he'd lost his belief in God and didn't believe in an afterlife. Paul had turned 75 the year before and had realized with a shock that he'd been around for three-quarters of a century. Since then, not a day passed by that Paul didn't think that, like a runner nearing the finish line, he was coming to the end of his life's journey. When you were young it was easy to dismiss religion and the usual notions of an afterlife. Paul didn't believe that there was a Heaven and a Hell, but the idea that once his life was over that was it was one he didn't like to dwell on.

In his mind, Paul reviewed the events of the day—the missing newspaper, the pool games with Sid, the moronic young bank teller, the printer fiasco, his annoyance at having to baby-sit his grandchildren the coming Sunday. Life's little annoyances. Was he becoming an old grouch? That's the way he thought of Sid. Did other people think the same of him? Was it resentment that the time he had left was much less than the time gone by that was making him so edgy? He shouldn't let himself get so upset over trivial matters, like the newspaper. He should be nicer. Well, not too nice. He went into the living room and watched television with Sally until eleven. When they were in bed, he turned to her as he did every night, kissed her and told her he loved her. She murmured something. Lying on his back, he thought, maybe instead of writing another "Observations" on life's little annoyances he should write one on life's little pleasures. There were some left, weren't they, even when you were 75 years old. There were Mark and Eric, his grandsons; they were a pleasure, most of the time. He'd think about it.

The Girl on the Train
(Fictionville)

"Thanks," said Paul Lerner. His wife Sally had just brought him a glass of orange juice.

"Do you want anything else?" she asked.

"No, that's fine."

:Did you take your medicine?"

"Yes, I told you I did."

"All right. Call if you need anything."

"I will. I will."

Paul sipped at the juice. It made his sore throat feel a little better. He was sitting in his bedroom chair. Sun poured through the window. He could have been out on the golf course if it wasn't for this damned cold.

He leafed through the morning paper; same old stuff. He read a few pages but the sun made him drowsy. He closed his eyes. For some reason, he'd been thinking on and off of his time in Germany, over 50 years ago, maybe because when he'd been drafted during Korea and sent over there it had been winter and it seemed he always had a cold.

What was her name? The girl on the train He'd been overseas for a few months and was coming back from his first weekend pass. He was stationed at Seventh Army Headquarters in Stuttgart. He was in a third-class compartment, sitting on a wooden, not very comfortable bench. The girl was sitting across from him, bundled up in her winter clothes. She had blonde hair and a round face with red cheeks and, even through her sweaters, he saw she had plump breasts. He knew some German and started a conversation with her. The other passengers in the compartment, a middle-aged couple, frowned. They didn't approve of a German girl talking to an American soldier.

He dozed off. When he woke up he thought he saw her name in his mind, but then it vanished like smoke. What had happened then? The middle-aged couple had gotten off and the girl had come over to sit beside him. She'd laughed at his bad German, then he'd kissed her. Then he'd found her plump breasts.

"Are you up?" asked Sally.

"Yes. What time is it?"

"It's almost noon. Do you want any lunch?"

"I don't have any appetite."

"You should eat something."

"Maybe later."

"Can I get you anything?"

"No, just leave me alone."

"You're very grouchy."

"You'd be grouchy too if you had this lousy cold."

"All right. Let me know if you get hungry."

"I will." He closed his eyes. He could hear the girl on the train's voice and feel her hands. He dozed again. When he woke up, the sun was gone. He felt cold. He found a blanket and pulled it over him.

"Are you up?"

"Yes."

"You slept almost the whole afternoon. Why are you smiling?"

"I just remembered something." They'd found a blanket overhead and wrapped it around themselves. Her name was Lisa. He'd jotted it down, and her address, on a scrap of paper. She'd gotten off at Heilbronn, about 20 miles before Stuttgart. If he hadn't lost that scrap of paper and had written her what would have happened? He'd have visited her and she'd have come up to Stuttgart. Several of the men in his unit had gone home with German wives. Probably just as well he'd lost that paper. But at least he'd remembered her name. Lisa.

"What did you remember?" asked Sally.

"It was nothing. I feel a little better, probably that long nap." he said. "Maybe I'll have some soup."

Playing Cupid
(Hackwriters)

Paul Lerner was a little late in arriving at the meeting room and saw that Travis Wyndham, President of the Boosters Committee, was already speaking. He looked around and was glad to see that Anne Lewis was there. Paul had introduced Anne, a widow, to a friend of his, Gary Palmer, a while ago in the hope that something would develop. He and his wife Sally had invited Anne and Gary to dinner and to play bridge a few times, but he hadn't seen them lately. He was curious as to how things were going. .

At age 75, Paul had tried to reduce his activities, but he hadn't been able to leave the Boosters, whose mission was to espouse the attractions of their Northern California retirement community. Paul had a certain reputation for wisdom. With his calm demeanor and soothing voice, he was able to mediate the quarrels that were inevitable in a community of crotchety old souls. At least, that was what some people had told him and this made him a prime candidate for committee service..

Wyndham finally ended his speech and the meeting adjourned. Paul sighed, stood up, went over to Anne Lewis, asked her how she was, then asked if she'd seen much of Gary lately...

"Oh, off and on," she replied. "We went dancing last week. In fact, I've been meaning to ask you and Sally over to have dinner with us and maybe play some bridge. Is Saturday good?"

"I think so. I'll have to check with Sally. She's the social planner in the family. I'll ask her to call you."

"Fine. Gary won some golf tournament and I'm sure he'll want to tell you all about it."

When Paul returned home he told Sally about Anne's invitation. Sally checked her calendar and said it was open..

"Anne and Gary seem to have hit it off," said Paul, with some satisfaction. Sally had been a little skeptical of his efforts at match-making, or "playing Cupid," as she called it..

"Let's wait and see. I'll give Anne a call right now.".

*   *   *

The dinner at Anne's on Saturday was very good; Anne was an excellent cook. As Anne had predicted, Gary told them all about his golf tournament victory, in more detail than Paul would have liked. Gary was a tall man in his sixties, a widower, with a florid face and wavy gray hair. He was fit and vigorous for his age, a low handicap golfer, still played tennis and liked to ballroom dance. He was a little flamboyant for Paul's taste, making sure everyone knew about his golfing prowess and showing off on the dance floor. But Anne's late husband, Tommy, had also been like that and Paul had thought that Gary and Anne would make a good pair.

After dinner, they played bridge. Gary and Anne had the better cards at first and Gary was all smiles as they won the first rubber. But then Gary overbid trying to make a grand slam and, as he tended to do, sulked for a while. After a few more hands though he'd gotten over it; the evening ended pleasantly and Anne told them that she and Gary were going dancing again that weekend.

When Paul and Sally returned home, Paul remarked that Gary and Anne looked as if they were becoming a couple. Perhaps they'd be attending a wedding pretty soon. "I'm not sure," said Anne. "Gary can be a little too much at times."

"But he and Anne like to do the same things—golf, dance, play bridge. I think they're a good match."

"Maybe they have too many interests in common. Maybe they're not different from each other enough."

"What do you mean?"

"Well, like us. I like to go out and do things. You'd just as soon stay home all day and read one of your books."

"We've just gone out to dinner and bridge," pointed out Paul.

"Only because you're playing Cupid.."

Paul shrugged. Sometimes Sally could be unreasonable.

*   *   *

Two weeks later, Paul saw Anne coming out of the retirement community's library. She held out her hand, showing him an engagement ring. "Congratulations," said Paul. "I knew you and Gary would hit it off."

"Oh, it's not Gary."

"Then who …?"

"Travis Wyndham. You know, the President of the Boosters Committee."

"What?"

"You seem surprised."

"I am. I'd never thought of him. I always thought he was such an old fuddy-duddy."

Anne smiled. "He is, in a way. Something like you. That's all to the good. I had enough excitement with Tommy. I want someone settled and stable."

"Have you told Gary?"

"Yes. I liked Gary but he's just too full of himself. Besides, I don't think he really wants to marry again. He's having too good a time with all the single ladies around here."

Paul shook his head. "Well, congratulations again."

"I'll send you and Sally a wedding invitation. I hope you'll be able to come."

Paul didn't see Sally until that evening when she came home from one of her club meetings. The first thing he did was tell her all about his encounter with Anne.

"Yes, I know," she said. "Anne was at the meeting."

"I suppose you were right," said Paul. "Gary wasn't the one for her. I feel a little foolish"

"Don't fret.. Your reputation for wisdom won't suffer. Anne credits you for getting her together with Travis Wyndham. If you hadn't recruited her for the Boosters Committee she might not have met him."

"That's right, I did recruit her. I didn't know I had a reputation for wisdom."

"Oh, you know people look upon you as a wise old man."

"Am I an old fuddy-duddy, too? That's what Anne told me I was."

"Hmm. You are pretty much, but a nice one. Now let's have some tea and we can decide what kind of wedding present we'll give."

A Friend for Life
(Clever Magazine)

My wife Sally was going over the list of neighbors to be invited to our party. "What do you think about that man who lives around the corner, you know, Sam Spivey?"

"The ornery old coot?," I said. "That's what everyone calls him. Nobody asks him any more. He's dirty and foul-mouthed, they said. He also insults everybody."

"Can he be that bad?" Sally tends to think the best of people. "We've never even met him."

"I'm just as glad he wasn't at the Campbell's party. I'm not sure I want to meet him."

We had moved into the Northern California retirement community two months ago. The community was run by an association and every neighborhood in the community had its own association, which had monthly get-togethers. Sally had been so enthusiastic after going to the Campbell's party that she'd volunteered to have the next one.

"We should at least ask him. He probably won't come anyway. I'm making flyers to announce the party. Someone should bring one over to Mr. Spivey.".

Uh, oh, I thought. "Who would that be?"

"Well, you're a man. It would be better coming from you."

I knew better than to argue with his wife's logic.

*   *   *

Good, I thought, it didn't look as if anyone was home. I bent down and slipped the flyer under the doormat. The door opened and I found himself looking at the belly of a man dressed in an undershirt and shorts. The legs under the shorts were bowed. I straightened up. Sam Spivey was unshaven and unkempt. He had a large red nose and beady-looking eyes. "What are you selling?" he demanded in a wheezy voice.

"Uh, I'm not selling anything. I'm Paul Lerner. My wife Sally and I moved in a couple of months ago. We're hosting the neighborhood party next week."

"Hah. They stopped asking me to those things a long time ago. They know I have no use for them. Bunch of SOBs. You met the Campbells yet?"

"Yes. They hosted the last neighborhood party."

"Bet they were all lovey-dovey. They fight all the time. How about the Masons?"

"I think they were there, too."

"He's carrying on with that widow up the street. Don't blame him. Wife's a nag."

I recalled the Masons as being a small, quiet couple who showed around pictures of their grandchildren. Spivey's accusation didn't seem likely.

"How about the Bakers? He parks his big RV in the street all the time. She walks their dogs and doesn't pick up after them. I don't let them get near my front yard."

I could see why he was known as the ornery old coot. "Well, look at the flyer and see if you want to come to our party."

"Hah." He slammed the door. That was that, I thought.

I told Sally about my encounter with Spivey. "I don't think he's coming. And he is an ornery old coot."

But, to our surprise, in the middle of our party, with a dozen or so of our neighbors circulating around the house, the doorbell rang and there was Sam Spivey. He had cleaned himself up but still had some beard stubble. "Thought I'd come and see what's going on," he said. Sally got him a drink and he went straight to the table and filled up a plate with food. Maybe that's what he'd really come for, I thought.

I was distracted by having to get some more ice and when I returned I saw Spivey holding forth to a group of couples. I moved in closer and realized he was telling a joke, a dirty one. As soon as he finished, the couples moved away. He then went around the room talking to anyone who'd listen about how bad the governing association of the community was and how they'd ignored all the letters he'd sent them. He then approached one of the single ladies. I don't know what he said to her, but she blushed and said something sharp to him. At this point, Sally rushed over to the rescue and led Spivey away. The party broke up soon after, much sooner, I expected, than if Spivey hadn't come.

The next afternoon, our doorbell rang. It was Spivey again. He had flowers and a box of chocolate, which he gave to Sally. "I appreciate your inviting me to your shindig," he said. "Had a helluva time. You're not like all those other SOB's."

"That's nice," said Sally. "Uh, we have to go out now. Thanks for the flowers and candy."

As far as I knew, we weren't going anywhere, but Spivey left and Sally looked at me. I shrugged.

The next week I was in the Lodge, the center of all community activities. Among other things, it had a restaurant and a pool room with four tables. The pool room was empty so I went in. I hadn't played for years and wondered if I might take it up again. I tried hitting a few balls.. Someone came in. A wheezy voice said, "Thought that was you." It was Spivey.. "I was here to put in a complaint about that damned cat always peeing in my yard. You a pool player?"

I explained I hadn't played for years. Spivey grabbed a cue. "Come on," he said. "Let's see what you can do.'

We played a game and he was surprisingly good. "Okay," he said. "See I have to teach you a few things. I'll meet you here next week, same time."

I said I wasn't sure what I'd be doing next week,. but he ignored my remark. "And I'm taking you and your missus out to dinner here. I'll make a reservation for Friday night, six o'clock.."

"I don't know what we're doing Friday." He ignored this too and left, saying, "See you soon."

When I returned home I described this latest encounter to Sally. "What have we done?" she said.

"I think we've made a friend for life."

A Day in the Life
(Magnus)

A day in the life on an 80-year old. Paul Lerner found it hard to believe that he was actually that age. When he'd turned 75, he'd realized with a shock that he'd been around for three-quarters of a century; that was a long time. The changes that had occurred during his lifetime were almost as many, maybe even more, than those that had taken place during his father's lifetime. Then, there'd been the radio, television, cars, airplanes, washers, dryers, air-conditioning, all the modern stuff we now take for granted. In Paul's generation, there'd come cell phones, iPods, Blackberries, Notebooks, blogs, and of course the computer along with the Worldwide Web. And now, after another five years, which had seemed to go by in a flash, he was 80. Incredible!

Paul lined up his shot, chalked his cue stick and bent over the cue ball. It was his once-a-week pool match with a friend and neighbor, Mike Wilson. When had they started playing? Paul had stopped playing serious tennis at age 75 so it must have been five years ago. Once Paul had played tennis three or four times a week. Now he shot pool three mornings a week, once with Mike, once with a group of other old tennis players and once with two other friends. The pool room, which had six tables, was in a building called The Lodge, the activity center of his Northern California retirement community. Paul was fond of saying that pool was much easier on the knees than tennis. He still played an occasional set of what he thought of as recreational tennis, just to keep his hand in and because old habits die hard.

It was funny, Paul often thought, that, although both he and Mike knew their pool games didn't matter a bit in the grand scheme of things they tried their hardest to win. Mike was, like most of their retirement community members, a golfer. He played pool only this one time a week. He still hated to lose, as did Paul. Why, knowing better, were they so competitive? Paul guessed that no matter how old and how much larger other things, such as sickness and death, loomed in their lives, the competitive fire never died. Maybe if it did you were ready to be carried away.

Paul straightened up, took a deep breath, his routine when facing an eight-ball shot, then bent over again, lined up his shot and brought his cue stick forward. The cue ball hit the eight at just the spot he'd aimed at; the eight ball went toward the side pocket, hesitated a second at the edge, then dropped in. Paul had won the game.

"Good shot," said Mike.

"Thanks," said Paul. "I guess that's it." He looked at his watch. It was almost noon. "I have to run some errands. I'll see you next Monday, if not before." Paul and his wife Sally usually met Mike and his wife Carol for lunch or dinner once a week..

*   *   *

Paul drove to the shopping center, only ten minutes away. His first errand was to deposit his monthly check from the senior newspaper that he wrote two columns for, one called Favorite Restaurants and one called Observations.. The bank never seemed to have enough tellers on hand at noon, the busiest time, and often had a long line of people waiting. This time there was miraculously no line; but each of the two tellers was dealing with a woman.Paul knew from prior experience not to be too optimistic. Sure enough, whatever the transactions, they seemed to go on forever. Finally, one of the women received her money and managed to get it into her pocketbook.

Paul stepped up to the window and gave the teller, a young man who looked barely out of high school, his check and a deposit slip. The young teller looked long and carefully at the two pieces of paper, as if he was trying to decipher some unintelligible code. Finally, he looked up and said, "How are you doing today, Paul?"

Paul? He was tempted to ask the teller if they'd met before, but Paul was from a polite generation, quite unlike the current one. "I'm doing fine," he said.

"Do you want to deposit this check?"

That's what I'm here for, Paul said, but, still polite, he said it to himself. The teller was one of those youngsters who treated senior citizens as if they were children. He was probably amazed that Paul could still dodder around. "Yes, that's right,." said Paul.

The teller punched what seemed to be a lot of numbers into his computer for such a simple matter. Finally, a piece of paper with the deposit amount came out and he handed it to Paul. "Is there anything else we can do for you today?"

Paul looked at the teller's name tag. "No, thanks, Teddy," he said. That took care of his banking business until the next month.

On to the supermarket.Somehow, probably because he liked fresh bread and rolls, Paul had taken over a lot of the shopping, going to the supermarket once a week. He got the usual milk and orange juice, some sodas, lunch meat and cheese for himself, potato chips, two bags of kitty litter (they were on sale), a box of strawberries and one of blueberries (supposed to be healthy) and the bread and rolls. For his wife Sally, he got a bag of salad, tomatoes and an avocado. Sally did the big shopping, the stuff for their dinners. He'd noticed that the cost of even his "little" shopping had been going up. Jessie, the checkout girl, who knew him by now, said, "How are you today, Mr. Lerner?" No "Paul" from her. . He told her he was fine. As usual, she asked if he wanted any help out, and as usual he answered, "Not yet."

In the parking lot, he backed out slowly. He'd become ultra-cautious in his driving. Some people drove like crazy in parking lots and he kept hearing stories of collisions. He also drove the short distance back to the retirement community slowly and cautiously. Once, when he'd drive up behind a car driven by an old guy wearing a cap, he'd go around it the first chance he got. Now, he reflected, he was the old guy in the cap.

When he arrived home, Sally put away the things he'd bought. She was having an early lunch. "What's on your agenda this afternoon?" he asked.

"Canasta. I just told you this morning."

"Right." Sally played canasta with three neighboring women once a week. She also usually had lunch "with the girls" once a week and went to various club meetings. The retirement community had a club for just about every imaginable activity. He didn't bother to keep up with her schedule; it was sufficient to be reminded every now and then.
"How's your teeth?"

"They seem to be okay."

Sally had taken a fall a month ago, resulting in a couple of loose teeth, which had to be pulled and so she had a new bridge. If advanced retirement was an occupation, then falling was an occupational hazard. Sally was five years younger than him. After the accident, everyone they'd talked to had a story about his or her own fall. Paul had taken Sally to their HMO's emergency room; she had cut her lip and it required some stitches. He'd driven there much faster than he usually drove, putting aside his usual caution. They'd been at the ER the entire afternoon. The stitches required about 15 minutes; the rest of the time was spent waiting out in a hallway. That was about par for their HMO.

"Do you think we should call Ken?" asked Sally Ken was their oldest son, age 45, which seemed impossible to Paul. How could he have a son that old? Ken had quit his job as a copywriter a few months ago and had been looking for employment since then, so far unsuccessfully. He'd quit because of a disagreement he'd had with a new supervisor, a woman, who'd started revising his work. Paul had strongly advised him to hold onto his old job until he could find a new one, but Ken had considered it a point of honor that he leave. He'd been scheduled for an interview at the beginning of the week, the third one with the same company, and had high hopes. Paul and Sally had been waiting for him to call with the result..

"Let's give him to the end of the week," said Paul. "Maybe he's still waiting to hear." He'd found that you never stopped worrying about your children, no matter how old you were and how old they were.

After Sally left, Paul went to his computer to check his e-mail. He had to admit he was at least a semi-computer junkie, checking for e-mails half a dozen times a day. He had an e-mail from Dave, the editor of an online magazine based in London which printed the short stories he sent them every month or so. The new issue, with his story, was up; the weather in London was the usual, wet. Paul regularly exchanged comments on the weather and sometimes on the political scene with Dave. The rest of his e-mail was the usual junk (or spam), which he deleted. It was time for lunch.

Paul made himself a sandwich with the fresh roll he'd bought, put it, some potato chips and a soda on a small tray and took it to the bedroom, where he put it on a lamp table next to his lazy-boy chair. He'd also taken the morning's newspaper and the Wall Street Journal with him. He sat in the chair and put up the footrest, wondering how he'd ever gotten along without a lazy-boy, one of the great inventions of his time. Using the remote, he turned the bedroom TV on to a cable news show. The news, if there was any squeezed in between the usual pundit-noise, would serve as a background while he ate and read.

Paul was reading a story in the morning paper about the state's budget deficit, up to $15 billion, when his big, black-and-white male cat Shandyman, jumped up into his lap, something he invariably did when Paul was trying to eat. Paul pushed his food out of Shandyman's reach and tried to continue reading while the cat walked back and forth across his lap. He automatically stroked Shandyman, who, fortunately was not a lap cat, or not for long. In a few minutes Shandyman jumped off and went to find something more interesting to do.

After the morning paper came the Wall Street Journal. Paul had starting reading this when the airline miles he'd accumulated on one of his credit cards were about to run out and he was offered the option of subscribing to a number of publications. His original subscription had run out, but he'd decided to pamper himself and so had renewed it for a year. If you couldn't afford a slight extravagance when you're 80, when could you?

Having eaten and read, Paul leaned back in the lazy-boy chair; time for the afternoon nap. Paul's father had taken a nap every afternoon when he was the same age and had lived to 98. Paul closed his eyes and in a few minutes nodded off. When he opened them, he looked at his watch and saw that half an hour had passed. Time to get back to the computer and do a little of what nowadays he called "work."

Paul had started writing for the monthly senior newspaper that went to his retirement community a year or so after moving there. After retiring, at age 62, he'd begun, through a series of accidents, doing free-lance articles for what was called the Neighbors section of the morning newspaper he'd just been reading. The senior paper editor had done an article on Paul because he'd started a New Yorkers Club, its members being people from New York City. When she learned that Paul wrote for Neighbors she'd invited him to submit a piece, which he did, entitling it "Observations after a Year in Sun City." She'd liked it and he'd been doing a monthly Observations ever since. The "Favorite Restaurants" column came shortly after, Paul having noticed that eating out was one of the retirees' favorite topics of conversation. The idea was that Paul (and Sally) would report on any restaurant they liked, and he also asked readers to write, or e-mail, him about places they liked. He hadn't expected to be still doing "Favorite Restaurants" but new places kept springing up in their area and so he kept writing about them.

He usually waited until a few days before deadline, the 15th of the month, to do his pieces, but Paul's cousin from New York had just called to tell him that Vic Herschkowitz, the reigning handball star of their youth, had died, at age 89, in Florida. That news had awakened a host of memories about growing up in the Bronx, going to the Crotona Park handball courts, then to the MacCombs Dam courts, where the top players were, riding the streetcar, taking a quarter to buy two hot dogs and a soda for lunch, actually seeing the great Herschkowitz play when one weekend he'd turned up at MacCombs Dam, something like Tiger Woods turning up at their golf course today.

He wanted to do an "Observations" on those handball days before the memories grew dim again. Besides, he and Sally were going on a trip the next week, to visit her brother in Seattle. He'd better get his columns done before the usual big packing began.

Paul ended his "Observations" by writing that in his last year of high school they'd started a handball team and that he'd been its captain for two seasons. He'd won a varsity letter, something he'd never have been able to do in any other sport. He wrote that he'd then gone on to college on a handball scholarship. This wasn't strictly true, but the teacher who'd coached the team was a graduate of the college and he'd steered Paul to it with a great recommendation. This reminded Paul that he'd been looking for his high school letter; he wanted to show it to his grandson Logan, Ken's son, who was ten years old. After finishing the article, which he called "Observations on a Minor Sport," Paul looked through his desk and then through his dresser in the bedroom, trying to find the letter, but it wasn't there.

Discouraged and annoyed, he knew he'd put the damned thing somewhere, Paul returned to his chair. He picked up the library book he'd been reading, but his mind was still on Vic Hershkowitz. He was glad that his old hero had lived to 89. In the last five years, Paul didn't think a day went by that he didn't reflect on mortality. Paul wasn't a religious person; he thought he hadn't been born with that particular gene. It had seemed clear to him from an early age that the world was as it seemed. The Earth was a minor planet in a vast universe billions of years old. Man had somehow evolved from earlier creatures. No supernatural force ruled over life or determined its outcomes. Look at all the twisting and turning used to explain the existence of suffering under God. The simple fact was that people, good and bad, suffered; there was no reason for it.

Eventually, Paul had given up trying to think about death. If there was something after, that would be fine, but that was unlikely. When he died, that would be the end. The consciousness which was his "I" couldn't imagine of its being extinguished but, like a flame, it would be.. He hoped he'd live to an old age, as his father had. For an 80-year old, there seemed to be nothing but to go on living, doing his writing, playing his pool, doing his best for Sally, his sons , his grandchildren, his friends, even a little bit for the world in general. What else could he do? Brooding about the impending end, which crept closer each day, wouldn't help, or change anything.

Sally returned from her card game at around five. She always had a medical report to give after her sessions with the girls. One of their neighbors had found she had breast cancer. It sometimes seemed that half the women in their retirement community had this malady. Another neighbor, one he knew only vaguely, had died of a stroke in the past week. This too was not unusual. As the retirees grew older more and more of them were passing away. He'd gone to at least half a dozen memorial services in the past year. More reminders of mortality.

As Sally had just gotten back, she made a light supper, ham and eggs and a fruit salad. They were increasingly having these light suppers, thought Paul, as they didn't seem to need to eat as much. Also, Sally was tired of cooking regular dinners, something that Paul couldn't blame her for. In fact, many, of not most, of the women in their community were tired of cooking. He supposed this accounted for the popularity of his "Favorite Restaurants" column in the senior newspaper. Because of the column, a lot of people thought he and Sally ate out all the time. This wasn't true. Most of the "favorite restaurants" came from e-mails sent by readers, something which Paul kept telling people, but to no avail. He and Sally did try to eat out once every few weeks, a treat that they'd been giving themselves ever since Paul had retired.

After supper, Paul went back to the computer and laid out his next month's "Favorite Restaurants" column, two new eating places that he'd been e-mailed about and a Mexican restaurant he and Sally ate at every few months whose owner always brought them a special appetizer when she was there. Well, you had to get a perk every now and then when you wrote about restaurants.

When he was finished, Paul went into the living room, where Sally was reading. She looked up and said, "Be thinking about what you want to wear in Seattle." Sally always prepared early for any trip, even if only for a weekend. They'd be staying in Seattle for eight days.

"I hope it's going to be a lot cooler there," said Paul. He had mixed feelings about going anywhere nowadays. He knew it was always good to have a little break from their retirement community routine. But it was also true that the older he'd become, the less he wanted to get away from that routine. Travel could be an ordeal, especially having to go by air. The flight would be short, but you had to get to the airport hours ahead of time, then there was the long security line when he'd have to empty his pockets and take off his shoes to insure he wasn't an 80-year old terrorist. "That reminds me, I better call Supershuttle tomorrow, and the newspaper." I'd better make a note of it, he thought, or I might forget. He went to his desk and jotted it down in his all-important date book. Then he thought of the little notebook he always took on trips; it had names and addresses and he put their airline schedules in it. He looked in his bottom desk drawer and there was the notebook, and under it was his high school handball letter.

He returned to the living room, holding up the letter for Sally to see. They talked some more about their upcoming trip. Sally's brother Jeff was ten years younger than she was. He and his wife Greta had moved from Orlando to the Seattle area about a year ago. Jeff was a retired veterinarian. He was an easygoing guy, a great sports fan. Paul had always considered Greta to be a little crazy. They'd already been told they'd have to take their shoes off when entering Jeff and Greta's new condo. Paul knew that Greta would have planned their visit down to the last minute. Well, that was okay. He'd just relax, with his shoes off, and leave everything to her.

Paul and Sally usually watched television from nine to eleven. They'd been catching up with old episodes of The Sopranos. Paul didn't agree with the critics that this was the greatest TV drama of all time. Basically, he thought, it was the same old glorification of gangsters that movies and television had been doing for years. The only difference was that the head mobster had panic attacks and saw a psychiatrist, who, in Paul's opinion, hadn't done him a lot of good. What made the show interesting was the good acting and trying to guess what gangster, or innocent civilian, would be "whacked" next.

They were in the middle of a "Sopranos" episode when the phone rang. Sally picked it up. "It's Ken," she said. Paul quickly went to his desk and picked up the other phone.

"Hi, Mom. Hi, Dad," said Ken. "I got the job."

Paul exhaled a sigh of relief. Ken then went to tell them that he'd been at his new employer's until late, then he'd taken Carol and the kids out to a pizza place to celebrate and this was the first chance he'd had to call them. Paul asked him some questions about the new job, then Sally asked if could come see their grandsons as she and Paul were leaving on their trip the next Monday. It was arranged that they would go over to Ken's house, which was not too far away, that Saturday. Paul told himself that he should remember to take his high school letter to show Logan.

When they were in bed, Paul kissed Sally and they both said, "I love you." It was a ritual they'd been doing for years. If he didn't wake up in the morning, thought Paul, his last words to Sally would be that he loved her. He closed his eyes. but he never went to sleep at once. He reviewed the day. The highlight of course had been his son's news that he'd gotten the job. Paul realized that he'd been getting increasingly anxious as Ken's period of unemployment stretched out. No, you never stopped worrying about your kids..

Then he'd gotten a start on his two articles. He'd look at the "Observations" and see what revisions had to be made. He'd write the "Favorite Restaurants." He'd print out both and show them to Sally, his unpaid editor. Tomorrow he'd also make his trip calls. Maybe he'd go to the library in the afternoon to get some books to read during the trip, if Greta allowed any time for this.

He thought about Vic Hershkowitz. He wondered how many of the other great handball players of his youth were still around. Maybe none. He wondered how long he himself would still be around. Just because he'd decided there was no point in thinking about mortality didn't mean he could stop himself from doing so, especially late at night. He had self-published three collections of his short stories in the last three years. Just to see if he could do it, he'd written a longer piece this year called "A Year in Retirement." It was a fictionalized memoir, in which he'd tried to put all of the things he'd learned in retirement. It came to 130 pages. All of the things he learned really hadn't amounted to very much. After this, maybe he'd put out a collection of his "Observations." Somehow, he felt, although he never articulated it to himself, that if he had a goal for the next year and the year after that he'd survive until then.

He'd never be able to believe that life was anything other than a series of random events. Still, maybe in the natural order of things, there were some currents or patterns, like ripples in the ocean, that gave some meaning or at least some order to life. Like his finding that old high school handball letter of his. It had been his cousin's telling him of Vic Hershkowitz, his memories of his handball days, the trip to Seattle, all combining so that the letter came to light.

Then there were the accidental events that had led him to become a writer. After his retirement lunch, he and Sally had gone to a store downtown where a teacher Sally had worked for was having a close-out sale. The teacher had told them she might be doing something for an alternative weekly newspaper published downtown and had asked Paul if he might be interested. This had led to his first free-lance writing job, unpaid, then he'd started writing for Neighbors, then for the senior newspaper. Maybe it wasn't all accidental; maybe it was meant to be. It would be nice to think so. At this point, Paul's thoughts began to break up, like images on a defective DVD. He turned on his side and was asleep. Another day was over.